A picture of deception . . .

Annabelle Lawson knew nothing about the breathtaking stranger she met on the train—only that he'd make an ideal model for the budding young artist . . . and that she desired him more than she believed possible. But after she'd been seduced, she learned that she'd also been betrayed. The man she thought she loved was really Magnus Wallis—a scoundrel like his father before him, the loathed cousin of Annabelle's benefactor.

A landscape of love . . .

No longer the naively romantic girl who would tumble for a rogue, Annabelle cannot avoid a reunion with the despicable Magnus, who wants to include her portraits in his new London gallery. She means to show him her coldest face—but upon seeing him again, her every intention melts from the heat of his touch. It is clear that Magnus still burns with love for her. But is he still the villain he once was, or can he be reformed into a man Annabelle can dare to love?

"Julianne MacLean's books should have 'keeper' stamped on them!"
Pamela Britton

By Julianne MacLean

PORTRAIT OF A LOVER
LOVE ACCORDING TO LILY
MY OWN PRIVATE HERO
AN AFFAIR MOST WICKED
TO MARRY THE DUKE

If You've Enjoyed This Book,
Be Sure to Read These Other
AVON ROMANTIC TREASURES

THE LORD NEXT DOOR *by Gayle Callen*
A MATTER OF TEMPTATION *by Lorraine Heath*
SCANDAL OF THE BLACK ROSE *by Debra Mullins*
THIS RAKE OF MINE *by Elizabeth Boyle*
AN UNLIKELY GOVERNESS *by Karen Ranney*

Coming Soon

PROMISE ME FOREVER *by Lorraine Heath*

JULIANNE MacLEAN

Portrait of a Lover

An Avon Romantic Treasure

AVON BOOKS
An Imprint of HarperCollinsPublishers

This is a work of fiction. Names, characters, places, and incidents are products of the author's imagination or are used fictitiously and are not to be construed as real. Any resemblance to actual events, locales, organizations, or persons, living or dead, is entirely coincidental.

AVON BOOKS
An Imprint of HarperCollins*Publishers*
10 East 53rd Street
New York, New York 10022-5299

Copyright © 2006 by Julianne MacLean
ISBN-13: 978-0-06-081935-4
ISBN-10: 0-06-081935-9
www.avonromance.com

First Avon Books paperback printing: March 2006

Avon Trademark Reg. U.S. Pat. Off. and in Other Countries, Marca Registrada, Hecho en U.S.A.
HarperCollins® is a registered trademark of HarperCollins Publishers Inc.

Printed in the U.S.A.

10 9 8 7 6 5 4 3 2 1

Acknowledgments

This book is dedicated to my former editor, Kelly Harms, who has begun a new chapter in her career. Kelly, you were a dream to work with and I will miss you, but I wish you great joy and happiness in every aspect of your life.

Special thanks also to Paige Wheeler, Nancy Berland, Paula Altenburg, and especially my critique partner and cousin, Michelle Phillips, for going the extra mile for me this time. Finally, thank you, Stephen, my real-life hero, for your true love and support, and Laura, for all the best hugs and kisses.

Prologue

June 19, 1892

Dear Annabelle,

You did not reply to my previous letter, so I have taken the liberty of writing again to request an appointment with you regarding the painting.

I implore you—please do not let the past dictate your decision in this regard. Come and meet me at the gallery before the exhibition. The painting deserves this recognition.

Magnus Wallis

Annabelle Lawson tipped her head back upon the rough bark of the oak tree on the hill and laid a hand upon her stomach. Her heart was pounding uncontrollably. She'd always feared this day would come—that after all these years, Magnus would be bold enough to contact her.

She took a deep, slow breath, telling herself that at least this way she'd been warned that he had returned to London. It would have been excruciating to meet him unexpectedly somewhere. Not that this wasn't excruciating enough on its own.

Meet me at the gallery.

Her stomach began to churn. He wanted to see her. But how could she see *him*? She had not forgiven him for what he'd done all those years ago. He'd ripped her heart to shreds and stomped on it. He'd treated her appallingly. Inexcusably. He was her brother's enemy, and he was vengeful. He had no heart of his own.

No. She could not see him. It would be too painful and agonizing to revisit all those feelings.

A cool breeze fluttered the letter in her hand, and Annabelle gazed beyond her easel, down the grassy hillside toward her home. Or rather, her brother's home, which she had been struggling to capture on canvas.

She folded the letter and stuffed it into her pocket. Picking up her palette and brush, she took a step forward, but stopped and laid a hand on her stomach again, waiting for the churning sensation to pass.

She had not felt anything quite so intense in years, she realized suddenly. Eight, to be exact, because that was the last time she had dealt with Magnus—the day he left England for America. Permanently.

She had been so very relieved that day. Relieved that he would disappear and never bother her or Whitby again. Whitby had made sure of it. He paid Magnus handsomely to leave, with an allowance forthcoming as long as he remained in America. Magnus knew that if he ever returned, the payments would cease.

But he was here now, wasn't he? Here on English soil, opening old wounds and causing her to question whether he had ever really been gone. Because the scars he had left were still etched sorely on her heart.

Forcing herself not to let those thoughts distract her any further, because she wanted this painting finished, she assessed and appraised her work.

It was nearly complete, but did not yet convey what she wished it to convey. Determined to get it right, she dipped her small flat bristle brush into the black paint and redefined the outline of the far side of the house. She tried to touch up the other side as well, then used her painting knife to delineate the lines she'd just added.

Annabelle stepped back again to examine the subtle changes.

Good God. She'd been working on this for what seemed like forever, and still she wasn't happy with it. It was dull; it evoked no emotion. Anyone could have painted it. Whitby would be just as well off with a photograph.

Letting out a frustrated sigh, she set her palette down upon her paint box and backed up against the tree. She continued to stare at the painting. What was wrong with it? What was missing?

The same thing that was missing from all her paintings, she supposed. Originality. Passion. Life. She never took chances with them and she was never happy with them, and she would tinker with them forever if she could.

Another breeze blew by, gusting through the leaves overhead. Annabelle spent a few more minutes staring with dissatisfaction at the painting, wondering what she could do to fix it, then at last shook her head and decided to give up. The truth of the matter was—she hadn't the slightest idea how to make it better without taking the chance of spoiling it. Best not to risk it.

Consequently, she cleaned her palette and brushes, set all her supplies into the paint box and closed it.

Perhaps Whitby would think it was fine. He always disagreed with her about her paintings, after all, and fought to convince her they were marvelous, when she invariably thought they were catastrophes.

Lying back on the grass to give the paint time to dry, she laced her fingers together over her stomach—which thankfully had settled somewhat—and crossed her legs at the ankles. She squinted up at the leaves against the bright white sky, listened to the whispery sound they made in the wind, and thought of the letter in her pocket again.

The painting deserves this recognition.

She realized then that she had been so shaken by the thought of seeing Magnus again, she hadn't considered the larger picture. He wanted to show one of her paintings in an exhibition.

No, not just any painting. He wanted to show *The Fisherman*—which she had not seen in thirteen years. She couldn't even remember what it looked like, and wasn't even sure she wanted to see it. She'd always regretted painting it and had wished it did not exist in the world. Many times over the years, she'd wished she could get it back and destroy it.

But *he* seemed to think it was praiseworthy.

Was it possible he was right, and this exhibition could be the key to her future as an artist? And if that was so, could she ignore this opportunity, because of her personal feelings toward Magnus?

Surely she was stronger than that, wasn't she? She knew the truth about him now, and she was a woman, no longer the naive girl she had once been so many years ago when she'd stepped on the train . . .

The Train

Thirteen years earlier . . .

Chapter 1

June 1879

"**T**hat shawl is entirely too young for her," Aunt Millicent said as she smoothed her skirts on the train seat. "She's turning seventy-five, after all. The color is too daring, and it's not even fashionable. Speaking of which, why in the world did you wear that hat? It's the worst thing I've ever seen. It looks like a purple haystack on your head."

As always, Annabelle ignored her aunt's narrow-minded taste in millinery, because she was not giving up the hat. It was satisfyingly unique.

"I suppose it suits our surroundings," she added with a self-important, haughty tone. She glanced around the Second Class carriage, looking down her nose in repugnance at the merchants and tradesmen.

Annabelle ignored her aunt's snobbery as well, for they'd had no choice about the traveling accommodations. First Class was full, and they couldn't possibly wait for another train, for they were already late for Aunt Sadie's birthday party as it was.

"The shawl is a very tasteful shade of blue, Auntie," Annabelle replied, trying to distract Millicent from her discontent. "It's like the sky. It will accentuate the vivid color of her eyes."

"Her eyes do not need to be noticed in that way. Not at her age."

Growing frustrated, for she knew Aunt Millicent wouldn't budge about the blue shawl, Annabelle turned her gaze toward the window. They were slowing down. The train was screeching to a halt at the Leicester station to pick up passengers.

Steam spurted and hissed from the engine as a crowd gathered on the platform. Annabelle looked down and smiled at a family—a young couple standing in the shade of the station overhang with their baby in a brand new pram. The woman, wearing a fashionable green plumed hat, raised a gloved hand and waved, and Annabelle waved cheerfully in return.

"Now *that* is a lovely hat," Aunt Millicent said, wagging a finger. "See how it fits in with all the others?"

Continuing to ignore her aunt's harangue, and thinking they might be stopped for more than a few minutes, Annabelle reached into her bag for the book she'd packed. She was leaning forward, quite distracted by the inconceivable mess inside the bag—when in the world had she put a cigar cutter in there?—when the door to their carriage suddenly swung open, startling her, for she was seated right next to it. She jolted upright.

"I do beg your pardon," a man said, stepping up and looking around the full carriage.

An elderly woman came along and entered behind him, and he helped her up, then gestured to the seats facing Annabelle and Millicent. "These appear to be the last available seats. If you don't mind?"

Naturally, Annabelle left it to her chaperone to respond, but even if she had been the one required to reply, she wasn't sure she would have been able to speak, for her heart was racing in her chest and her mouth felt strangely tingly inside. Because the man standing before her, removing his black overcoat right in front of her eyes was, in a word, magnificent.

The elderly woman behind him removed her coat, too, but Annabelle was only aware of the man—tall, broad-shouldered, and dark. His hair was shiny black, his eyes dark brown. He turned to face her again, and she had to struggle to keep her eyes downcast, though she did glance up briefly to observe the fine lines of his shoulders and back as he assisted the elderly woman by hanging her coat with his on a nearby hook.

Then all at once he turned and glanced down at Annabelle's feet—his eyes lingering there for a moment.

For the first time in her life Annabelle was embarrassed by her boots. They were made for boys, and they were absolutely *not* fashionable, but they were so much more comfortable than ladies' boots, especially when she spent most of her time tramping around the countryside with her easel under her arm.

She quickly drew her feet under her skirts.

When the man finally took the seat facing her, he smiled politely, first at Aunt Millicent, who was looking down her long, aristocratic nose suspiciously at him, then at Annabelle, who managed to smile casually in return.

She hoped she wasn't blushing. That would be mortifying.

Determined not to stare, she raised her book and opened it, pretending to read. Yes, pretending, because she could hardly concentrate with such a handsome man sitting not three feet away from her, facing her squarely.

Trains could be so decidedly awkward sometimes.

The train blew its whistle and they lurched forward, rocking back and forth as the locomotive began to slowly move away from the station. Annabelle looked out the window at the young family again, and watched them through the spiraling coal dust until she couldn't see them anymore.

Soon they were under way, the pistons hammering fast beneath them as they gained speed on the tracks.

Feeling the chugging sensation beneath the soles of her boots, Annabelle peered over the top of her book to steal another glance at the man across from her. He was gazing absently out the window, so she recalled her artist's mantra—*there is no substitute for close observation*—and studied his face more meticulously.

Of course, it was pure perfection—a straight nose, a strong chiseled jaw, and high cheekbones. Yet, along with all those sharp, manly angles was a set of full, moist lips that looked quite agreeably soft.

What she wouldn't give to paint him.

It was an odd thought, because she never painted people. She only did landscapes, preferably rugged ones, which was perhaps where this marked fascination came from. He, too, was rugged, like the jagged English coastlines that captured her imagination more than any other place or thing. She loved the sound of the sea, surging and crashing up against the rocks, and she loved to try and capture the unfathomable depths and distances that were an intrinsic part of the ocean.

She couldn't explain it, but strangely, this man made her body feel the same way. He made her blood quicken, made her mind tick like a clock wound too tight. Just looking at him made her feel happy to be alive, when there were so many beautiful, wondrous things to comprehend.

Though of course he was not a thing. He was a man.

Just then the beautiful, wondrous man gazed directly at her, and she froze, caught in the embarrassing circumstance of ogling.

She almost panicked and lifted her book to cover her face, but that would have been childish, and she was not a child. She was twenty-one.

Instead, she smiled politely and lowered her book to her lap, lowering her gaze along with it. It was at that instant she noticed she had been reading the same page for the past ten minutes.

"Are you all going to Edinburgh?" the elderly lady asked, causing Annabelle to look up again. "I'm going to Newcastle."

The wrinkles on the lady's face were in happy

places, at the outside of her eyes, suggesting a lifetime spent smiling.

The handsome gentleman replied, "I'm going past Edinburgh and on to Perth."

The woman leaned closer, raising a hand to her ear. "Where?"

"Perth!"

The woman sat for a few seconds, as if trying to decipher what she'd heard, then nodded. "Oh, yes, yes! I once had an uncle in Perth."

The handsome gentleman looked curiously at Annabelle and her aunt, waiting for them to respond to the question as well, but Aunt Millicent turned her face away, no doubt finding the exchange intrusive.

The elderly woman then turned to the gentleman beside her and began a conversation about whom she was going to visit in Edinburgh—her daughter and children—and how long she would be there, but it was a rather awkward conversation, as the woman was almost completely deaf and had to hold her hand up to her ear every time the man spoke.

The two of them were shouting by the end of it, and when they finally stopped talking, Annabelle glanced up and found herself sharing an amused grin with the handsome man.

It was not a grin at the expense of the elderly lady; they were not making fun of her. On the contrary, Annabelle recognized a look of compassion in the gentleman's dark eyes. He, like she, was able to see the humor in life sometimes. *What a dear lady*, they both seemed to be saying to each other.

Afterward, Annabelle lowered her gaze to the book again, but the printed words on the page held little allure. For one thing, she was still on the same page as before, and for another, her dancing thoughts were making it difficult to make sense of the story in her brain.

This was going to be a very long trip indeed, she thought as she crossed her legs at the ankles and struggled not to look up again.

To be honest, she was afraid to, because—good God in heaven—she could sense that the intriguing man was now ogling her.

About an hour into the journey the train was chugging along at full speed across the rolling English countryside, the sun was beaming in through the windows, and Aunt Millicent's head was beginning to nod. Millicent resisted sleep as best she could, jerking her head up every time it fell forward, but it wasn't long before her eyes dropped closed and her mouth fell open. She tipped her head back on the upholstered seat and at last began to snore.

Annabelle noticed her aunt's open book sliding off her lap, so she reached for it and carefully dragged it from her aunt's limp grasp. She put the ribbon in place to mark the page and set it on the seat between them before returning to her own book.

She was just becoming absorbed in the story when she was interrupted by an unexpected question.

"Suspenseful?" the man across from her asked.

She lifted her gaze. "I beg your pardon?"

He pointed at her book.

Glancing at the other elderly lady, who was writing a letter and didn't seem to be aware of any conversation, Annabelle paused uncertainly for a moment before replying. The man was a stranger, after all.

"My apologies," he said after a few seconds, apparently realizing that he'd made her uncomfortable. He went back to his own book.

Annabelle immediately regretted her hesitation. She hadn't meant to be rude. "No apologies necessary," she said, closing her book over her finger, which she used to keep her page.

The man's gaze met hers again, making her feel strangely giddy.

"It's been very suspenseful," she said. "Have you read it?" She showed him the cover.

"Can't say that I have." He closed his own book and set it on the seat beside him, then held out a hand. "May I?"

Annabelle passed the book to him. She noted the distance between their knees . . . a foot, or perhaps two at most, which gave her a rather naughty little thrill.

He flipped through her book—using his own finger to keep her page—then handed it back. "I must pick that one up. I like a good mystery."

Gracious, he was exquisite to look at, she thought. A famous sculptor couldn't have created anything more beautiful. She'd never seen such magnetic eyes before. How old was he? Late twenties perhaps?

Annabelle glanced down at his hand and noted he wore no wedding ring. A deep feminine element of her being rejoiced.

She noted also that his hands were large and rough-looking. He was no idle gentleman, that was certain, and the idea of his male strength and ruggedness thrilled her beyond all.

"Are you on your way somewhere, or returning home?" he asked, his voice deep, yet soft at the same time. Just the sound of it made her feel womanly.

"We're going to my great aunt's seventy-fifth birthday party. She lives near Newcastle. And yourself?"

"Business." His eyes roamed over her face from the top of her head down to her chin, and it felt like a sensuous caress.

She couldn't deny that she secretly enjoyed it, which felt rather wicked and exciting.

A short time later, Aunt Millicent was snoring like a dairy farmer, and Annabelle had relaxed significantly regarding her conversation with the gentleman seated across from her, even though she didn't know him at all and they had not been properly introduced and he was very handsome and she was . . . Well . . . she was young and unmarried and painfully aware of his attractiveness.

"What kind of business are you in?" she boldly asked.

"I'm a clerk in a bank."

"You live in London, I presume?"

Another bold question. Annabelle glanced prudently at her aunt. Still dead to the world, thank heavens.

"Yes. My mother is currently residing with me, and it's just the two of us. My father passed away a number of years ago."

"That is very good of you to care for your mother. She's a lucky woman, to have you for a son."

"As is your mother, to have such a lovely daughter." He glanced at Aunt Millicent, whose mouth was still hanging open. She twitched and slapped herself on the cheek.

Annabelle grinned. "She's my aunt, actually."

"Ah."

"I never knew my mother," Annabelle blurted out, realizing too late that such a personal admission was even bolder than her earlier questions. She didn't even know this man's name. Yet something made her continue. Perhaps it was the transitory nature of the circumstances. She would probably never see him again after today.

"I'm sorry to hear that," he said.

"She died when I was not quite a year old," Annabelle continued, "and my father passed away a year later. So I was adopted and raised by my mother's closest friend. They had known each other since they were children."

He smiled warmly. "You were very fortunate to have such good people in your life."

"Indeed I was. My adoptive parents are gone now, but I still have my older brother Whitby— *adoptive* brother, that is—to care for me, and of course, Aunt Millicent, who has been living with us since I debuted in society."

He tilted his head to the side. "You were raised by the *Earl* of Whitby?"

"Yes."

He stared at her for a long moment, appearing utterly staggered. Then his voice softened with an odd hint of resignation. "Well. It seems I am in esteemed company this morning."

He was looking at her differently. The fire in his eyes had gone out.

Perhaps he thought she did not wish to be speaking to him because she was the sister of an earl, and he was a bank clerk. She wanted more than anything to assure him that was not the case.

"I am hardly that," she explained. "My parents were simple country people."

"It matters little what your parents were. I can see you are a charming, intelligent woman all on your own."

Annabelle's cheeks felt hot all of a sudden.

"I've embarrassed you," he said, with an almost melancholy tone. "Please forgive me. My only excuse is that I couldn't help myself. I was lost in thought, in awe of your friendly, open manner."

She raised an arched brow. "Who's being charming now?"

He stared at her for a few more seconds before he quietly laughed. Annabelle laughed, too.

A moment later she leaned back and eyed him lightheartedly. "So tell me, sir, what do you do when you're not banking? I see you like to read."

For a brief moment he looked as if he weren't sure he should continue conversing with her in this manner, then he seemed to let go of his reservations and laid his hand on top of the closed book. "Yes, reading is an enjoyable pastime, but what I really like to do is fish."

"Fish?"

He nodded. "Nothing can compare to the experience of rowing a boat across a calm lake at dawn, when the air is crisp and your nose is chilled, and steam is rising from the water. Then you cast your line and hear the sound of it slicing through the air, and the hook hits the water with a quiet splash. Everything is so peaceful in the morning, and the sky has a certain glow."

Annabelle imagined what he had described. She could see herself sitting in his boat. It was a lovely thought.

"You make it sound wonderful," she said. "I've never been fishing before."

"No?" His eyes were warm and his smile calm, almost soothing. "Perhaps one day someone will take you."

Annabelle recognized the romance in his voice. He was telling her in no uncertain terms that he wished *he* could be the one to take her.

Desire burned through her body as she imagined seeing this man again in such a private setting, being alone with him in a rowboat, sharing such a moment.

Heavens, no one had ever flirted with her like this before. None of the young men she had danced with at balls or spoken to at assemblies had been anything like this man, who seemed mature and capable and so much more sure of himself compared to them. Even his physical presence was more manly. He was tall and broad through the chest and shoulders. His legs looked more muscular, and his hands . . . Well, she'd already noticed how attractive and strong they were.

But there was something else about him, too, something that stirred her blood and excited her in a way she'd never experienced before. It was the way he looked at her—as if he found her the most beautiful creature in the world.

"I would like that very much," she replied breathlessly.

His eyes traveled from her face down the front of her bodice to her knees, then back up again before he slowly leaned forward. "Please allow me this impropriety," he whispered, glancing briefly at Aunt Millicent, who was still snoring. "But may I ask your name?"

Annabelle experienced a surge of both apprehension and excitement. The whole tone of their exchange was highly improper and very wicked. She would never be speaking to him this way if Aunt Millicent were awake, or if the elderly lady beside him could hear what they were saying. Thankfully, she had barely looked up from her correspondence.

Annabelle shifted nervously in her seat, then whispered in return, "It's Annabelle. Annabelle Lawson."

He continued to stare at her face, almost entranced, as if he didn't know what to make of her or what to say next.

"And what is your name, sir, if I may be so bold?" The fact that she had also whispered the question gave the whole conversation an air of secrecy and subterfuge. It was without a doubt the single most exciting conversation of her life.

He leaned forward even more. "John Edwards."

A long, lingering, and delightfully sensuous gaze passed between them. Their faces were scandalously close.

"So tell me, Miss Lawson, what do *you* like to do when you're not talking to strangers on trains?"

Annabelle smirked at him. "I paint."

"Do you indeed? You're an artist. I should have guessed."

"How would you guess such a thing?"

"Don't all artists have deeply tortured souls?"

Annabelle laughed out loud, and Aunt Millicent stirred beside her. Both Annabelle and Mr. Edwards quickly sat back as Millicent opened her eyes, stared dazedly up at the ceiling, then closed them again and drifted back to sleep.

Mr. Edwards swiped a hand over his brow, as if to say, *That was close.*

Annabelle shook her head with mock disapproval, then leaned forward again. Mr. Edwards did the same.

"Let me assure you," she said, "I am not tortured."

"Are you certain?" he asked with a teasing glint in his eyes. "You don't feel wretchedly miserable or trapped? As if the life you are supposed to lead is beyond your reach and nothing has meaning?"

He was toying with her, of course, but she could not deny her astonishment that he had hit the mark exactly, because yes, sometimes she did indeed feel trapped. Especially when her aunt dressed her up like all the other London girls and paraded her around at balls—because she was not like other girls. She hated the Season, she had no interest in fancy gowns and heeled shoes, she had a strange fascination with Egyptian mummies, and she had a cow for a pet.

To be honest, there were times when she was truly screaming inside her head, trying to fit into this polished, patrician world, and not be a disappointment to her family, who had taken her in and loved her like one of their own. She felt she owed so much to them.

But she could not possibly express such an unconventional sentiment to Mr. Edwards.

"I paint landscapes," she told him. "And I would describe my experience of painting in the same way you describe fishing. Nothing compares to the bliss of standing before a view of an autumn forest, setting up my easel and contemplating the first brushstroke. Though my favorite thing to paint is the coastline. Unfortunately, we don't live on the coast—though I wish desperately that we did—so I must content myself with the countryside most of the time."

He pointed a finger at her. "See? You are tortured after all. Frustrated by the geography of your existence."

She laughed. "Yes, I suppose so. You win."

He watched her laugh, and she could see as plain as day a gleam of desire in his eyes.

Oh, how he flattered her, just by the way he looked at her. She didn't think she'd ever felt so beautiful before.

"I wish you could paint me fishing," he said. "I would hang the painting over my mantel, and every time I looked at it, I would feel content."

Content because it would make him think of fishing? Or because it would make him think of *her*?

She supposed she would never know the answer to that.

"I'd enjoy painting you," she said openly. "I've never painted a fisherman before."

"Perhaps one day we'll make it happen. We'll take your paints and a blank canvas out to my favorite fishing hole."

Annabelle gazed out the window, feeling dreamy. "Wouldn't that be splendid," she replied as she imagined such a wonderful day.

It wasn't long, however, before reality settled in and she had to accept that it would *not* happen. Ever. He was not the kind of man her aunt would approve of. He was a stranger on a train, after all, and he worked as a bank clerk.

As she watched the trees fly by outside the window—so fast she could barely focus on them— she was distressed by the extent of her disappointment. She was not free to do as she wished, for she was a London *debutante*.

Oh, how she hated that word.

If only her life were just a little different. She could only imagine all the things she would do.

Thinking such a thing made her feel guilty, however, for she had been blessed with so many privileges. She was grateful for her life. Truly she was. She had no right to feel frustrated.

Chapter 2

Magnus Wallis sat across from Miss Annabelle Lawson on the fast steam train to Newcastle and cursed the cards he had been dealt all his life—today in particular.

He had not asked to meet her. If he had known who she was, he most definitely would have waited for the next train. But *bloody hell*, he had not known, and he'd been attracted to her the very first instant he'd noticed her—with her wild, frizzy, honey-gold hair and that outlandish purple hat.

He'd known immediately that she was one of a kind, perhaps a bit of a rebel. Not just because of her unconventional attire—not to mention those intriguing black boots—but because her eyes were so full of life, as wild and blue as the irrepressible sea.

And now he was in very deep, completely over his head as a matter of fact. He was sitting forward, listening to her describe her art with passion and hunger, gesturing with her hands as she spoke, her luscious smile dazzling and intoxicating.

All this, after he'd lied to her and given her a false name.

Magnus shuddered inwardly. He shouldn't have done it. He'd known it was wrong, even as he was speaking the words, but he just couldn't stomach the possibility that she would recoil in horror, which she would surely do if she knew who he was.

Her aunt would probably go into convulsions, for he was Magnus Wallis, Whitby's contemptible, undesirable cousin, whom they all blamed for Whitby's brother's death. They thought he was a monster—just like his father—and all his life he'd been feared and loathed and shut out by the very people who had given Miss Lawson a home.

Lovely Miss Lawson . . .

All at once he found himself glancing down for a brief, appreciative moment at her extravagant bosom, which heaved enticingly as she took a deep breath to continue talking. He thought of their earlier conversation about going fishing together, and imagined teaching her how to bait the hook and cast the line, then imagined her standing in front of her easel, dabbing paint on a fresh canvas.

God, he wanted nothing more than to disembark from this train at the next stop and lead her out of here by the hand. To pretend they were two very different people. To continue talking like this—openly and passionately.

But no . . . That could never be, because she was a member of that family. She had been raised within their walls, while he had been tossed over them, and she was under Whitby's protection. Magnus knew she was untouchable, as far as he was concerned. He should not even be speaking to her. Nothing could come of it but frustration.

Yet he was still drinking in her every word, wasn't he? Still eyeing her full, sumptuous mouth and stealing glances at her lavish breasts, which continued to rise and fall with her enchanting enthusiasm. She was a delicious young beauty, to be sure, and God help him, he was a hot-blooded man.

He was indeed in way over his head.

When Aunt Millicent woke, Annabelle checked her timepiece to discover it was closing in upon noon.

The elderly lady beside Mr. Edwards had fallen asleep some time ago, so he and Annabelle had been free to chat for over an hour about everything imaginable—art, politics, books, the theatre, the pleasures and trappings of society, trains and coaches, the view outside the window.

They shared many interests, and when they did not agree on something, they each respected the other's opinion and expressed a general feeling of enlightenment at having never considered such a viewpoint before.

Overall, Annabelle found Mr. Edwards to be the most fascinating, intriguing man she had ever met, and she could quite decisively say she was enraptured. She felt as if she had found the perfect companion—someone she could converse with about anything, even subject matters her aunt considered inappropriate *genteel* conversation.

Perhaps this strange freedom she felt stemmed from the fact that Mr. Edwards lived outside her world. He was not bound by the same constraints as she. He was different, to be sure. He made her feel alive and alert, and more consciously aware of the physicality of her being. Her heart raced with excitement over a certain word he spoke or a particular way he moved. She could feel her skin tingling with arousal. She could hear her heart pounding in her ears.

And she did not want this train ride to end.

So it was with great disappointment that

Annabelle watched her aunt awaken from her nap. Aunt Millicent smacked her lips a few times and gave a sleepy little whimper.

Without uttering a word, Mr. Edwards stopped talking, calmly reached for his book and opened it on his lap before Millicent had even realized she was awake.

"Good heavens, what time is it?" she asked.

"It's almost noon," Annabelle replied, trying not to reveal her disappointment.

Mr. Edwards did not even glance up. He behaved as if he hadn't heard the question.

Aunt Millicent nevertheless eyed him suspiciously when she noticed the other lady asleep. She glanced at him and Annabelle, looking concerned.

Perhaps her aunt did not want to admit she'd been negligent in regards to her duty, or perhaps she believed that Annabelle and Mr. Edwards had both been sitting in silence, reading the entire time.

Whatever she thought, thankfully, she asked no questions.

After the train made a brief stop in Sheffield, where everyone got off for lunch, they were soon chugging noisily down the tracks again. Aunt Millicent was knitting with impressive vigor, making it necessary for Annabelle and Mr. Edwards to ignore each other.

Having already lost interest in her book,

Annabelle rested her forehead against the cool glass, gazing dreamily at the white sheep dotting the green countryside. The train rocked back and forth, smoothly at times, jerkily at others, and she might have fallen asleep herself if the elderly lady next to Mr. Edwards had not spoken up.

"What a lovely lunch," she said as she shifted in her seat. "Did you enjoy your meal as well?" she asked Aunt Millicent.

"Yes, thank you!" Millicent shouted in reply, nodding in an exaggerated fashion.

"That's good, dear," the lady said. She leaned her cane up against the seat and smiled at everyone, then reached into her reticule for her book of crosswords.

At that moment, Mr. Edwards grinned at Annabelle, his heated gaze raking boldly downward.

Heart jolting with a wicked thrill that settled in the pit of her belly, Annabelle glanced quickly at her aunt, certain that if her conservative chaperone had seen the decadent spark in Mr. Edwards's eyes just now, she would pick up the older lady's cane and knock him over the head with it.

But Aunt Millicent was not looking at Mr. Edwards. She was absorbed in her knitting.

When Annabelle glanced back at him, he appeared amused by the whole situation—the two of them sitting across from each other with a clear attraction neither of them could pretend didn't exist, yet unable to converse the way they would have liked to. And they both knew Aunt Millicent was not about to encourage an introduction that could, God forbid, lead to an unwanted acquaintance.

So the next two hours passed in almost complete silence, except for once or twice when the elderly lady asked a question, and everyone looked up from their books or knitting to contribute. The train made a few stops along the way, and everyone got off to stretch their legs.

Then at last, late in the afternoon, Aunt Millicent's head began to nod again, and she went out like a wet candle.

Annabelle glanced across at the other lady, who had also fallen asleep. Then she found herself smiling eagerly at Mr. Edwards, who had just set his book down. He leaned forward and rested his elbows on his knees, clasping his large hands together in front of him.

With breath held, Annabelle waited for him to say something, but he took his time before he raised a finger and gestured for her to come closer. She quivered beneath the teasing glimmer in his seductive, dark eyes.

Laying her book down as well, Annabelle leaned forward. She and Mr. Edwards swayed from side to side with the rocking of the train, their faces only inches apart. His eyes roamed from the top of her head to her nose and lips, then to her frizzy hair and purple hat.

She studied his face, too—his strong cheek-bones, the shadow of stubble along his jaw and chin, and the depths of his dark eyes. She gazed at him with more than an artist's appreciation for male beauty. She was just a woman now, and he was so impossibly handsome in her eyes, it hurt just to look at him . . .

At last he spoke, in a low, husky voice, almost a whisper. Just the sound of it made Annabelle's skin tingle deliciously with gooseflesh.

"How daring are you?" he asked.

Annabelle swallowed, shocked by the spell he'd cast over her—there was no other word for it—and she couldn't believe her own blatant disregard for the concept of consequences. She felt as if she would blindly follow this man to the door and jump off the train into a slimy green swamp if he suggested it. If it meant she could be alone with him for just five minutes.

That scared her a little.

"What do you have in mind?" she asked never-theless, curious, while at the same time struggling to hold tight to her common sense, murky as it was at the present moment.

He hesitated before he began to explain in a

quiet voice. "Miss Lawson, all day I've been dreading the moment we'll have to get off this train."

"So have I," she blurted out, before she had a chance to think rationally.

The two ladies were snoring beside them. Nevertheless, Mr. Edwards quickly confirmed their lowered lids before he reached for Annabelle's gloved hand, turned it over, then slid his fingers up to the sensitive inside of her bare wrist. With the tip of his finger, he drew tiny feathery circles over the delicate blue veins . . .

Annabelle's body went weak from his touch. She had never been so quickly enamored with a man before, nor had she ever experienced the true, aching cadence of lust. She had not understood its power.

"I can't let you go," he whispered, "knowing I will never see you again. Meet me somewhere. Anywhere. Could you do that?"

Annabelle panicked as she considered it. What he was suggesting was beyond improper, yet she wanted it with urgent desperation.

"Do you mean alone? I'm not sure that would be . . ." She didn't know what to say next.

He hesitated, then bowed his head and shook it. "I'm sorry, Miss Lawson. I'm tactless. Of course it's not ·possible to meet alone, and you should throw me off the train for even thinking such a thing." He looked up, his eyes apologetic. "Forgive me. Is there another way?"

Staring into his dark, passionate eyes, she found herself leaning suddenly toward caution. Attractive though he was, he was still a stranger, and she found herself questioning his integrity. Was he testing how far he could go with her? And when he'd sensed her reluctance—because she was a well-bred young lady—was that the only reason he was retreating, and behaving slightly more respectably?

Perhaps he made a habit of taking advantage of young women he met on trains. Perhaps he only wanted to steal her overstuffed reticule.

Aunt Millicent twitched and snorted.

Annabelle immediately pulled her hand out of Mr. Edwards's grasp, as anxiety cooled her thoughts. She was being rushed into a decision. Her aunt could awaken at any moment . . .

Which was why she answered so quickly, whispering, "Perhaps somewhere we could be properly introduced."

Though she didn't know why she should even bother with such a formality. Even if this man's intentions were honorable, her aunt would never encourage such a match. She was very ambitious. Aunt Millicent knew Annabelle would have a substantial dowry, thanks to her generous brother, Whitby, and she was searching among the aristocracy for a husband for Annabelle. Even though Annabelle was not truly one of them.

"Where?" Mr. Edwards asked, staring intently at her. "A shop perhaps. But no, what would be the point? We'd only say hello and good-bye again."

Annabelle experienced a sudden flash of fear. Indeed, what *would* be the point in seeing him again, unless she intended to defy her family and run away with him and live the modest life of a bank clerk's wife?

Oh, good gracious. She was getting ahead of herself. She'd met a handsome man on a train. She'd known him only a few hours, and already she was plotting an elopement, despite the fact that she was slightly wary and had just wondered if he wanted to steal her reticule. She had best regain control of her senses.

"Perhaps it's not a good idea," she said. "I couldn't deceive my aunt that way."

His gaze fell upon Millicent for a long moment before he nodded, almost in defeat. He leaned back. "Of course. You're right. I shouldn't have suggested it."

She recognized the disappointment in his eyes. He was surrendering to the reality of their situation—that he was not a suitable acquaintance for her—and all Annabelle's suspicions about his integrity fell away, because she felt positively beastly over the direction this was heading. She had enjoyed their conversation so very much. He *was* the kind of man she would wish to know. He was intelligent, polite and interesting, not to forget handsome and exciting—so much more so than all the young lords she'd been dancing with of late. She did not wish him to think she considered him beneath her. She did not. But her family would certainly not support any—

Just then the steam whistle blew and Aunt Millicent sat straight up, eyes wide. Annabelle sucked in a breath, while Mr. Edwards calmly turned his head toward the window.

"What time is it?" Millicent asked, looking around, confused.

"It's just past three," Annabelle replied.

"I think I fell asleep for a few minutes."

"Did you?"

Annabelle struggled to smile casually at her aunt. She and Mr. Edwards glanced briefly at one another.

"We should be arriving soon," Millicent said, running a hand over her hair, patting down some untucked strands. "Thank goodness. It was a rather tedious trip, don't you think?"

"Yes, Auntie," Annabelle lied.

In a matter of minutes the train was slowing down, but Annabelle's heart was racing faster and faster, for she was about to disembark and never see Mr. Edwards again. She had just rejected him, and surely he was under the impression that she did not wish to see him again, that she did not trust him, nor find him interesting or appealing.

Though she did not know him well enough to trust him, she certainly *did* find him appealing, in every possible way.

With the slow lumbering of the locomotive and the noisy screech of the brakes, Annabelle felt more and more as if the walls of the train were closing in on her. She was running out of time, and soon she would have to say good-bye to Mr. Edwards for good.

If that happened, she knew she would always wonder what would have become of them if they'd had more time to get to know each other . . .

Aunt Millicent leaned forward and shouted to the older lady, "We're pulling into the station!"

The woman jumped and awakened. "Oh, we're here, are we? Thank you, dear." She reached shakily for her cane.

Annabelle was breathing hard now. This was it. They would be getting off in a few short minutes.

She glanced across at Mr. Edwards. He returned her steady gaze.

"Don't forget your book," Aunt Millicent said, picking it up off the seat and handing it to Annabelle.

"Does anyone see my pen?" the older lady

asked, appearing flustered as she searched around her seat. "My grandson gave it to me. Did it fall on the floor?"

Everyone leaned forward to look. Then Annabelle was struck by a thought. Well, not so much of a thought. It was more of an involuntary action. She reached into her own reticule for her pen and sketch pad, and while everyone was distracted by the older lady's panic, she scribbled something on a small corner of the pad and ripped it out.

The pen was soon located by Mr. Edwards, who had spotted it under Aunt Millicent's feet. Annabelle quickly crumpled the note in her hand.

She knew she was doing something rash and imprudent, but she couldn't help herself. She could not get off this train and say good-bye forever to Mr. Edwards. She could not explain it. She simply had to see him again, even if it was only to discover he was an unscrupulous character. At least then she would know.

A short time later the train screeched to a halt at the station and they all stood.

"It was a pleasure traveling with you," the older lady said to Annabelle and Aunt Millicent.

"Indeed it was," Millicent replied.

One of the uniformed guards opened the door and helped the elderly lady down first, and as soon as Millicent took the first step down, Annabelle turned and discreetly slipped her crumpled note into Mr. Edwards's hand.

He glanced up, surprised at first, then his eyes filled instantly with a flirtatious spark of understanding that sent Annabelle's senses whirling. He held her for a moment in the pounding allure of his gaze.

That instant, she knew she *had* to see him again. She simply *had* to, and she prayed he would understand what she had written in the note and would not let her down.

Physically wrenching herself away, she turned for the door, seizing the opportunity to steal just one more backward glance at him before she left the train.

Magnus watched Miss Lawson walk the length of the platform until she was gone from view, then he immediately opened the tiny, crumpled note and read it.

Bloody hell . . .

He stuffed the note into his breast pocket.

What had he done? What the devil was wrong with him?

Sitting forward, he dropped his head into his hands, raking his fingers through his hair. He could never have her. Never, never, never. She came from that *world*. She lived with—and loved—the very people he despised, the people who despised him equally in return.

He still could barely comprehend that she was one of them, because she was so undeniably different, and for most of the day he had practically forgotten the connection. He supposed he'd been distracted by the shining, disturbingly lovely blue of her eyes.

Magnus sat back again and gazed with weariness out the window at the mulling crowd on the platform. The uniformed guard blew his whistle, signaling that it was time to depart.

This was a wretched predicament indeed, he thought, recalling the pleasure of stroking her slender wrist and the *dis*pleasure of having to resist touching his lips to it.

His actions had been beyond reproach, to say the least, but he hadn't been able to stop himself.

No, he should not see her again. He should not, for on top of everything, he had lied to her about who he was.

The best thing to do was put her from his mind. Forcefully. Permanently. He was a strong man. He could do it.

But as the train pulled away from the station, damned if he wasn't thinking about her luscious full lips again, and feeling most inconveniently aroused.

Chapter 3

1892

Struggling to banish such painful memories of her unforgettable first love, Annabelle gazed upward at the swaying branches of the oak tree and listened to the leaves fluttering in the wind. She covered her face with both hands.

A lump formed in her throat. She swallowed hard over it, trying to suppress it, but couldn't, because it had been years since she'd recalled that day in such vivid detail, when she had met Magnus for the first time on the train.

Yes, that had been his real name. It had not been John Edwards, as he'd led her to believe.

These days, she only remembered the unpleasant things about Magnus, because she had forced herself to forget the way he had made her feel when she first met him. Forced herself to forget how handsome he had been, how charming and polite with the elderly lady, and how her body had responded to him.

He had awakened every passion that existed within her, when she had not even known she possessed such passions to begin with. She had never been in love before.

Nor since. It had been thirteen long years, and she was a woman now—an experienced, sensible woman—no longer the girl who had stepped on a train believing in love and romance and the private mate of one's soul. Those beliefs had been very dangerous, and had set her up for a tremendously painful and damaging fall . . .

She dropped her hands to her sides and squeezed the cool, green grass between her fingers. It hurt to remember all this. Why was she doing it? Because she knew she would have to see him again?

His letter angered her suddenly. Why was he

back here, thinking he could write to her as if none of it had happened?

Well, it *had* happened . . . all the lies and betrayals.

She rolled over onto her stomach and rested her chin on her hands. She watched a bee land in a patch of clover a few feet away. The bee collected some nectar, then buzzed away, searching for more.

Annabelle inhaled the scents of the grass and earth, so close to her nose. She closed her eyes and again thought of the letter in her pocket. She also thought of the first one he'd written a few weeks ago, when he arrived in London, which she had not answered. It was locked away in the cedar box in her desk . . .

She could feel the key to the box, which she wore on a long chain around her neck inside a locket, pressing uncomfortably between her breasts.

Annabelle sighed and rolled over onto her back again. She had started something today with these memories, and somehow she knew that if she were going to see him again, she would need to remember everything, especially how he had hurt her. She could not forget that. She would need to strengthen her guard.

So she forced herself to go back to the two excruciating weeks that had followed that first day on the train, the weeks she had spent longing to see Mr. Edwards—*Magnus*—again. She had thought of nothing but his face and his hands and the sound of his voice. She had dreamed of being reunited with him, being held in his arms, and finally running away with him.

Oh, she had been so young and innocent . . .

Paintings

Chapter 4

August 1879

The crumpled up note Annabelle had placed in Mr. Edwards's hand had said:

> *National Gallery*
> *Two weeks, 2 P.M.*
> *Dupre*

The day had finally come.

There she stood, pacing back and forth in front of Dupre's painting, while her brother Whitby was elsewhere in the gallery, moving along at his own pace.

Whitby and Annabelle had come here many times in the past, and thankfully he had learned to give her time alone to admire the art. Which was why she had chosen this place.

Annabelle checked her timepiece, praying Mr. Edwards had understood what her note meant and would be able to find her. Her heart began to pound when she noted the time. It was two P.M. She nervously glanced around at the other patrons.

Oh, she hated this. She hated worrying that he would not come, or that he had met another young lady on another train and forgotten all about her, while she had spent the past two weeks dreaming of nothing but him.

She anxiously squeezed her reticule in her hand. The wretched truth was that what she felt for Mr. Edwards two weeks ago had proliferated into an ardent, sweeping desire more powerful than anything she'd ever known. She had butterflies in her belly constantly, and was either deliriously happy with the dream that he, too, was missing her, or was inconsolably miserable, thinking she would never see him again.

The logical part of her brain realized that perhaps she had begun to idealize him. She was probably romanticizing their conversations and overestimating the level of desire he felt for *her*.

Yet she could not stop herself from believing that she loved him, like no woman had ever loved before.

She chuckled rather bitterly, finding some humor in the fact that she was finally grasping what the poets had been going on about for centuries.

An older couple wandered into the room, and Annabelle made an effort to look as if she were just another gallery patron, admiring the paintings at her leisure. She stood before the Dupre, staring at it: *Willows, with a Man Fishing*.

It was not a large painting. It was not even twelve inches wide, but it was a good choice for today—rather brilliant in its romanticism, she had to admit. It was a painting she wanted very much to show Mr. Edwards. She wanted to explain that the Barbizon style was very different from the way she painted, and if she were ever to paint him in his boat the way they had discussed on the train, she would approach the trees and the water very differently.

Though that took nothing away from how she felt about this painting. She had always admired it for its quietness and intimacy.

She turned away from the Dupre, glancing discreetly around the room, hearing only the echoed sounds of a woman's heels as she walked quickly through another room, and the whispers of the other patrons quietly discussing the works of art.

It was ten minutes past two.

Annabelle tapped her gloved hand upon her thigh. She was beginning to lose hope. He wasn't going to come.

No, she mustn't jump to conclusions. He was only ten minutes late. He could be dashing up the front steps of the gallery at this very instant, as eager to finally see her as she was to see him.

She took a deep, steadying breath. Oh, how she yearned to see him. She was growing tired of picturing him in her mind. She wanted the real man—tall and strong and smiling at her. She wanted so badly to be alone with him right now . . .

And so it was that two more hours passed, every minute painstakingly slow, and when a man finally entered the room where the Dupre was located and spoke Annabelle's name with affection, she was barely able to keep the tears from her eyes. Tears of disappointment, heartbreak, anger. For the man coming to fetch her and take her home was her brother, Whitby.

Over the next fortnight, Annabelle grew to despise the Dupre painting, each day hating it more than the last. She didn't want to think about it; she was irritated on the days Cook served fish for dinner, and most of all, she was angry with herself for becoming so deeply infatuated with a man who had evidently toyed with her feelings and taken some perverse pleasure in leading her to believe there was something special between them, when there was no such thing.

She had fallen victim to the charms of a thoughtless man, who no doubt flirted with every woman he stumbled across and had probably ruined more than his fair share of young innocents. He probably had a whole host of illegitimate children, too. Maybe he wasn't even a bank clerk. Maybe he was one of those confidence men. Or worse good heavens—a stage actor.

She held firmly to the certain belief that he was a rake of the worst kind, until on the fifteenth day there was a surprise waiting for her in the formal gardens at her country house in Bedfordshire—that surprise being Mr. Edwards himself.

Annabelle had taken a walk to be alone, and lo and behold, there he was, waiting for her beyond the tall lilac hedge, leaning at his ease against one of the columns of the open rotunda.

Heart throbbing suddenly in her chest, she stopped dead in her tracks, not quite ready to believe she was seeing properly. But then he pushed away from the column, removed his hat and held it at his side, and she knew it was really him.

He was wearing the same black jacket and trousers he had worn on the train. He looked exactly the same, just how she remembered him, tall and handsome and so darkly appealing.

Annabelle struggled to comprehend what she was feeling. One part of her wanted to stick her nose in the air and storm off, for she was so angry with him for not being there to meet her that day in the gallery.

But another part of her was melting into a puddle of forgiveness right here on the grass, because he had found her. He had come all the way to her brother's country house. He had not forgotten her. Perhaps he'd had a good reason not to be there that day. She had certainly considered that over the past two weeks, but found it easier and safer to presume otherwise, for she had not wished to continue pining away for a man she would most likely never see again.

But here he was . . .

Magnus held his hat in a firm grip, his breath ragged, his mind in turmoil. It had been a full month since he'd seen Miss Lawson, and part of him had hoped that when he came here today, her effect on him might have diminished.

But no, it had not. Seeing her now in her clumsy black boots and wildly knotted hair—her eyes as vivid and piercing as he remembered—sent him dangerously out of control with wanting her.

He knew then, with devastating certainty, that he had failed in his valiant struggle to forget her.

"Miss Lawson," he said in an apologetic tone, because any fool could have seen she was angry with him. "Hello."

When she made no greeting in reply, he cut straight to the point. "I came to tell you I'm sorry . . . For not being at the gallery that day."

At least part of it was true. He *was* sorry. Sorry for disappointing her.

But the truth was—he *had* been there. Unfortunately, Whitby had been there, too, so Magnus had been forced to retreat in order to avoid a confrontation with his enemy.

Not that he feared confrontations with Whitby. He could handle himself, and there might even be a very serious confrontation about Annabelle sometime in the near future. In fact, over the past two weeks Magnus had begun to dream about it. He'd never been more determined to take what he wanted from his powerful, influential cousin, who had always enjoyed keeping him in his place.

Because this time what Magnus wanted was Miss Lawson.

Blood quickening in his veins, he slowly, cautiously, approached her as if she were a deer who might bolt at any second.

Finally she spoke, her expression cool and stern. "I waited for two hours."

He nodded, because he knew how long she had waited. "I swear to you, I wanted to be there. I thought of nothing else after we parted on the train. I was counting the days until I could see you again, but on my way to meet you, I . . ."

"You what?"

He narrowed his gaze, considering whether he should speak the truth and tell her his real name, after tearing himself apart about it for the past month.

I withdrew because my name is Magnus, and I am Whitby's cousin. The one he loathes. Why am I loathed, you ask? Because I am my father's son, and surely you've heard the disturbing stories about my father's madness . . .

He tried to imagine her response. She would probably be aghast. She would run back to the house and call out the dogs.

Just then he experienced a twinge in his stomach—that old familiar shame and agony from his childhood, when he had been rejected and spat upon in the streets by those who knew that he and his father were banished by an earl. He'd been called a lunatic. A son of the devil.

No, he couldn't tell her. Not now, when he was standing on thin ice to begin with . . .

"I had concerns," he tried to explain, struggling

to choose his words carefully, while pushing all thoughts of his childhood to the back of his mind.

Suddenly he was aware of nothing but the need to conquer, to hasten forth into an overrun battlefield, swinging his sword at an oncoming charge of enemy soldiers. He would do anything to have her—to win her heart and take her for his own.

Swallowing hard, forcing his brain to formulate the right words so as not to scare her off, he continued what he had begun to say. "I had concerns about our situation. I'm not someone your family would approve of."

It was the truth.

Annabelle stared uncertainly at him, her freckled cheeks flushing pink as she wet her full lips, until Magnus couldn't resist her anymore. He'd been having erotic dreams about this woman for a month, and here she was at last, standing before him in the flesh. She was a unique, beguiling beauty, a sweet, ripe maiden, and he simply had to touch her.

Moving closer, he raised her gloved hand to his lips and gently kissed each knuckle. Somehow, she would belong to him. No matter what it took.

Annabelle did not pull her hand away. She stood motionless, watching the top of Mr. Edwards's head while he dropped leisurely kisses across the back of her hand. His lips were soft and tantalizing. She could feel the moist heat of his breath through the thin fabric of her glove.

She had to scramble to keep her head, for her body was aching and burning to be even closer to him, to step into his arms and feel his chest pressing against her breasts. She felt dizzy, intoxicated by something far more potent than wine.

Somehow, however, she managed to withstand the pounding force of her desires. She could not give into those feelings, not so easily when she was still hurt by his failure to meet her that day, and she still knew so little about him.

A moment later he gazed intently into her eyes. "I wish you would speak, Miss Lawson."

"I don't know what to say. I was very disappointed when you did not come."

Something in his manner changed. His eyes glimmered with a sensual light and his voice softened, like a caress. "I wanted to see you, but there was another far more serious problem."

"What was that?" she asked, feeling shaky with longing.

"I wanted only to be alone with you, and I was plotting ways to steal you away and take you home with me—to my bed."

His bed.

Annabelle knew she should have been scandalized. He had said something very wicked, something no gentleman should ever say to a well-bred young lady like Annabelle Lawson.

But surprisingly, she was not scandalized, because it filled her with a strange inner excitement that caused a passionate fluttering in her belly. And if she was understanding him correctly, he had not shown up that day because he had wanted her *too much*, and had not trusted himself to resist her.

Forgiving him today was suddenly becoming very probable.

"Why did you wait until now to tell me this?" she asked, nevertheless. "I've just spent the past two weeks thinking all kinds of hateful things— like how many ways there are to push a man like you out of a fishing boat."

He looked down at her hand in his and rubbed his thumb over her knuckles. "You had every right to be angry with me, and I probably deserve to swim with the fish." He hesitated a moment before continuing in a quieter voice that was almost a whisper. "To be frank, Miss Lawson, I wasn't *ever* going to tell you. I was never going to see you again, because I wanted to do the right thing. I didn't want to complicate your life. I am not from your world, remember."

It was true, and she had known it would be complicated. He was not the kind of man her brother or aunt would accept as a husband for her, despite the fact that her parents were who they were. Whitby considered her his sister, and he was an earl.

"We could have been friends," she said.

"Do you really think so? You and me?" He shook his head. "Even if we could be, I believe I would rather pound my forehead against a brick wall than spend every day trying to resist kissing you, then God forbid, congratulate you, while I watched another man take you as his wife."

Annabelle shook inwardly. Was he really saying all this? They barely knew each other. No man had ever spoken so candidly to her before.

Mr. Edwards was either impossibly rakish and arrogant, or he was utterly and hopelessly in love with her.

She placed an open hand on her chest. This did not seem real. She felt as if she were standing in the pages of a fairy tale. It was certainly magical enough.

Except that he was, unfortunately, not a prince.

"I don't know what to make of you," she said, stepping onto the cement floor of the rotunda and walking to its center. "You say you want to do the right thing, yet here you are, skulking around in my garden, telling me you wanted to take me to your bed."

Still holding his hat in his hand, he followed her into the shade of the tiny sanctuary and leaned a shoulder against one of the columns. "I'm afraid you're right. I've behaved deplorably, but only because I've lost my bloody mind over you. And that, my dear, is the truth."

She turned to face him. He was gazing at her with blinding charismatic splendor, confidently amorous, as if he wanted to unbutton her bodice and thought she might be of a mind to let him do it.

Heavens above, he *was* arrogant, but it stirred her blood like nothing she'd ever known.

"Mr. Edwards," she said very primly, lifting her chin and squaring her shoulders, "will you not even *try* to disguise the fact that you are attempting to seduce me?"

She couldn't help it—her lips betrayed her with a hint of a smile. And she had been trying so hard to be properly virtuous . . .

He grinned at her in return, and with a sharply honed, animal-like instinct she couldn't even begin to fathom, he seemed to perceive her willingness to flirt. Somehow, instinctively, he knew she was surrendering to him.

But she supposed he was surrendering to her, too, for even she, in all her innocence, could not have missed the unmistakable spark that had flared between them from the first moment they'd made eye contact on the train. It had been blazing hotter every day since, hot enough to make him leave London for the countryside, just to see her again. In secret. She quivered with pleasure at the thought of it.

"Seduce you," he said, narrowing his eyes, as if he was pondering such a suggestion for the first time. "I suppose I am, but I simply cannot help myself. You are so very enticing." He took a step away from the column and sauntered toward her. "This is all very wicked, isn't it? I'll wager right now you're wishing you'd never met me."

"No, that's not what I'm wishing," she replied, revealing the truth without caring about the inappropriateness of it, or the consequences.

Then she strove to be sensible. She had never behaved like this in her life. "You know . . . I should return to the house, because this *is* wicked, and I should not be out here with you."

But she probably couldn't leave if she tried. Her feet were stuck to the ground.

"No, don't go," he said.

They were both breathing hard now. "But I feel nervous all of a sudden."

He moved forward, closing the last small distance between them, disarming her with his dazzling sexual brawn. "Do you indeed?"

She considered it a moment. "To be honest, I'm not sure. Perhaps what I'm feeling is not nervousness, but rather . . ."

Oh, she didn't know what it was.

"Excitement?" he suggested.

She wet her trembling lips. "I'm not entirely sure."

With a slow smile, he backed her up against the column and rested a forearm against it, just over her head. Her heart was pounding like a drum now, so fast she thought it was going to bounce right out of her chest.

He brushed his forefinger across her temple and leaned in close, whispering in her ear, "Have you never been excited by a man before?"

She swallowed, finding it increasingly difficult to breathe. "Only once, by a man on a train."

He smiled at that, his face now barely an inch away. She could feel his breath on the tip of her nose.

"Are you flirting with me, Miss Lawson?" he asked in a husky voice that gave her shivers.

Her knees were going weak. They might as well be made of cream. She closed her eyes. "I don't know. Am I?"

Yes, she was. To pretend otherwise would be futile, for her body was tingling with a thousand sensations she couldn't begin to understand.

Was this normal? Was it normal to feel so instantly aroused and enraptured by a man you barely knew? A man who was completely unsuitable for you?

"I think you are," he said with a hint of amusement, his whisper a hot, moist breath on her lips.

She'd been kissed only once before in her life—

by a naughty young man when she was sixteen. He'd surprised her and stolen the kiss behind the stable, then ran away. His lips had been cold from the winter air, and tightly puckered. That had been a swift, unexpected kiss that she giggled about afterward.

This was nothing like that. Mr. Edwards was not trying to surprise her. He was preparing her, teasing her and patiently drawing out the intensity of the moment. She could feel the heat of his lips already, as he brushed the tip of his nose lightly like a feather over her cheeks.

He *was* going to kiss her. She knew it, and she wanted him to. No amount of propriety or common sense could keep her from letting him do it.

He touched his nose to hers and gently whispered, "Miss Lawson, since I met you, I haven't been able to stop thinking of you, though I've certainly tried, and I anticipate this situation is going to become exceedingly complicated."

"Yes," she replied.

"If you are not completely certain of your feelings for me, tell me now and I will go. I'll walk away and I'll never bother you again. But if you truly want this as much as I do, then you must be prepared for a difficult time."

He pulled back slightly to allow her a moment to think about it, but he was still leaning that strong arm on the column over her head. His hand was relaxed, bent at the wrist, his finger still playing in the loose hair at her temple.

She knew she should be contemplating the issue at hand and what the future would hold—but all she could feel was the magnificent bliss of his body so close to hers.

"I can't tell you to go," she said. "I know I should, but I can't. Not today."

For a long moment he gazed into her eyes, as if *he* were still contemplating it, attempting to convince himself he should leave, regardless of her response just now. Then he looked down at her moist lips.

She waited, breath held, heart thundering in her ears. Reason and logic floated away. All that existed in her mind was the awareness of need—a fierce, fiery need . . .

Then at last his lips found hers in a hot, wet, open-mouthed kiss that sent an erotic yearning straight down to her core. His full lips parted hers. His tongue swept smoothly into her mouth—probing, plunging ever so slowly and gently. The kiss was soft and sensuous, and he groaned huskily at the pleasure of it.

He leaned into her at the same moment his arms came down and slid around her waist. Annabelle made no conscious movements. Everything was instinctive, as if her body had a separate mind of its own. Her arms wrapped around his neck and somehow her lips knew exactly how to kiss him.

Her hips knew how to push against his, and her hands knew how to travel down the firm muscles of his back and pull him even closer.

He brought the kiss to a gradual finish, drawing his lips from hers but maintaining the intimate link of their bodies.

"Now I'm done for," he whispered, caressing her cheek with a finger.

"So am I. My heart is racing. What are we going to do?"

He rested his forehead upon hers. "I have no idea. Perhaps you should think further about this."

"I don't need to think. I just want to see you again."

"Your brother would never approve."

"Let me deal with that when the time comes. If it comes."

His body went still. "You think he'd be reasonable?"

Annabelle recognized the doubt in his voice. She detected a hint of bitterness as well. He did not believe there was hope.

"My brother cares for me very deeply," she explained. "He wants me to be happy."

But in all honesty, she was not sure he would permit her to marry someone like Mr. Edwards. Whitby would surely think him a very shrewd fortune hunter who was greatly overstepping society's bounds.

Mr. Edwards stepped back, looking almost ashamed of himself for doing something he knew he should not be doing. He seemed to be wrestling with the idea that he was taking something he had no right to take, and he looked almost guilt-ridden.

Annabelle took his face in both her hands. "Meet me at the lake tomorrow. There's a boat at the north end. We'll take it to the island and have lunch there."

"You can get away like that?" he asked, still looking doubtful.

She began to worry that he would change his mind again and fail to appear, that he would leave her waiting like he had at the gallery. He seemed so very hesitant.

"I'll bring my paint box and a canvas," she replied, finding herself willing to take the risk. "No one will expect me back for hours."

He turned his back on her and walked to the other side of the rotunda, staring off into the distance, at the lush green hills and dense forests. "This is a beautiful place."

Annabelle swallowed hard over a lump of apprehension that had risen in her throat. There was something melancholy in Mr. Edwards's voice, and she feared she would not see him again after today. She couldn't let that happen.

She crossed to stand beside him. "Yes, it is. I've been very happy here, but it doesn't mean everything to me."

He shifted his gaze to her upturned face. "It should. You're lucky to have lived a life like this, to have had so much. Not everyone is so blessed."

She was more than aware of that, and felt guilty for being disloyal to her brother, who had done so much for her. Yet she could not turn away from this.

Mr. Edwards shook his head. "This is insane. You know that, don't you?"

"Yes, I know it, but I don't care. I've only ever been frustrated with my life as it is anyway." Again she felt guilty for saying such things when she had been given so much, but she wanted so very badly to be free, even just for a day.

He chuckled softly, almost bitterly. "I don't quite understand that, but I certainly admire your spirit."

"Does that mean you'll be there tomorrow?"

Placing his hat back on his head, he faced her. "What time?"

She breathed a sigh of relief. "Two o'clock. But you had best not keep me waiting. I won't forgive you a second time."

She started to back away, but he caught her

hand. With a seductive glint in his eye, he said, "One more kiss."

Annabelle grinned mischievously. "Not until tomorrow."

"Is that your way of making sure I'll be there?"

"Maybe. Or maybe I just don't *want* to kiss you."

Still holding her hand while she leaned away from him, tugging, he looked at her as if he were completely besotted, and Annabelle's heart leaped with delight and a burning impatience for the next day.

He smiled and placed his hand on his chest, as if she'd shot an arrow straight into his heart. "You're killing me."

She dashed forward, rose up on her toes and kissed him quickly on the cheek. "There. Now go. Sneak out of here before someone sees you."

He followed her to the edge of the rotunda and leaned against a column again, watching her leave. "Don't worry. I'll be very sneaky."

And not really understanding the hidden truths in that statement, Annabelle darted excitedly back to the house.

Chapter 5

~~~OCO~~~

"**Y**ou didn't keep me waiting this time," Annabelle said as she emerged from the path through the woods and spotted Mr. Edwards already sitting in the rowboat, which was tied to the small dock. He sat on the floor of the boat, leaning his elbows on the transom seat, his hands relaxed at the wrists. He looked as if he'd been there for a while.

"You said you wouldn't forgive me a second time, so I was careful not to be late," he replied. He rose and stepped onto the dock, the boat rocking and dipping as he did so.

Annabelle stopped on the grassy bank, feeling her breath catch in her throat at the full sight of him. Wearing that familiar black jacket and trousers, he looked every bit as striking and manly, walking toward her with a wickedly flirtatious glimmer in his eye.

He reached her on the bank, his appreciative gaze gliding smoothly down her body as he took the easel and paint box out of her hands. "You carried this here on your own?"

Heart already atwitter from the aura of his sexually charged appeal, Annabelle was acutely aware of his fingers brushing over hers and how it made her skin tingle. "I'm used to it. I carry these everywhere."

She also wore a lunch sack strapped across her chest, so while he placed her painting supplies in the boat, she lifted the sack over her head. "I brought sandwiches, and I even snuck a bottle of wine from the cellar."

He turned to face her, his head snapping back in surprise. "My word, I hadn't taken you for such an adventurer, Miss Lawson. Do you *like* to take risks?"

"To tell you the truth, I never get the chance."

He walked toward her again—his dark, seductive eyes never veering from hers—and took the lunch sack out of her hands.

He raised a doubtful eyebrow. "I find that hard to believe."

His voice was laced with deliciously wicked teasing, and his look was so electrifying, Annabelle felt a rush of pink stain her cheeks.

How in the world was she going to survive this without having a nervous fit?

After he set everything in the boat, he looked out across the lake. "That's the island?"

Annabelle raised a hand to shade her eyes. "Yes. There's a good spot to drag the boat onto the beach on the other side."

"Right, then." He held out a hand and led her down the length of the dock, then assisted her into the boat.

"You brought your fishing gear," she said, noticing the rod and creel as she sat down. "Can you show me how it's done?"

"That was the idea." Mr. Edwards untied the boat and stepped in with remarkable agility. Then he sat down, picked up the oars and glanced over his shoulder before starting to row.

Annabelle sat quietly watching him steer the boat, listening to the sounds of the water lapping up against the sides and the oars creaking in the oarlocks. She could feel the boat propelled forward with each strong, swift stroke.

As soon as he had them slicing through the water in a straight line, he focused his attention on Annabelle, and they watched each other in silence. For her, it was a strangely erotic moment, as they were staring unreservedly at one another, studying faces and eyes and lips, feeling no need to look away.

Annabelle had never stared at anyone like that before. In any other situation, it would not be considered polite, but this was like no other situation she'd ever been in. She was here with this man outside of all rules and social graces. She was here out of sheer natural desire, and no one—*no one*—knew they were together.

"Did you come from London this morning?" she asked when they reached the center of the lake, where the water was deep.

He was still rowing fast and hard, his big hands gripping the oar handles tightly, the muscles of his shoulders straining. "Yes. I caught the early train."

"And you'll take the train back tonight?"

He nodded. "I have to be at my desk at nine tomorrow morning."

He had to be at his desk . . .

"I'm trying to imagine you at work," she said. "Do you talk to many people? Do you arrange loans?"

He looked over his shoulder again to see how much farther they had to go. "No, I work with numbers. I record figures, balance deposits, that sort of thing."

"Do you enjoy it?"

"Not really."

Annabelle's brow furrowed as she digested the flatness of his reply. She shook her head at him. "Why do you do something you don't enjoy? Why not try something else?"

He looked over his shoulder again. "I need the income," he said bluntly, seeming strangely distant.

"Yes, but you never considered being a fisherman, for instance?"

"I enjoy fishing too much," he said. "I wouldn't want to turn it into work."

He stopped rowing and pushed forward on the oars to slow the boat in the middle of the lake. His subtle aloofness from a moment ago faded away. "This looks like a good spot, if you'd like to give it a go before lunch."

"Give it a go?" Annabelle asked, suggestively raising an eyebrow.

He reached for his fishing pole, which was lying flat along the side of the boat, and smirked at her. "That's enough flirting, Miss Lawson, if you please. I'm going to teach you how to fish. Hold this."

She chuckled while he handed the rod to her, then reached past her to drop the anchor over the transom.

"I hope you won't mind baiting the hook. Do worms bother you?"

Annabelle gazed blankly at him for a moment, until he faced her again with a smile.

"I was teasing," he said. "I'll handle that part."

He reached for a small tin box with a lid, opened it and showed Annabelle what was inside.

"Very appetizing," she said, looking at a mass of squirming worms in a pit of dark earth.

He reached for the rod, which Annabelle handed over. "Watch out, the hook is sharp." Then he proceeded to harpoon a most unfortunate wiggly worm. Annabelle made a face, which Mr. Edwards seemed to find amusing. "You wanted me to show you," he said teasingly, as if to say *I told you so.*

"Yes, I did, didn't I? What could I have been thinking?"

Mr. Edwards wound the reel, then cast his line in an arc, sending the hook and worm sailing through the air. They plopped onto the water's surface, and he wound the reel again. As soon as he had everything set up, he passed the rod to her.

"Hold it right here. Both hands."

She took the rod and wrapped her hands around the well-worn cork handle. Feeling rather silly, just sitting there holding the rod, she glanced wryly at him. "Now what do I do?"

"Reel it in slowly to drag the bait. Not too fast."

Annabelle followed his instructions.

"Look, there's a falcon," Mr. Edwards quietly said, pointing over the treetops on the other side of the lake.

"I see him. Look how graceful he is."

They smiled at each other, and Annabelle felt like she was floating, until Mr. Edwards touched the rod. "You can jiggle it every now and again, like this. That's right. Now reel it in a little more."

"How will I know if I've caught one?" she asked, struggling to focus on the matter at hand.

"You'll know. You'll feel it."

She continued to slowly bring the hook back to the boat, and when it came out of the water, there was no fish, nor was there a worm swinging on the line.

"Where did he go?"

"He appears to have made his escape." Mr. Edwards reached for the line and speared another worm on the hook. "Would you like to cast this time?"

"I'd love to."

"All right, let me see . . ."

The boat rocked as he leaned forward and reeled the hook up to the end of the rod. Then his large, warm hands curled around hers. Annabelle felt a quivering of excitement in her belly, just from his nearness. He was so much of a man, so strong and capable. She remembered the intoxicating sensation of his lips touching hers the day before, and wondered with fiery anticipation if he would kiss her again today.

"Hold it here," he said, seemingly unaware of

her thoughts about his lips. "Then tip it back, but be careful not to snag your clothing. That's it. Now swing the rod forward so the hook goes as far as you can cast it."

She did as he instructed, hearing the whizzing sound of the reel spinning and the line slicing through the air, then the quiet splash of the hook and bait as it hit the water.

"Well done," he said softly. "Now bring it in like you did last time and—"

Just then, the rod tugged in Annabelle's hands, and a sprightly thrill zipped up her spine. "I think I caught something!"

The rod was pulling and bending and she began to squeal. "What do I do?"

"Reel it in!" he said, laughing.

"Oh!" She panicked and began winding the reel at an alarmingly fast pace, and the rod continued to tug and pull in her hands. "Oh, my goodness! Here!"

Before she knew what she was about, she was trying to pass the rod back to Mr. Edwards.

"You're doing fine!" he said, raising both hands in front of him. "Just keep reeling."

She squealed again, and suddenly, the fish at the end of the line flew up out of the water and flopped around in the air. Annabelle was swinging the rod back and forth in all directions, and the boat was rocking. "Help!"

Mr. Edwards laughed and finally took the rod from her. A brief second later the fish was in the boat, bouncing around while Annabelle was still screaming. The fish flopped onto her feet until Mr. Edwards finally grabbed hold of him.

"It's a perch—and a dodgy one at that."

Hands braced on the seat, Annabelle met his gaze. They stared at each other intensely before they both burst out laughing.

"I thought you said fishing was a relaxing affair!" Annabelle managed to say between chortles.

"And quiet!" he replied. "I can't say I've ever had a fishing experience quite like this."

They continued to laugh until Mr. Edwards realized he was still holding the fish. He freed it from the hook, then tossed it back into the lake with a splash.

"What are you doing? That was my first fish!"

Mr. Edwards could barely speak, for all his laughing. "I don't quite know how to break it to you, Miss Lawson, but he was too small. He'll be better off maturing a bit before he succumbs to the sad fate of becoming someone's dinner."

Annabelle was laughing so hard, she had to bend forward and hold onto her stomach.

"Are you all right?" he asked.

"Never better. But what are you doing? We just got started."

He was closing the bait box and setting the rod

back down in the boat. "There's not much point casting again, Miss Lawson. We've surely scared every fish within a ten mile radius all the way to Kingdom Come."

Annabelle continued to laugh while he drew up the anchor, still chuckling as he set it in the boat and picked up the oars. "We'll have lunch— *quietly, please*—then try again later."

Annabelle wiped the tears from her eyes and watched Mr. Edwards steer the boat toward the island. "That was so much fun."

"It's not usually as exciting as all that, but at least you experienced the thrill of the nibble."

She grinned. "It's rather addictive. I can't wait to try it again."

"Patience, my dear. You will."

Annabelle managed to calm her laughter as the boat coasted along smoothly. She leaned to the side and let her fingers glide through the cold water.

"This boat rows like a dream," he said.

Annabelle admired the graceful movement of his muscular arms. "You're a strong oarsman."

"Lots of practice."

He winked at her, and another thrill zipped up Annabelle's spine, just as it had when she hooked the fish.

She had never met a man more exciting than Mr. Edwards, and that very awareness inspired a sensation of dread—because they were forced to sneak around like this and meet in secret. But perhaps that was part of the excitement.

Within minutes he was dipping the oars into the shallow water, pushing on the gravel as the boat scraped onto the shore. He hopped out with a splash and pulled the heavy boat—with Annabelle in it—up onto the beach.

Annabelle passed the lunch and her painting supplies to him, then stood up and put her hands on his shoulders. He grabbed hold of her under the arms, lifted her out of the boat, and deposited her effortlessly onto the dry shore.

"Thank you," she said, grinning up at him before she turned to pick up the lunch sack. "Shall we head in that direction? There's a nice clearing where we can set down the blanket."

"Lead the way."

They crossed the beach to the path, which led through the woods, and Annabelle marveled at how her body was drumming with sensation from the mere sound of his shoes on the footpath behind her.

They arrived at the grassy clearing. She retrieved the white picnic blanket from the sack, along with the food and wine. "I didn't bring wineglasses because I was afraid they would break. The best I could do was a couple of tin coffee cups."

"Ah, but I adore a practical woman."

He took the folded blanket from her and spread it out on the grass, where they sat down together and enjoyed a delicious lunch of turkey sandwiches, boiled eggs, and shortbread cookies for dessert.

Afterward, Mr. Edwards stretched out on his side and leaned on one elbow. "So tell me, did you bring your painting supplies as a mere ruse, or did you truly intend to be an artist today?"

"That depends," she replied, "on whether or not I feel inspired." She was feeling the effects of the wine, to be sure. She wondered if it was obvious to Mr. Edwards.

"*Are* you inspired?"

She brought the cup to her lips and regarded him over the rim as she sipped. "Yes."

A simple answer. Direct, and probably scandalously delivered.

He sat up. "What do you wish to paint?"

She leaned forward. "You."

"How?"

Under the current tone of their exchange, she could easily have said, *Nude, here on the blanket*. But she'd already been daring enough as it was.

Besides, ever since she met him, she had been thinking of only one way to paint him . . .

"In the boat. I want to paint you fishing, like we talked about on the train."

He inclined his head at her. "I thought you wanted to experience the thrill of the nibble again."

"I do, but first I want to paint *you* experiencing it."

He smiled at her again. "You are lovely, Miss Lawson."

"Thank you, Mr. Edwards," she replied, enjoying how he flattered her.

He glanced at her easel, lying folded on the grass. "How long will it take you? Because I have a train to catch."

"Well, I'll sketch you today, and maybe have time to block in some of the color, but we'll have to come back another day if you want me to finish it."

He took a slow sip of wine. "I like the idea of you sketching me."

"You'll like the finished piece even more when it's hanging over your mantel."

His dark eyebrows lifted. "You intend to give it to me?"

"Of course."

"I'd have to pay you," he said.

Annabelle smiled warmly at him. "No, it would be a gift."

"And what did I do to deserve such a thing?"

Annabelle thought carefully about how she should answer that, then decided she would simply be honest.

"You've inspired me. I was bored before I met you—bored and frustrated."

He gazed at her for a long moment in the warm sunshine, looking almost puzzled. "How could you be bored? You have everything."

Annabelle gazed up at the treetops that circled the clearing and watched a blackbird flutter into the sky. "I don't mean to sound ungrateful. It's just that sometimes I feel like a bit of a misfit. Maybe it's because I wasn't born into this life. My parents weren't aristocrats, so I've never really felt like I belonged, and I'm just not like other women my age. I don't like to gossip about people, nor do I like to shop—unless it's for paints or brushes—and I wear these ugly boots." She lifted her foot to show him. "And I have a cow for a pet, who often accompanies me when I go trekking over the countryside to paint."

He studied her with smiling eyes. "What's your cow's name?"

"Helen of Troy. But I just call her Helen."

Mr. Edwards smiled.

Annabelle glanced at him. "You probably think I'm strange now, don't you? I'm sure my aunt thinks so. She calls me eccentric."

"No, I don't think you're strange," he replied with a chuckle, "because I often feel the same way—that I don't belong."

"Why? You seem very normal to me."

He shrugged, and she had the distinct feeling he was not telling her everything.

Not wanting to pry, she made a joke instead. "So here we are, a couple of misfits."

"A couple of misfits indeed. Maybe that's why we are friends."

Friends. But it was so much more than that.

Annabelle and Mr. Edwards continued to sip the wine while they munched on the shortbread cookies, talking about everything from his work to her family life, until they knew they had to pack up and she had to start sketching.

They walked to the beach, where Annabelle set up her easel. She looked around at the lake, up at the sun to see where it was and which way the shadows were falling, then pointed. "Can you row out there? Not too far. I want you close enough so I can see the details of you and the fishing pole."

He pushed the boat out a few feet, then hopped in, causing it to rock until he was settled. He picked up the oars and pushed off the gravel bottom as he turned the boat around.

"Aren't you worried I'll leave you here?" he asked with a sly grin. "How do you know you can trust me?"

"I guess I'll find out."

He began to row hard in the direction she had

suggested, while she unpacked her canvas and sketching pencils.

"That's far enough!" she shouted, hearing her voice echo across the lake. "Come back a little closer!"

He rowed in a circle and headed back toward her. "How's this?"

"Perfect! Now drop the anchor and catch some fish!"

While he hooked the bait and cast his line, she began sketching the lake and woods on the other side, capturing the rough lines of the background, then the shape and dimensions of the boat. She worked hardest on Mr. Edwards, the lines of his shoulders and arms, the position of his head, but he was difficult to capture because the boat was always changing direction.

He fished for about a half hour while Annabelle sketched him. He caught two trout, which he proudly presented when he rowed back to the island.

"Thank you for posing for me," Annabelle said, tucking the picture into her bag.

He hopped out of the rowboat and dragged it onto the beach. "I do beg your pardon, but aren't you going to show me your masterpiece?"

She grinned impishly. "Not yet. It's just the sketch."

"But I'm curious."

She packed away her pencils. "That's unfortunate, because you're not going to see it until it's completed."

"Completed?" He sauntered slowly toward her, and Annabelle found herself gazing at the full height of him—from his head down to his boots and back up again. He was so handsome, he took her breath away.

"Just one peek," he said.

"No, I told you, not until it's finished."

He raised an eyebrow and lowered his chin, smirking.

Annabelle's stomach spun like a top as he drew closer, looking as if he intended to wrestle it out of her grasp. And win.

Clutching the bag to her chest, she backed up a few steps, knowing he was going to follow.

And oh, how she wanted him to.

Nevertheless, she wagged a finger at him teasingly. "No, Mr. Edwards."

He stopped before her, anticipation brimming in his dark eyes. Then she laughed and bolted. She managed only about ten strides, however, before he caught her around the waist and scooped her up into his arms like a bride.

He dropped to his knees and planted her flat on her back in the grass—almost knocking the wind out of her while she laughed. He had the bag in his hand within seconds, holding it high over his head where she couldn't reach it.

"Mr. Edwards!" she called out in mock effrontery, while he grinned down at her.

"I'll give it back in exchange for a kiss."

She had wondered when he would ask for one. He'd been a perfect gentleman all day, and she, quite frankly, had been waiting for him to behave otherwise. She'd been dreaming of it since the moment he'd left her on the rotunda the day before.

"You, sir, are a scoundrel."

He smiled devilishly. "A cunning one, if I do say so myself."

She tried not to smile. She wanted to be cunning, too, but God help her, she was turning to mush beneath the heat of his gaze. Staring up at his handsome face in the sunlight, she would have given him anything he asked.

"Just one," she replied, even though she wanted more than that, but if she let him take more, he could easily take everything. And she possessed enough common sense not to let that happen. At least not yet.

His expression went slowly from playful to serious as he set down the art case and repeated her words. "Just one."

Annabelle wet her lips. He wet his, too, then

lowered his head, kissing her gently, chastely, before drawing back and gazing down at her for what seemed a very long time.

"Perhaps one more," she said breathlessly.

He kissed her again, and this time Annabelle cupped the back of his head in her hand, delighting in the heady sensation of his lips parting, his tongue sliding into her mouth and meeting hers.

She let out a tiny whimper and let her other hand slide around his waist and travel up under his jacket over the coarse wool of his waistcoat. She could feel the firm, strong muscles of his back. Then, before she realized what she was doing, she had parted her legs, and he had settled himself snugly between them.

His breathing changed, and he rested a hand on her hip while he moved over her, his body pulsing gently.

Annabelle wanted to devour him with her mouth—to wrap her arms and legs around him—but before she had a chance, he broke the kiss.

Appearing flustered, he said, "Are you aware that you're on an island alone with me, Miss Lawson?"

She felt confused . . . bewildered . . . "Yes, I'm aware."

His chest rose and fell with a deep breath. "How do you know you can trust me?"

"That's the second time you've asked me that."

His eyes clouded over suddenly. Gone was the desire she'd seen in them only seconds ago.

Rolling off her, he sat up and rested an arm on his raised knee. "I must be raving mad."

Annabelle sat up, too. "Why?"

He shook his head, taking a long time to answer. "I've never been in a situation quite like this before. It's easy to forget who we are in a place like this."

"I haven't forgotten who we are," Annabelle insisted. "We're just people. And I'm happier now than I was before I met you."

He glanced back at her with a hint of disdain that surprised her. "Because you were bored in that *palace* of yours?"

Annabelle was taken aback. For a moment she wasn't sure where his anger was coming from, but then she understood—or thought she did—and inched closer to him. She put her hands on his shoulders. "I'm not just amusing myself with you, if that's what you think."

"Then what are you doing? Because you know your family would never approve of me." He raked a hand through his hair and spoke harshly. "You shouldn't have come here with me today. You should have looked down your nose at me on the train, like your aunt did. Believe me, it wouldn't have fazed me. I'm quite used to it."

She stared at him, bemused, while he waited for

her to say something. When she did not—because she didn't know what to say—he shook his head and stood.

"Why *did* you come here with me today?" he asked. "What were you thinking? I'm a stranger to you."

She gazed up at him uncertainly. "I don't understand why you're angry with me all of a sudden. Did I do something wrong?"

He glanced down at her briefly while he paced, then turned his back on her and looked across the lake. He rested his hands on his hips.

"Mr. Edwards?"

He faced her and spoke tersely. "I apologize. You did nothing wrong. I am just struggling with the logic of what we are doing. By all rights, you are forbidden to me, Miss Lawson. *Forbidden.* Do you understand that?" He gestured down at her with a hand. "But you're so bloody hard to resist."

Growing increasingly uneasy, Annabelle tugged her skirts down to cover her ankles and boots. Perhaps he was right. Perhaps it *had* been extremely imprudent of her to row out to a private island in secret with a man her family would never approve of.

"We should go," he said flatly. "I don't want to miss my train." He offered his hand to her.

She gathered her skirts and took his hand, letting him pull her to her feet. "Will I get to finish the painting?"

She didn't know why she was asking him that now. She supposed that despite the rising tension between them, she couldn't bear the thought that she would never see him again.

He considered it for a moment, and then, as if he could read her mind, answered the real question she was asking. "I enjoyed myself with you today, Miss Lawson. More than I should have. I suppose my dilemma lies in the fact that I don't wish to hand myself over to you, only to be casually tossed away someday in the future because I am beneath you. And we both know I am."

Annabelle felt her brow furrow with both surprise and umbrage. "I'm not like that. I would never treat a person in such a cavalier manner. I don't *toss* people away."

He stared intently at her for a long moment. "But your family might. It happens all the time."

She narrowed her eyes at him. "Did someone toss you away once? A woman? Did you love her?"

She didn't know where that bold question had come from. All she knew was that she wanted to understand Mr. Edwards in the deepest way possible.

After a long pause he shook his head. "No, there was no woman. At least no one I've ever . . ." He didn't finish.

Annabelle was surprised at how relieved she was to hear that he was not carrying a torch for someone. Perhaps she would be his first love.

He was certainly hers. She knew it already, because she had never felt like this before. Ever. She hadn't even known such extreme emotions were possible.

"I want to finish the painting," she firmly said.

He wet his lips and didn't answer right away. His chest was heaving with indecision. Then at last he said in a quiet voice, "So do I."

Annabelle inhaled deeply with another wave of relief. "When?"

"Next Sunday? Same time?"

A whole week seemed too long to wait to see him again. She would go insane. But in the end she agreed because there was no way around it. He had his clerkship in London.

She would simply have to accept that she would spend the next seven days dreaming of him, and fighting the insurmountable fear that he would leave her standing at the lake, waiting and waiting again, just as he had at the gallery.

Chapter 6

⎯⎯⎯⎯✺⎯⎯⎯⎯

The following Sunday, Annabelle arrived at the lake and was pleased to discover she would not be kept waiting—for there in the boat, casually lounging back, was Mr. Edwards.

And he was there waiting for her every Sunday afternoon for the next six weeks.

It was the happiest, most romantic summer of her life. Mr. Edwards always brought two fishing poles, and he and Annabelle spent countless hours sitting in the small boat, bobbing up and down in the waves, enjoying the summer heat and the peaceful outdoors.

It wasn't *all* peaceful and relaxing, of course. One particular afternoon they argued when Mr. Edwards tried to show her how to gut a fish.

Annabelle proudly won the argument, drawing the line at hooking a worm, which she had become quite an expert at, she could not deny. She no longer squealed for any reason, not even when a floppy trout landed with a *splat* on her boots in the boat.

And though they spoke of nearly every subject under the sun that summer, they never mentioned the argument they'd had that first day, nor did they speak of the future. If Mr. Edwards talked about his work, it was only to relay an amusing story about a coworker or customer, never to draw attention to the differences in their social positions. Perhaps they simply wished to enjoy themselves and forget how their lives differed. Or perhaps they preferred to imagine that those lazy summer afternoons would never end.

Annabelle wished they wouldn't. She wished it most ardently when she and Mr. Edwards stretched out on the picnic blanket after their lunches, their heads together as they stared up at the sky, watching the puffy clouds drift by at a snail's pace. They would pick out shapes of things and watch the blackbirds soar freely against the blue.

And that was always the time he would kiss her, his lips moist and soft as they met hers, tasting like red wine. All he had to do was lean toward her and her entire body would purr with the passion-filled delight of his presence and the overpowering desire for more.

But despite her feverish longings, Mr. Edwards consistently refused to do anything more than just kiss, and never for more than a few minutes. Each time, he explained that he wanted her to have choices, in case she later changed her mind about him.

"I won't," she always said.

"You might," he always replied.

So their physical intimacies made little progress. And it was not until the summer's end that she fully understood why.

It was the last Sunday in August.

Magnus leaned a shoulder against the old English oak on the hill, which overlooked Century House, Annabelle's opulent home—an aristocratic mansion of unparalleled grandeur, set amidst terraced formal gardens and magnificent fountains.

He stood for a long time just looking at it, while his emotions were tearing him apart inside—for the summer was at an end. The sunlight and shadows had changed, the air had turned crisp, and today . . .

Today was the day Annabelle would finish the painting.

He glanced down and kicked his booted toe against a large exposed tree root. He thought about what he had been doing all summer—spending romantic afternoons with Annabelle, charming her into falling in love with him, never telling her who he really was.

He had suffered for it each and every minute, constantly vowing he would tell her the following week. But then she would arrive at the dock with her easel, all smiles and playful teasing, and he had never been able to say the words. He hadn't been able to bear the thought of her reacting to him with revulsion.

Just one more day, he'd tell himself. If he could just make her love him a little more, it wouldn't matter when he told her. She would forgive him for keeping the truth from her, and love him regardless. He'd wanted only to wait until they were stronger.

But now, on this day, he found himself facing the reality of what their future would be, even if she did forgive him. He thought of the bed he'd gotten out of that morning—the coarse, wool blanket and the mattress full of holes. He'd gotten dressed, then shoveled the coal into the stove himself, but not until after he tramped down the road at dawn to purchase a jug of milk from the worn-out dairymaid.

He thought of the breakfast he'd eaten—the same breakfast he ate every day of his life: bland porridge in a chipped bowl.

And his mother was run-down and depressed again, drinking too much as usual. The previous night, he had returned home to find her in a drunken swoon with her head on the kitchen table, a half-empty bottle of whiskey in front of her.

He quietly slid the bottle out of her loose grip and poured it out in the muddy yard, knowing he'd never hear the end of it when she woke, but he followed through nonetheless.

Magnus lifted his weary gaze and looked down the hill at Century House again, and imagined Annabelle waking this morning under clean, white embroidered sheets, eating a breakfast prepared by a devoted kitchen staff. Her maid would have helped her dress and knotted her hair, and another set of maids would have cleaned out the grate in her fireplace, swept her polished floor, and fluffed her feathery pillows.

It was a world very different from his.

He felt nauseous all of a sudden, and slid down the side of the tree to sit on the ground. Resting his elbows on his knees, he raked both hands through his hair.

What did he think he was doing? How could he be so selfish, thinking he could take Annabelle away from the life she knew and force her to alienate her family, then drag her down into the hell that was *his* life?

He supposed the problem was that he felt something for her that he'd never felt for any other woman. He loved her laughter, her intelligence, her nonconformity. She inspired him with her artistic creativity, challenged him and made him think, and she made him feel at ease and at home—which was something he rarely felt with anyone.

He had grown to care for her so very deeply and devotedly that it was now much more than a simple matter of lust. What concerned him today was her welfare and well-being. Her future happiness.

Yet with his feelings as profound and passionate as they were, he wasn't entirely certain he could be noble and self-sacrificing enough to do the right thing—which was undoubtedly to give her up.

"Are you ready to see it?" Annabelle asked later that afternoon, meeting Mr. Edwards at the water's edge as he dragged the heavy boat onto the beach.

"I've been ready for six weeks," he replied.

She had noticed with some concern that he'd seemed downtrodden most of the day. He was not his usual flirtatious self, and had been very quiet.

During lunch she'd asked him if he was all right, and he'd assured her he was just tired after a long, busy week. She had accepted his explanation, hiding her fear that it might be something more.

"Well, come and see it, then," she said, holding out her arm. "But close your eyes." She took him by the hand and led him to the easel. "All right. You can look now."

Mr. Edwards opened his eyes and stared at her painting for the longest time while she watched him apprehensively. His eyes moved over the details in the center of the canvas, then he studied every corner.

At last he looked at Annabelle, who warmed at the tenderness and wonderment in his expression.

"What do you think?" she asked hesitantly.

He slowly approached. "It's beautiful, Annabelle. Too beautiful to give to me. It should be in a gallery somewhere."

She shook her head. "I'm not famous enough to be in a gallery."

"You should be. You *will* be."

Annabelle smiled, dumbfounded by the astounding pride and elation that came from knowing someone truly appreciated her work.

No. He more than appreciated it. He was awestruck. Not just with the painting, but with her.

All at once she wanted to shout out loud across the lake and hear her voice echo back in return.

She was so happy to be with him, and so proud of this piece! It was beyond a doubt the best thing she'd ever done.

"Can I assume you like it?" she asked.

He came to her. "I more than like it. I love it. It has movement, yet stillness at the same time. And the reflections in the water . . ." He returned to stand before the painting, and moved his hand over it as he spoke. "They look so real, yet when you study them, you are struck by the fact that you are seeing only the surface of the water, and there are deep, unknown depths beyond. It's the most incredible thing anyone's ever given me. I'm not worthy of it."

"Of course you are."

He returned to her and cupped her cheek in his large, warm hand, stroking with his thumb. His touch gave her shivers.

Slowly he lowered his lips to hers and kissed her while he held her face in both his hands. The kiss deepened, and Annabelle reveled in the taste of his tongue and the hot wetness of his mouth closing over hers. She let out a small whimper as she wrapped her arms around his broad shoulders, feeling all at once flooded with a rush of need so strong, she feared she would never be able to let him go.

She wanted more. She knew there was more. So much more . . .

He dragged his lips from hers and whispered, "No, Annabelle."

But she refused to take no for an answer. She cupped his face in her hands. "Please, just this once."

She could see in his eyes that he was straining to resist her, but soon he gave up the fight and kissed down the side of her neck.

Annabelle began backing up toward the trees, leading him by the hand. This time he did not resist. He followed willingly, his eyes laden with desire. As soon as she reached the shade of a tall oak tree where the scents of pine and chamomile were thick in the air, she sat down on her knees in the grass, still holding his hand as she looked up at him.

He hesitated, but only briefly before he knelt down before her and eased her onto her back. His body and mouth covered hers, and emotions welled up inside her.

She wanted to tell him she loved him, but she was afraid, because she knew if she did, he would stop. He would remember their impossible situation—that she was forbidden to him, just as he was to her. He would stop kissing her like he always did.

Suddenly driven by a sense of urgency, she reached for his hand and held it firmly to her breast.

Their gazes locked.

Annabelle's body quaked with both excitement and fear as she recognized the passion in his eyes and felt his physical strength as a man. He was heavy on top of her, powerful and aroused, pressing his hips into hers, looking as if he wanted to take her completely—and if he decided to, there would be nothing she could do to stop him.

But she did not want to stop him.

She could see, however, that he wished to stop himself. It was clear in his eyes, so she quickly parted her legs and wrapped them around his hips.

The rock-hard stiffness of his arousal pressed against the pulsing ache between her thighs, and she took in a deep, shuddering breath.

"This is dangerous, Annabelle," he said, his voice strained with a firm warning.

"But please don't stop."

She wiggled her hips, her body flooding with a willful desire for pleasures beyond anything she knew. She wanted to give herself to him completely and love him forever, and those emotions were so strong, her awareness of duty and responsibility to her family meant nothing.

Something about the way she moved must have aroused him further, because he lowered his weight upon her and covered her mouth again with a deep, rough kiss that threatened to steal her soul.

She moaned huskily as his tongue drove into her mouth. It was nothing like any of the other gentle, tender kisses on the picnic blanket. This was powerful and demanding and it was the start of something new. She felt as if she'd just been dropped onto a moving train.

Annabelle slid her hands down his broad back, lifted the back of his jacket and tugged his shirt from the waistband of his trousers. She massaged the strong muscles at his lower back, marveling at the smoothness of his skin and wanting to touch the rest of him, everywhere.

He groaned and rolled off her slightly to lean on one elbow while he quickly unbuttoned her bodice. Then Annabelle unhooked her corset in the front, feeling a pleasurable freedom as it came loose. He slid a warm hand up under her chemise.

It was shocking—the feel of his hand upon her bare belly, then her breast. No one had ever touched her there before, and when his thumb stroked her nipple and his mouth came down upon hers again, she whimpered at the throbbing lust spreading through her body. It was incomprehensible, and the intimacy of his caress only made her love him more. She kissed him deeply and affectionately, wanting to show him with her body just how much she loved him.

Then Mr. Edwards raised her chemise and took

one of her nipples into his mouth, and Annabelle thought she might die from the ecstasy of it—his tongue and lips and the feel of his hot breath upon her wet skin. She let out another little whimper.

"God, Annabelle," he said, resting his forehead upon her chest, "I want you, but I can't take you. I can't."

"Yes, you can. Please don't stop."

He paused there in silence for the longest time, his shoulders heaving as if he were out of breath from rowing the distance of the lake. A squirrel chirped somewhere in the distance.

For a moment Annabelle thought he was going to stop, as he always had before, but no . . .

He moved quickly and decisively, inching down and tugging her skirts upward until he found the tapes that fastened her drawers.

Lying flat on her back with her legs parted, Annabelle put a hand over her eyes, allowing him to remove her drawers, then her stockings and boots, not knowing what would come next.

Suddenly she was exposed to the cool air. Her legs were bare and still parted, her skirts bunched up around her waist.

Her heart began to pound with trepidation. This was happening so fast. Was he going to plunge into her right now and take her virginity? He could if he wanted to. She had told him to do it.

But was she really ready?

Before she had a chance to think anything through, he moved down between her legs and began kissing her knees, then her thighs, then his mouth traveled up to the place where her desire was centered and he stroked her with his tongue. Annabelle gasped in shock, but the shock quickly passed as pleasure consumed her. She took his head in her hands as a mad passion ripped through her body like a summer storm.

"What are you doing to me?" she asked breathlessly, all doubts and fears vanishing in an instant.

He made no reply. He only reached a hand up to hold hers.

She squeezed it, squeezing her legs together, too, cupping his head between her bare thighs. Annabelle bit her lip as all her muscles clenched and tightened. She lifted her head off the ground, shutting her eyes and blocking out the rest of the world. All she knew was the blinding heat of sensation—his mouth and tongue driving her to the wild realms of hot, tingling mayhem.

And wild mayhem it was, as waves of pleasure crashed and washed over her moments later. Her flesh throbbed and quivered. She cried out, tears spilling from her eyes. Annabelle grabbed for his head again, cupping it in both hands while he continued to drive her through the fierce, spiraling completion.

He did not stop until she went limp and her

arms fell open onto the grass. Then he pulled her skirts down, before he lay beside her, leaning up on one elbow.

Finally, Annabelle opened her eyes and turned her head to look at him.

"What did you do to me?" she asked, her voice weak and listless.

He kissed her tenderly on the lips, his hand caressing her cheek. Then he slowly drew back. "You had an orgasm."

She looked up at the white puffy clouds in the sky. "I never knew of such a thing."

"Well, now you do," he said, smiling, his voice quiet and gentle.

He rested his hand on her belly, and for a long time they lay in silence, relaxing and listening to the ducks quacking on the lake, until Annabelle's breathing returned to normal.

Mr. Edwards gazed out across the water and said, "I think I deserve a medal."

"Why?" she asked, laughing.

"Because you're still a virgin."

A breeze blew through the trees behind them, and Annabelle's face grew serious. "It wouldn't matter if I wasn't."

And she meant it. She wanted him to be the one.

She rolled onto her side to face him. "I wish I could do that to you. Touch you and give you that kind of pleasure."

Annabelle reached for the front of his trousers, but he quickly caught her wrist in his hand.

"No."

"Why not?"

"Because I'd lose my medal, and you'd lose something else more important than your virginity. You'd lose your freedom to make choices."

"Regarding a husband?" she asked.

"Yes, and I will not take that away from you."

Annabelle bristled. She wasn't entirely sure if he was doing this for *her*, or if it was a more selfish rationale. Perhaps he did not want to be obligated.

She kept her hand where it was, poised over his arousal, and he continued to hold her wrist, keeping her at bay until she finally gave up.

"What are we going to do," she asked in a desperate haze as she sat up and hugged her knees to her chest, "now that the painting is done? I don't want to say good-bye."

He sat up, too, resting his elbows on his knees and linking his hands together.

But he said nothing.

"You could come and pay a call," she suggested. "I could talk to my brother. I believe if he could come to know you, he would admire you as much as I do."

Mr. Edwards took a moment before he rose to his feet and walked to the edge of the woods, leaning a hand upon the rough bark of an elm. "No."

Annabelle was baffled by the firmness of his reply. "Why not? I would talk to Whitby first."

Mr. Edwards shook his head and walked toward the water, where he bent down, picked up a rock, and pitched it hard, as far as he could into the lake. "I remember the way your aunt looked at me on the train."

"I would talk to her, too," Annabelle argued. "I would make her understand."

He faced her. "Understand what? That you've been lying to her all summer? Sneaking off to meet a bank clerk alone on a secluded island? I'm sure she'd be happy to hear it." He turned toward the lake again. "No, Annabelle, they'll never understand."

A sick feeling moved into the pit of her stomach. "You're not even willing to try?"

He looked over his shoulder at her, tilting his head as if he thought she was very foolish.

She had seen him look that way only once before—the first time they had come here—and today she sensed there was a side of him she did not know very well. A darker side.

It worried her. She wanted suddenly to see where he lived, to see his home and his mother. This summer had been nothing but a fantasy after all, for real life was not an endless string of leisurely Sunday afternoons . . .

"We should go," he said flatly, just like he had said that first day, when they'd argued. "I can't miss my train."

"Why do you do that?" she asked pointedly. "You always want to leave when things get . . ." She didn't know what they were exactly, but she knew something was different.

He went to pack up her easel and paints, while she sat bewildered on the grass, watching him. What had just happened? A moment ago he'd looked at her with desire in his eyes. Now all he wanted to do was get away from her.

"I don't care what they think anyway," she blurted out, referring to her family, as she pulled on her stockings, drawers, and boots.

He was crouching down, putting paint tubes back into the box, ignoring what she'd said. He didn't even look up.

Annabelle walked to him. "Did you hear me? I said I don't care what they think. I'd run away with you if you wanted."

He went instantly still.

He closed his eyes briefly, then opened them and looked up at her. "You don't know what you're saying. You don't even know me."

"Yes, I do."

"No. You *don't*."

He returned to his task, quickly dropping the

brushes into the box and closing it. He slid the box into her bag, then walked to the boat and set it inside.

Annabelle stood watching him, feeling hurt and confused. "I don't understand. Did you just come here every Sunday because you wanted a painting of yourself, and now that you have it, you're done with me? Or did you grow bored with me?"

She could feel her heart breaking as she spoke the words. He wanted to end it. She could feel it coming.

He folded the easel and carried it and the painting to the boat, then came back for the lunch sack. "You know that's not true. I've enjoyed this as much as you have, but maybe we should be sensible and take some time to think about everything."

He returned to the boat and stood by it, waiting for Annabelle to get in, but she couldn't move. She was in shock over this change in him. It was as if the beautiful bubble of their love had just burst in front of her eyes.

"I don't need to think about it," she said, "but obviously you do." She strode toward him. "Just tell me why."

He did not respond. He simply gestured toward the boat. "Get in please, Annabelle."

"No. Not until you tell me why you're acting this way. Do you not care about me? Have I become dull?"

"You're not dull," he replied, sounding frustrated as he struggled for words. "It has just become too complicated, and I don't like things complicated. Now get in the boat please."

She was fuming now. She couldn't believe this was happening. How could a person change so quickly? What was wrong with him? And why had he let things go so far today if he wanted to end it? Why had he touched her like that and made her love him even more?

"Have you met someone else?" she asked, barely able to keep her voice from breaking.

"No." His tone was firm.

Not knowing what to say, because she was too angry to speak, Annabelle got in. She braced her hands on the seat, while he pushed the boat over the gravel and into the water. Climbing inside, he picked up the oars, never meeting her gaze as he turned the boat around.

Annabelle glanced down at the painting. She had worked so hard on it.

Soon they were coasting swiftly through the water, the boat propelled forward with every strong, forceful stroke. Mr. Edwards glanced at her occasionally while he rowed, but neither of them spoke. They both sat in angry silence, crossing the lake.

When they approached the dock, Annabelle grabbed hold of the post while Mr. Edwards climbed out and tied the rope.

As soon as the boat was secure, she handed the painting and all the gear to him. He offered a hand to help her out, but she ignored it, awkwardly gathering her skirts in a fist while she climbed onto the dock without assistance.

"Annabelle . . ." he said, watching her pick up her things.

She did not speak to him. She couldn't. She was too angry.

She drew the lunch sack over her shoulder, along with her art case, then clumsily managed to get the easel under her arm.

"I'm leaving," she said as she started up the length of the dock. "You better get going. You don't want to miss your train."

She heard him take a few steps to follow. "Annabelle, wait."

Her foot landed on the grassy bank before she stopped and turned. He was standing on the dock with the lake and their private island behind him. It looked so very far away.

Annabelle waited for him to say what he wished to say, but all he did was spread his hands wide in a shrugging gesture. Then he dropped them to his sides.

The noncommittal message infuriated her even more, and she could feel her cheeks coloring, her muscles clenching with fury.

"That's it?" she asked, shifting her load, barely

managing to cope with the heavy easel under her arm.

He did not respond.

She looked away for a moment and shook her head. She had thought their time together had been special, but clearly she was wrong. All she'd been to him was a casual summertime affair, and now he wanted out.

"You've got your painting," she said icily. "The summer's over, and I think it's obvious that our friendship is over, too, because I for one *do* like things complicated."

When he still said nothing and did not even argue the point of their friendship coming to an end, Annabelle's anger mixed with heartache and disillusionment, and she had to fight not to let those feelings overtake her. As hard as it was to walk away from him—when a part of her wanted to drop everything, run back and beg and plead with him not to end it—she had to be strong. She was heartbroken, but she would not be pathetic.

She raised her chin and strove to keep her voice steady as she spoke over the painful lump in her throat. "Good-bye, Mr. Edwards. I will ask you not to contact me again."

With that, she headed for the path toward home, still thinking he might follow to say he was sorry. She wanted him to. The whole way along the path she listened for his footsteps, hoping, praying, he would change his mind and come running after her.

But he did not come running. The woods were quiet as she tramped along the footpath, forcing herself to accept the truth—that she had been very wrong when she thought he loved her. He had been using her for his own pleasure and amusement. *Especially today.*

Annabelle walked as fast as she could, fighting the tears that were filling her eyes, but as soon as she reached the private depths of the forest, she couldn't go any farther.

She stopped on the path, dropped to her knees and wept into her hands.

Chapter 7

During the week that followed the painful end of her summer affair, Annabelle kept mostly to herself. She slept late, feeling no desire to get out of bed, and she excused herself from her aunt's company in the afternoons to nap in her bedchamber, though she never really napped. She merely lay in her bed, experiencing extreme—and sometimes conflicting—degrees of emotion.

One minute she hated Mr. Edwards like she'd never hated anything or anyone.

The next minute she missed him desperately

and longed to see him again—to touch him, to feel his hands on her body, to taste his kiss. She wanted to hear his voice and his laughter. She wanted to sit in the boat with him and watch him row.

Most of all she wanted to feel the joy and freedom she had felt when she was with him. She had never felt more alive, or more herself.

Annabelle cried many tears that week, and on the following Sunday she did what she'd promised herself she would not do. She ran through the woods to the lake, whizzing past bushes and branches, hoping he had missed her, too, and would be there.

But when she emerged from the shady path to discover the boat empty, bobbing up and down upon the choppy water and knocking against the dock, she hated herself for being so weak. She hated herself even more for waiting there all afternoon, hoping he would appear and apologize for their argument.

It had been a sad, humiliating afternoon.

But it was nothing compared to the final time she saw him two weeks later, on a rainy Monday morning in London, when she had experienced one of the most traumatic events of her life . . .

Hopping out of a hansom cab and into a puddle—after sneaking out of her brother's Mayfair mansion without her chaperone—Annabelle made her way across the cobbled street to the bank where Mr. Edwards had told her he worked. She dashed quickly through the rain to the front door.

Stopping under the overhang to catch her breath, she lowered the hood of her cloak and paused there a moment, looking down at her muddy skirts.

She didn't know what she was doing here. She knew better than to try and see Mr. Edwards again, after he'd made it more than clear he wanted to cut her loose. But she couldn't help it. She had spent the past three weeks wondering what had killed it for him, and she began to cling to the belief that he felt he was not good enough for her and thought he was doing the right thing by ending it.

If that was all it was, she would convince him it was *not* the right thing. She would convince him that he *was* good enough, no matter what her family thought.

She took a deep breath and swallowed hard, straining to hold onto her courage. All she wanted was an honest answer, even if the truth was not what she wanted to hear. If she had that, she believed she would have an easier time getting over him.

Just then, an older gentleman in a dark coat and top hat came running to reach the shelter of the overhang and paused a moment, brushing the raindrops off his shoulders before pulling the door open. He smiled at Annabelle and gestured for her to enter first.

"Thank you," she replied, forcing herself to cross the threshold.

Once inside, she glanced around the large bank and up at the high ceiling and brass chandelier. The floors were shiny black-and-white marble, and the desks and counters were all dark tiger oak.

There was a general echoing chaos of masculine voices, all speaking at the same time, and a bell rang from somewhere, signaling something. Toward the back, at least two-dozen desks were arranged in rows, and each had its own lamp.

Feeling suddenly uncomfortable and out of place, she was about to turn and walk out when a young man in a bright blue tie approached.

"Good morning," he said. "Do you have an appointment?"

Annabelle squeezed her reticule in front of her and tried to appear relaxed. "No. I'm looking for someone. Mr. Edwards. John Edwards."

The young man's brow furrowed. "Is he a customer? Were you supposed to meet him here?"

She shook her head. "No. He works here, but he's not expecting me."

The man glanced uncertainly around at the array of desks at the back. "I don't believe I know a John Edwards. Is he new?"

Her heart was beginning to pound. She shouldn't have come here alone, she thought, and certainly not to see her former secret lover. She felt as if this man knew she was sneaking around and doing something very wrong, and he was about to blow a whistle and turn her in.

"No, he's been working here for two years," she explained.

"Two years," the man replied with some confusion. "You're sure that's his name? Because there is no John Edwards here. What does he look like? Or perhaps you have the wrong bank."

Annabelle began to feel a sickening knot tighten in her stomach. He had told her he worked here. Had he lied about that? But why would he lie? And if he did not work here, where did he work? How would she ever find him again?

Just then something drew her attention away from the young man before her, as if someone had called her name, though no one had.

Her gaze swung toward the back corner of the bank, where it remained fixed on the man walking toward her. All the sounds of the bank faded away, leaving only the whisper of her blood in her veins. The whole world seemed to disappear for a moment while she stood immobile, watching the man—Mr. Edwards—walk toward her.

He did not look pleased.

"Here he comes," she said in a fog, barely aware of the young man leaving her side and moving away.

Mr. Edwards came to a slow stop before her and spoke flatly without emotion. "What are you doing here?" He glanced uneasily at a coworker who was watching them. The coworker quickly went about his business.

Annabelle fought a feeling of intimidation as she looked up at her former love.

There was no softness in his eyes, only displeasure. If she did not know him, she would believe him a cruel man. Perhaps he was. Perhaps that was why her heart was pounding and her hands were trembling. She actually felt afraid of him. This was not what she had expected.

"I just wanted to talk to you," she managed to say in a deceptively confident and assertive voice.

"About what?" he replied icily, as if she were a great bother to him and he had no time for her. It was shocking to her, the way this was unfolding.

All at once anger filled her. He had no cause to be so rude to her, to make her feel so troublesome. All she wanted was a few minutes of his time.

She squared her shoulders and copied his icy tone. "That man said there was no John Edwards here. Why would he tell me that?"

He stared down at her for a long moment before moving past her toward the door and indicating for her to follow. "I don't want to talk about this here."

Still shocked by his inconceivable rudeness, Annabelle followed him outside, where they stood in front of the bank window. The rain poured hard on the street beyond the shelter of the overhang, hissing as it misted on the ground.

"I just want to understand what happened," Annabelle said, determined to get this over with as quickly as possible. "And why that man didn't know you as John Edwards."

"Let it go, Annabelle. This sort of thing happens all the time. Flirtations occur, and then they come to an end."

"Flirtations?" She could not control her voice. She had practically shouted the word. "Was that all it was to you? Because it was much more than that to me. I fell in *love* with you."

Something flashed through his eyes. Regret? Anguish?

No. It was shock. Love was a strong word.

"That's why I had to end it," he said. "It went further than I had intended it to go."

"Than you *intended*?" Her stomach was whirling with dread and anxiety as she contemplated what he was saying. "So even in the beginning, you just wanted a casual affair?"

He paused, his brow furrowing as if he were in physical pain. "Yes."

"But when you came to see me that first time in my garden, you led me to believe it was much more than that. Were you toying with me? Is that something you do? Lead women on, only to discard them when their feelings become *complicated*?"

Annabelle realized she was clenching her fists.

"Lower your voice, please," he whispered, glancing around. "It had to end, there was no way around it. I thought it more kind to end it sooner rather than later."

"More kind? I never wanted your pity."

"No, you wanted something else. You wanted too much, and I always knew it could never happen. You must have known that yourself."

"No! I told you I didn't care what my family thought."

He was quiet for a moment. "You need to let it go, Annabelle, and move on. Forget about me."

He turned to leave, but she grabbed hold of his arm. "Wait a minute. I don't believe you. You *did* love me. I couldn't have been so wrong about that."

Oh, that sounded pathetic. She wished she could take it back.

He glanced around. "Let go, Annabelle. Please. You're making a spectacle of yourself."

A spectacle? That did it. She could have throttled him.

"No, I will not let go! Tell me why you ended it. The real reason, and I want the truth!"

The rain came down harder suddenly, roaring on the roof of the overhang and pouring onto the ground like a thick curtain beside them. But neither of them noticed. Their eyes were locked on each other's, while this painful scene played out.

Magnus was having trouble breathing, and knowing that the time had come, that he *had* to tell Annabelle the truth, he nearly fell to his knees in despair.

He didn't want to hurt her, nor did he want to lose her forever, but he couldn't let her go on thinking they could be together. He couldn't do that to her. He couldn't rip her from her beautiful, glittering life and put her in the middle of a war between himself and Whitby. For if she defied her brother, she would be exiled to hell, just like he had been.

He pulled his arm from her grasp as a shame-filled wretchedness flared in his gut. He should never have started this. He should have changed seats on the train that first day, as soon as he'd learned who she was. He shouldn't have let himself be pulled in.

His voice shook when he spoke. "Fine. You want the truth? Here it is. My name isn't John Edwards. It's Magnus. I am Whitby's cousin."

*   *   *

Annabelle felt her eyes grow wide. It seemed her thoughts were draining out of her and washing away in the muddy flow of water down the street. She was stunned.

Cousin Magnus? No, he couldn't be . . . It wasn't possible.

"Have you heard of me?" he asked. "Do you know that Whitby's father and my father were twins?"

Yes, she did know. She knew the whole sordid story about Magnus's father being sent away as a young boy because he was violent and dangerous. He had threatened the very life of his brother—Whitby's father. But she couldn't speak. Her brain was muddled, her mouth didn't seem to be working.

"It's a vile story, isn't it?" he said, his voice low and controlled, but seething with resentment. "My father was cut off from your high-browed family as I have always been, and it is no secret your brother and I despise each other."

"Why didn't you tell me?" Annabelle asked in a numb, shaken stupor.

"Because I knew it would cut our summer short, and . . ."

Magnus hesitated. A knife plunging into his heart would have been less painful to him than what he was about to say to Annabelle.

But he had to say it, because if he didn't, she might cling to some tiny shred of hope. He had to make sure she would let go of that and never come back here. For her sake.

"And I was enjoying a very satisfying jab at Whitby," he ground out.

Annabelle's face went pale, and her voice trembled when she finally spoke. "You were *using* me?"

He paused again, his jaw clenching. "Every minute we were together."

"But I loved you."

"I'm sorry to hear that, because I didn't love you."

He nearly choked on the words.

Annabelle sucked in a breath. There it was. The cold, hard truth, and hearing it spoken aloud felt like a plank across her chest. It knocked the wind out of her.

He was staring at her, his eyes dark and expressionless. "I didn't want to say it, Annabelle, but you forced me to. So there it is. Now you should go."

Annabelle thought about what she knew of Magnus. She'd heard that he had inherited his father's jealous, violent nature, and that he was responsible for the death of Whitby's older brother. John, the heir to the earldom before Whitby, had been found dead in Hyde Park when he was sixteen. His head was cracked open on a rock, and everyone knew he and Magnus had seen each other that day and fought, as they always did.

Magnus had a bloody nose when they caught up with him afterward, but of course he denied having anything to do with what happened. They'd had no proof, and it was concluded that John was simply thrown from his horse.

John. John Edwards. Whitby's first name was Edward . . .

Her mind spinning with horrifying revelations, Annabelle felt faint and unsteady on her feet. "I can't believe I was sneaking around behind Whitby's back to be with *you*."

Magnus stiffened visibly, then his expression turned to a cold mask of stone. "But you were, and I helped you do it."

Annabelle could barely think or breathe. She had believed herself in love with a bank clerk named John Edwards, but it had all been a lie. He was her brother's enemy, and had used her and manipulated her for the sole purpose of vengeance.

"Whitby is right," she said, glaring at him with hatred and loathing. "You *are* a monster."

She turned to leave, the rain pelting her face as she stepped out from under the overhang.

"Are you going to tell him about us?" he shouted after her. "I hope you do. I only wish I could be there to see his face."

Because Magnus never hated Whitby more than he did at that moment.

Hearing that, Annabelle stopped. She didn't

care that she was standing ankle deep in a puddle, nor that she hadn't bothered to pull up her hood and her tiny hat was soaking up the rain. She turned on her heel, marched back to Magnus, and slapped him hard across the face.

He took the punishing strike without flinching, then bowed his head very low.

"I will tell him," she said, "because I won't give you the satisfaction of knowing there is a secret between my brother and me, or that you know something he doesn't. And God help you when he finds out."

That was the last time she had ever seen or spoken to Magnus, her brother's enemy.

And from that day forward, he was *her* enemy, too.

Chapter 8

⁓⦿⦿⁓

June 1892

Annabelle opened her eyes and found herself still lying on her back, staring groggily up at the quiet leaves of the oak tree. The wind had died down and the sun had almost disappeared beyond the horizon. How long had she been asleep?

She sat up and reached for the timepiece in her pocket. The gold hands indicated seven-fifteen.

Annabelle scrambled to her feet, packed up her easel and painting, and started down the hill in a hurry with everything in tow. She didn't want to miss dinner. If she did, everyone would be worried about her, for she never stayed out this late, unless she was painting a sunset.

But she hadn't been painting a sunset today, had she? No, she had been remembering the past.

She entered the house at the back and climbed the main staircase to her rooms, then rang for her maid, Josephine. Annabelle had already removed her bodice and overskirts herself when Josephine knocked and entered.

"Thank goodness you're back, Miss Lawson. I was concerned."

"No need to be. I fell asleep on the hill under the oak tree while the paint was drying."

Josephine disappeared into the dressing room and quickly returned with Annabelle's dark green dinner gown. Annabelle stepped into it and turned, so Josephine could fasten it in the back.

"Your hair," her maid said, looking flustered.

Annabelle started pulling the pins out herself, while Josephine fastened the last few hooks at the back of her dress.

A minute later Annabelle was sitting in front of her mirror, watching her maid pull her troublesome, frizzy hair into a knot on top of her head.

"The green earrings?" Josephine asked.

"Yes."

Josephine was passing them to her when the

loud dinner gong rang, signaling the family to gather in the drawing room. Annabelle and Josephine exchanged a relieved glance. They had been very fast and efficient.

Rising from the chair, Annabelle smoothed out her skirts, while Josephine picked up Annabelle's afternoon dress, which was draped over the foot of the bed.

"Wait!" Annabelle said, hurrying to reach into the pocket of the skirt before Josephine took it away. "I need something." She reached in for the folded letter, then managed to feign a smile. "You can have it now."

As soon as Josephine was gone, Annabelle took the tiny key out of the locket around her neck and walked to her desk. She sat down and pulled her miniature cedar chest out of the top drawer, set it in front of her on the desktop and inserted the key into the lock. When the box clicked open, she raised the lid and stared at the first letter from Magnus, which she'd received almost two weeks ago.

She touched a finger to her lips.

He had written to tell her he'd returned to London and purchased a gallery, and that he wished to meet with her. Naturally, she had not replied, for she'd been in shock, for one thing. Secondly, she had not wished to meet with him, just as she did not wish to meet with him now.

A knock sounded at her door and she jumped,

then slammed the box shut, for she had not told anyone about the letters. Though she certainly should have. She should have informed Whitby. The fact that she had not done so had been troubling her for two weeks. It was not like her to keep things from her brother. But so many things about Magnus were secreted away in her heart. So much of what had happened that summer she would never share with anyone.

"Who is it?" she asked.

"It's Lily."

Annabelle quickly shoved the box back into her desk drawer and shut it. "Come in!"

The door swung open and her brother's wife entered with a hand on her swollen belly, for she was due to deliver her fifth child in the next few weeks. "I saw you coming in late, and wondered if you needed any help preparing for dinner."

"Oh, no, I'm fine," Annabelle replied, her hands fidgeting on the desk. "Josephine was very astute. She had my gown ready and waiting for me."

Lily approached and rested a hand on the corner post of Annabelle's bed. She appeared hesitant, and her eyes held a hint of concern as she tilted her head to the side.

"Forgive me, Annabelle, but I must ask—are you all right? You've not seemed yourself over the past few weeks."

She should have known she could not hide her

feelings from Lily, for they were best friends, and had been for the past eight years, since the day Lily married Whitby. Indeed, she had confided in Lily then, about what occurred with Magnus, but this new development with the letters, she had kept to herself.

Leaning back in her chair, Annabelle sat in silence for a moment, then opened her drawer and reached for the cedar box. Setting it on the desk, she removed the two letters and handed them over.

"What are these?" Lily asked.

"They're from Magnus."

Lily gasped in astonishment, then fumbled with the letters, hurrying to read what they said.

"He's in London!" she blurted out. "He can't do that. The allowance from Whitby requires that—"

"I know," Annabelle cut in. "I don't understand it. I don't know what he's trying to accomplish."

Lily considered it, then moved toward an upholstered chair. With one hand on her belly, the other reaching behind her, she lowered herself onto the cushioned seat. "Have you replied?"

"Of course not. I was in shock, and I certainly don't wish to see him, or have any contact with him whatsoever."

Lily's cheeks paled as she considered the broader ramifications of this.

"Honestly, I can't believe this is happening," Annabelle said. "I'd thought he was gone forever. For the past eight years it was almost as if he didn't exist. I've been content living here with you and Whitby and the children, and thought all that was behind me, but now he's come back and . . ." She didn't quite know how to say it. She didn't even fully understand it herself. "I'm afraid he's stirring up old feelings."

Lily's eyes clouded with worry. "What kinds of feelings?"

Annabelle thought about how she'd just spent an entire afternoon reliving the past, feeling the excitement, the joys, and the overwhelming pain of the heartbreak.

"Mostly my anger toward him," she replied. "Today I was recalling that summer we spent together, and I . . ." She hesitated, fighting to keep her voice steady. "I was so in love with him, Lily."

Lily gave her a consoling look. "I know you were."

Annabelle felt tears threaten, but forcibly crushed them. She stood and walked to the window. "Of course that was before I knew the truth about him—that he was lying to me and using me to satisfy his vindictiveness. He was so cruel that day at the bank. It's remarkable how quickly love can change to hate."

Lily was still holding onto the letters. She flipped through them again. "What do you think he really wants? He can't just be here to open a gallery. There must be a more personal motivation."

Annabelle raised an incredulous eyebrow. "He's a tyrant. He's probably here to enact another ruthless scheme."

Lily ran a hand over her belly. "I met him once in the village, remember? Eight years ago, just before he left for America. It was five years after he'd jilted you, and I know you and Whitby thought I was naive, but I didn't find him tyrannical."

"That's his talent," Annabelle explained. "He knows how to charm when he needs to, but he can knock you onto your back the very next instant. And are you forgetting that your coach overturned immediately after you encountered him?"

"There was no proof he was involved," Lily argued. "And he denied it to Whitby. It could have been a coincidence."

"Just like there was no proof about how Whitby's brother John ended up with his skull cracked open on a rock when he was sixteen?"

Lily dropped her gaze. "Oh, Annabelle. Must you."

Annabelle closed her eyes, feeling ashamed for saying such harsh things. She faced her sister-in-law. "I'm sorry, Lily. That was my anger spouting out of me."

"It's all right. I understand."

Annabelle went to sit across from Lily on the sofa. She rubbed the back of her neck to ease the tension she was feeling.

Lily handed the letters back. "Have you considered," she said, "that no matter what Magnus's motives are, this is an opportunity for you to be included in an art exhibition? It's something you've always wanted, and at least this time you would know who you're dealing with."

For some unknown reason, Annabelle laughed. "But of all the paintings I've done, he wants to show the one I never wanted to see again."

"Which one is that?"

Though Annabelle had confided in Lily about many things, she never told her—or anyone—that she had painted Magnus that summer. She supposed she had not wanted to talk about it because, unlike the painful memories, it was something she could not erase.

"It's a painting I did of him that summer, while he was in the boat, fishing. But I hate that painting, Lily. It's not representative of my work. It's artificial because I was painting a lie, and what I really want is to get it back and destroy it. Perhaps I could buy it back from him, or even give him another in exchange."

Lily pursed her lips. "That's a possibility."

For a long moment Annabelle thought about

everything, then she spoke in a gentle tone. "Do you know why I've never married? Because I have never been able to trust a man who was trying to be charming."

Lily's lips curled up in a grin. "All men try to be charming when they wish to impress you."

"I know that, but I believe I will always be suspicious and skeptical regardless. When a man is attentive or looks at me with interest, I feel immediately contemptuous of him. It's my downfall. My weakness. It's why I'm thirty-four and gathering dust on a shelf."

"In that case," Lily said, "you should definitely go. You're older and wiser now, and skeptical, as you say. This time, you know who and what you're dealing with. You'll be able to tell whether Magnus is sincere or seeking further vengeance. You'll see it in his eyes."

Annabelle leaned back on the sofa. "I don't know. I can't conceive of it—actually seeing him again, discussing an art exhibition, of all things."

"If it makes you feel any better," Lily said, "ask if he'll show another one of your paintings, but at least go and find out his true purpose."

It was difficult to imagine walking into a gallery and seeing Magnus face-to-face again after all these years. What would he look like? Annabelle wondered. Perhaps his hair would be speckled with gray. Perhaps he'd grown fat. She could only hope.

Either way, Lily was right. She was older and wiser now. She would see through his charm this time, and most assuredly the love she once felt for him no longer existed. For thirteen years she had felt nothing for him but hatred.

"All right, I'll go," she said. "Under one condition. You can't tell Whitby."

Lily sucked in a breath. "I beg your pardon? I can't keep a secret from him. We share everything."

"Please, Lily. Just this once, because if he knows Magnus is in London, he'll try to talk me out of going, and he'll go straight to Magnus himself. And you know what happened the last time, when I told him what Magnus had done."

"Yes."

Of course Lily knew. Years ago, Annabelle had told her sister-in-law how Whitby had taken his coach out in the dead of night and gone to Magnus's home. He'd pounded on the door, and when Magnus answered, Whitby grabbed him by the lapels and shoved him across the entryway, up against the opposite wall. Heated words were exchanged, threats delivered, and Whitby had punched Magnus.

From what Annabelle had been told, Magnus took the blow and did not fight back, and after a second persuasive punch in the stomach, he doubled over, fell to his hands and knees on the floor and said simply to Whitby, "There. Now get out."

Even now, when Annabelle imagined that row, she cringed. Perhaps it was the unsettling idea of her brother conducting himself with brutality, because there was no man in the world more kind and loving than he. She knew that without a doubt. His fury must have been exceedingly potent that day.

Aside from that, she could not deny she disliked the image of Magnus being beaten, despite his appalling treatment of her. It made her feel slightly ill.

"Please don't tell Whitby yet," she said to Lily again. "Just wait until I see Magnus, then I'll tell him immediately afterward. You have my word."

Lily shifted her posture, her expression strained with misgivings. "I'll *try* not to say anything, but I can't promise it. Now let's go to dinner. I could eat a team of horses, harness and all."

Lily pushed herself out of the chair and made for the door, but Annabelle went to her desk. "I'll join you in a few minutes. First, I want to send a note to Magnus and tell him I will meet him, before I change my mind."

Lily left the room, and Annabelle put both his letters back into the box, dipped her pen in ink and began to write.

Mr. Wallis,

I received your letters, but have one request. I would like to offer another painting to you in exchange for The Fisherman, *as I would like to have it back. I will bring, for your perusal, a selection of my other works to your gallery on Tuesday. I hope you will find one of them suitable for your exhibition.*

Sincerely,
Annabelle Lawson

Two days later Annabelle's letter arrived at the Grand Hotel in London and was delivered up the stairs on a gold-trimmed salver—to the largest, most luxurious suite in the building.

Magnus Wallis answered the door and accepted the letter, then carried it toward the roaring fire in the marble hearth, where he stood for a moment, staring at the penmanship.

At last he tore it open, his heart pounding violently with curiosity and anticipation as his eyes scanned over it.

She was coming. Tomorrow.

Exhilaration flooded through his veins at the mere thought of seeing her again, after all these years. He tipped his head back and closed his eyes, and labored to slow his breathing.

A moment later he set the letter on the red cushioned chair and crossed to the sideboard, where he poured himself a brandy. He swirled it around in his glass a few times before taking a sip, wondering what the hell he would say to her when she first walked into his gallery. There were a thousand things he wanted to say, but he knew he would have to tread carefully.

He supposed, since she was coming to discuss the exhibition, he would have to address that particular issue first and convince her to let him show *The Fisherman*, because he knew it would garner a superb response. He'd been waiting a long time to show it to the public.

He was disappointed, however, that she wanted it back. What did she mean to do with it? he wondered uneasily. Did she have a plan for it, or did she simply not wish *him* to have it?

Sweeping that notion away—for it would do him no good tonight—Magnus continued to stand over the sideboard, staring at the wall. He took another sip of his drink. A log dropped in the grate, but he barely noticed because he was thinking only of one thing—Annabelle's pain and anger outside the bank that horrific day thirteen years ago, and his own unbearable agony.

He had wronged her and he knew that, but he'd wronged himself as well, for he had not believed himself worthy of her.

Downing the rest of his drink, he reminded himself that everything was different now. He had made something of himself in America, and finally put the misery and indignity of his old life behind him.

But most importantly, he had crossed an ocean for Annabelle, and this time nothing was going to stand in his way.

She didn't know it yet, but this time, no matter what it took, no matter how long, he was going to fight for her. And he would be relentless in that fight—forever—until the glorious, blessed day she was his.

Chapter 9

When Tuesday finally came, Annabelle rode the train to London for her dreaded meeting with Magnus, and spent the entire trip rehearsing what she was going to say and how she would say it.

She had already decided she would speak of nothing but the exhibition, and she would be aloof, indifferent, somewhat cool—so he would know she did not trust him—but not to the point of rudeness, for he was a gallery owner, after all, and possibly her *entrée* to the exclusive London art world.

She hoped she could convey those things, and not let him see that she was nervous. Or tense. Or still affected by what had happened in the past.

Glancing down at the fashionable heeled boots she'd borrowed from Lily, which were unreasonably tight and uncomfortable, she wondered with a frown who she was trying to delude. She was beyond nervous or tense or affected. She was terrified. Terrified that she would take one look at Magnus and remember the inescapable attraction and the forbidden pleasures, and feel the heartbreaking, devastating loss of those wonders all over again.

Oh, she was dreading this. She took a deep, shaky breath and let it out slowly, and promised herself that she would only remember that which was foul.

The train slowly chugged into the London station, and Annabelle got up and lugged her large case down the aisle. She stepped onto the noisy platform, where dozens of people were waving and shouting hello to other passengers, then she walked through the crowd and out onto the street, where she climbed into one of the hansom cabs lined up outside.

"Two twelve Regent Street, please," she told the driver, who closed the door and returned to his seat. Soon they were on their way, clattering through the busy streets of London.

Annabelle glanced down at her black case and suddenly felt a pang of nervous butterflies. She wondered if she was being foolish, trying to get *The Fisherman* back. It was hardly the act of an indifferent woman . . .

A short time later the cab pulled up in front of the gallery, which on the outside looked like any other shop. It had a large paned window and a sign over the door that read, UMBRELLAS BY MAILLET, but the paint was faded and the space looked as if it had been empty for quite some time. Was this supposed to be the gallery?

Annabelle frowned. Perhaps she had been gullible to trust him even this much. Perhaps the gallery itself was another ruse, another deception.

She got out and paid the driver, then walked to the front door. Standing before it, she placed a gloved hand on her belly and took a few deep breaths to try and shoo those maddening butterflies away before she went inside.

Gathering her nerve at last, Annabelle entered and stopped just inside to look around the large, open space.

The walls were painted soft white. She could smell the fresh paint and sawdust, and the floors were newly polished oak. Supplies were littered on the floor in the far corner—a saw and sawhorse, a carpenter's box full of tools, a few cans of paint, and brushes.

There was a large maple desk at the back, which looked like it had just been delivered, and when she looked up, she saw that the lights were yet to come, for there were a few holes in the ceiling with new wiring.

So it *was* going to be a gallery . . .

Annabelle could not deny that it would probably be marvelous when everything was finished. And the location—in the most exclusive shopping district of London—was simply inspired. It was perfect for an unknown artist just starting out.

Wondering if Magnus was there, perhaps beyond the door at the back, she cleared her throat. The sound echoed off the walls.

"Hello!" she called out. She took a few uncertain steps forward, and her heart began to pound fast and hard against her ribs.

There didn't appear to be anyone there, so she paused to consider what to do. Perhaps she should just wait. Perhaps Magnus had stepped out for a moment.

Just then the door at the back clicked open. Annabelle sucked in a little breath and gave her bodice a quick tug at the bottom to make sure she was neat and tidy and confident. But the door stopped only halfway, as if the person behind it weren't quite ready to come out.

Finding this more than a little disconcerting— she just wanted to get this dreaded meeting over with!—she took another step forward and spoke in a firm, assertive voice. "It's Annabelle Lawson."

At last the door opened all the way and a man stepped out from behind it. He wore a black suit and tie, his hair was thick and wavy, and he was striding slowly across the gallery toward her.

In the space of a single heartbeat Annabelle knew it was him—Magnus—and her breath caught in her throat.

Watching him approach, her gaze locked on his intense dark eyes and she immediately fell into a numb stupor, for he looked exactly the same— still strikingly handsome, still wielding a raw, charismatic power no other man in the world could rival.

All at once her heart boomed like thunder in her head, and she seemed to lose feeling in her arms and legs. All she could do was struggle to breathe, and fight to remember how he had once used, hurt, and deceived her.

He came to stand before her with his hands at his sides, and despite all her preconceived plans to act aloof and speak of nothing but business, something utterly inappropriate spewed out of her mouth.

"What are you doing in London, Magnus?" she asked, powerless to hide her antagonism. "You promised never to come back, and Whitby pays you to stay away."

Oh, good God, Annabelle. She'd surely lost her mind.

He was speechless for a moment, and she thought she saw a loss of composure in his eyes. And no wonder. He probably hadn't expected her to bring up the past, at least not in the first five seconds. She hadn't expected it herself.

"I am aware I'm in breach of that contract," he said firmly, recovering himself. "But I intend to terminate it while I'm here. I don't want your brother's money, and if I want to come to England, dammit, I'm going to come."

Annabelle raised her chin, taking a moment to try and regain her own composure, which seemed to have drained down into her tight boots.

"Why *did* you come?" she asked. "To trick me again? To try for another jab at Whitby?"

She was beginning to think she should slap her hand over her mouth to prevent herself from talking. What was wrong with her? She'd intended to speak only of business matters.

Surprisingly, Magnus veered completely away from the argumentative tone of their exchange and shook his head, his voice low as he spoke with a deep, almost forceful sincerity. "*No, Annabelle.* I don't give a damn about Whitby."

His response shook her from the inside out. She felt the full power of his emotions, the potent pull of his resolve. He was determined to convince her she was wrong, and shockingly, every impulse in her body wanted to hear more.

All at once she felt as if her best intentions to remain "on guard" were no match for the strength of his will, or the power of his desires, whatever they were. Her heart was racing and she was perspiring, and she wanted only to flee.

"Maybe this was a mistake," she said. "I think I should go." She turned to leave, but he followed.

"Wait. Just hear me out."

"Hear you out?" What in God's name did he want to say?

"*Please*, Annabelle."

She stopped with her back to him, her hand on the door handle, wondering uneasily why she was not already outside on the street, hailing a cab. Because she hated Magnus—now more than ever—for showing her how much of a hold he still had upon her. Just the sight of him had knocked all her best laid plans out of her mind and turned her into a blathering idiot, a pathetic woman, still pining away over a thirteen-year-old heartbreak.

He moved to the door and stood beside her. Blood pulsing through her veins, she could feel his eyes studying her face, and it took considerable effort to turn her gaze toward him. She managed it, however, and strove to maintain a steadfast glare that told him he could not take advantage of her in any way.

Eyes fixed on her, he slowly brought a hand up

to place over hers on the doorknob, then gently lifted it off.

Annabelle snatched her hand back. She did not want him to touch her.

"Please, hear me out," he said one more time.

Annabelle labored to quiet the mad workings of her body, but it wasn't easy when she was so shaken by the fact that this meeting—which was supposed to be about an art exhibition—had spiraled so swiftly out of control.

"What is it you need to say?" she asked with impatience, noticing for the first time some differences in his appearance. He'd developed lines around his eyes, and he was dressed differently. Expensively.

His broad shoulders rose and fell with a deep intake of breath. "Will you come away from the door?"

She took a moment to consider it, then did not even try to hide her lack of enthusiasm as she turned around.

"Perhaps we could go into my office," he said. "I have chairs, and I could make you a cup of tea."

"I don't want to go into your office," she replied.

"Please," he said again, holding up a hand to direct her toward the back.

For a long moment Annabelle stared at him, for she did not want to do anything he asked of her, but in the end she did move away from the door—albeit reluctantly—for no reason but one. She had come here to learn his intentions and his reasons for returning to London, and if she did not learn those things, she would leave here feeling very much in the dark. And she did not wish to be in the dark. That had been her downfall with him the last time. All summer long.

Not waiting for him to ask again, Annabelle set down her art case, crossed to the back and entered the office. It was a small room, but impeccably furnished, with a new sofa and two matching chairs on a Persian rug, and an empty space at the other end, presumably for the desk outside the door.

Magnus entered behind her and walked to the cabinet in the corner. He opened one of the doors and withdrew a kettle.

"How are you going to make tea?" Annabelle asked. "You have no stove."

"It's an electric kettle," he replied. "I picked it up in Chicago last year."

Annabelle watched him plug it into the newly wired outlet on the wall. An electric kettle. What a brilliant invention. In any other circumstances she would have asked questions about it, but at present she was in no mood to talk about kettles, even if they *were* electric.

While he bent forward to withdraw cups and saucers from the bottom of the cabinet, Annabelle took note of his finely made black suit and how it complimented his strong, muscled form. He was, and always would be, an attractive man who moved with a masculine grace all his own, and she hated the fact that she could still think so. Hence she decided it would be better not to look at all. She turned to face the window.

It was at that moment she saw it.

The painting.

It was hanging on the wall adjacent to the window.

Annabelle froze on the spot, her gaze moving slowly across the canvas as she took in the dramatic mix of color, the light and delicate shadows. She could almost hear the fishing line slicing through the air, the hook landing on the water. She could smell the lake, the worms in the bait box, and the smelly trout.

Barely aware of the teacups clinking on the saucers behind her, she moved closer to the painting, her emotions welling up inside her.

God in heaven. It was unlike anything she'd ever done before or since, she realized with a strange feeling of despair as she stared at it. She couldn't believe *she* was the artist.

Suddenly Magnus was standing beside her, gazing down at her profile. She hadn't even heard him approach.

"There it is," he said, turning his eyes toward

the painting as well. "I know you said you'd like to exchange it for another piece, but I'd really rather not."

Suddenly she remembered that she had wanted to destroy it, and she could have wept at the thought. What had she been thinking? She couldn't possibly, not after seeing it again.

"I'd forgotten what it looked like," she said in a haze.

They both stood in silence, staring at the painting, while the clock ticked steadily on the opposite wall. Then Annabelle remembered where she was and with whom she was standing.

"I'm surprised you kept it," she said with bite. "I thought you would have sold it by now."

His tone was calm and disturbingly tender. "I could never sell it. Not in a thousand years, for any price."

It was a flattering reply, but Annabelle didn't trust it.

Saying nothing more, she went to sit on the sofa. Magnus took a seat in one of the chairs, facing her. They sat in awkward silence for a moment before Magnus spoke.

"You look well," he said.

So they were going to engage in small talk, were they?

"Thank you," she replied coolly. "I've been keeping busy."

"Painting?"

As he sat back waiting for her answer, Annabelle wondered why they were doing this. They were surely beyond normal social graces, especially after all the angry words they'd already spoken. Well, the angry words *she* had spoken.

Perhaps he was seeking to bring some normalcy to this conversation, which might not be such a bad thing. She did not wish to be unnerved. She wanted to be as calm and indifferent as he appeared to be.

"Yes, I paint often," she replied at last, "and I spend a great deal of time with my nieces and nephews."

He was nodding, looking genuinely interested, but she did not trust that, either.

"And how is Lady Whitby?" he asked.

"Very well. She and Whitby are expecting their fifth child in a few weeks."

"Ah. That's wonderful."

Annabelle felt her brow furrow with dismay. Magnus had been her family's enemy for as long as she could remember, and he'd been accused of causing the death of Whitby's older brother. Yet he was asking after them like an old friend, acting as if he cared.

Which he could not possibly. He was a villain. A hateful human being. And this was ridiculous.

Yet when another awkward silence descended upon the room, Annabelle found herself slipping into the familiar safety of polite conversation again, because she could not bear the noise of her heart drumming in her ears while he simply looked at her.

"America agrees with you?" she asked without enthusiasm.

"Yes. I have a house in New York and another in South Carolina. I prefer the southern weather in the winter months."

She pondered this news. He had two homes, and he'd purchased this space, furnished it with some very fine pieces, and his clothes . . . Well, he looked immaculate, with shiny Italian leather shoes and a shirt that was clearly made of the finest linen money could buy.

What had he been doing since he left England?

He must have seen the question in her eyes, for he answered what she was thinking. "I'm in business in America. Shortly after I arrived there, I discovered I had a knack for buying and selling property."

He was leaning an elbow on the armrest, his forefinger resting on his temple. He appeared very relaxed now, with one long leg crossed over the other, gazing calmly at her.

Annabelle knew he was doing this just to ride out her shock from seeing him, and despite her agitation, she found herself breathing slower. Perhaps that was a good thing. She felt more in control now. She was more rational. She could do this.

"I started out by purchasing a building not much bigger than this one," he continued, "which had a good location but was run-down. I rebuilt it almost from scratch, doing most of the work myself, and sold it for a profit. Then I did the same thing again with a bigger building each time, and now here I am."

"Congratulations," she said, only because it was the appropriate thing to say.

She looked around the room. "Did you do all this work yourself?"

"Most of it, yes," he said, "which I greatly enjoyed, because I haven't done this sort of thing in a while. The projects became too complex, and there were too many at once. I have people now who do this for me."

"I see." She was quiet for a moment, pondering what he had just told her, thinking about this building. "Why a gallery?"

He inclined his head at her. "I have an interest in art."

"You didn't when I knew you," she said, raising an accusing eyebrow. "You knew nothing about it when I met you on the train."

He did not seem surprised or shaken by her tone. He remained cool and collected. "No, but since then I've acquired an appreciation."

Another tense silence enveloped the room. Annabelle could almost feel the weight of her painting hanging on the wall behind her. She turned around and glanced at it.

When she looked back at Magnus, he was watching her intently. His gaze went from her eyes to the painting over her head, then back to her eyes again.

"Someday that'll be in the National Gallery," he said. "Or perhaps in the Met in New York."

"I hardly think so," she replied, even though she knew the painting was exceptional. More than exceptional, and it felt strange to think such a thing, because she never marveled at any of her other paintings. She was always so critical of her own work. But this one . . .

She still couldn't believe she had painted it.

"Is this your first gallery?" she asked, wanting suddenly to redirect the conversation back to him. She didn't want to talk about herself or her life or her work as an artist.

"No. I own two others in New York. They're labors of love."

Labors of love? For pity's sake, this whole conversation was insane. This was Magnus. Magnus!

Annabelle strove to get her head on straight and decided it was time to take control of this meeting and find out the real reason why he had come back, and why he'd wanted her to hear him out.

"Magnus," she said, closing her eyes briefly, her voice still cool and faintly antagonistic. "Let's get to the heart of it, shall we? What is it you want to say to me?"

Annabelle waited for him to answer, while he gazed at her with steady, penetrating eyes. Finally he leaned forward in his chair and spoke.

"I returned to London," he said, "because I have some regrets about what happened between us, and I wanted you to know that."

Annabelle squeezed her hands together on her lap. Her brain couldn't seem to process what he'd just said to her. He had regrets? Magnus? Magnus had regrets?

She could have laughed out loud, but that would have required her to smile, which just wasn't possible right now. She was far too tense.

"How interesting," she said. "But I'm afraid I'm having a hard time believing you."

He nodded his understanding and lounged back again as if he hadn't a care in the world. "I knew you would."

"You knew I would?" He was entirely too confident, so she scoffed out loud. "You treated me appallingly, Magnus. You used me and discarded me, knowing from the very beginning that you were going to break my heart, but you didn't care in the least. So you must forgive me for finding it difficult to believe that a man as heartless and unfeeling as you might be remorseful."

Oh, it had felt so good to say all that.

His eyes smoldered with resolve. "I am not heartless, Annabelle, and I mean to prove that to you."

She laughed. "How are you going to do that?"

"Well, to start with, I can tell you that I'm sorry, that I never meant to hurt you."

Annabelle's mouth fell open. Perhaps she was being a tad vindictive herself, but good God! Did he think he could just come here and say he didn't mean it, and she would simply smile and say, *How kind of you*, and he would be absolved?

"It took you thirteen years to realize that you'd been unscrupulous, and that I deserved an apology?" Her anger was rising up inside her again.

He spoke with vehemence. "I was not unscrupulous, but merely stupid. And it did not take me until now to realize I'd wronged you. I knew it all along."

"So why come here and apologize *now*?"

She stood up. This was absurd. She wanted to leave.

He stood, too. "Sit down, Annabelle. Please. Let me finish."

She hesitated, fighting to subdue her temper, then reluctantly did as he asked.

"How can you tell me you were not unscrupulous," she asked, "after what you said to me that day outside the bank, when you told me that you'd been using me all along?"

She frowned at him and leaned back on the sofa, remembering his brutal, merciless words.

I was enjoying a very satisfying jab at Whitby . . .

I didn't love you . . .

Just thinking of it made her breath come short. He had cut her so deeply. There had been no kindness in his manner. He had not even tried to be gentle about it.

"I thought it was my only choice to say those things to you," he said. "But none of it was true. I did care for you, and I was never using you for vengeance upon Whitby. I ended it because I was your family's enemy, and I knew I could not provide for you. I said what I said because I knew you loved me, and I believed it was the only way to make you forget me."

She stared at him in astonishment. "So now you're telling me you lied to me outside the bank?" She threw her arms up in the air. "I'm afraid I'm getting rather tangled up in all the different lies on different days."

She heard the kettle hissing on the side table.

"Your water is boiling," she said.

He glanced up, then rose to pour the water into the silver teapot. He carried the small round tray to the coffee table between them and set it down.

Annabelle leaned forward to pour her own tea. "Aren't you going to have any?" she asked, sitting back.

He blinked slowly. "No."

Exhausted and weary from this trying conversation, Annabelle brought the fine china cup to her lips, but the tea was too hot to drink, so she set it back down and contemplated what Magnus was saying to her.

All her life she had been told certain things about him and his father—that they were both dangerous and conniving. Magnus had proven that sentiment to be true. He'd even admitted it that day in front of the bank, so how could she trust anything he said to her now?

Suddenly in no mood to drink tea, Annabelle stood and walked to the window, which looked out onto a narrow lane. She focused not on what was outside, but on the window itself—the way the little bubbles in the glass held the light.

Then she heard Magnus rising from his chair, too, and heard his quiet footfalls across the Persian carpet. Just the sound of his approach caused a fire to burn through her body, and she remembered all too well the excitement of being with him on the lake, and in the woods on the island, and how she had melted from the bliss of his presence alone.

He still possessed that same power, that same magnetic pull, and she hated that she was affected by it all over again.

Fighting hard to quench the memories—

because she could not let him use his charm to trick her again—she squared her shoulders.

He came to stand beside her, so immensely disturbing to her in every way, but she refused to look at him. She did not take her eyes off the glass.

"Annabelle," he said in a soft, tender whisper, "I know you don't want to hear this, but I must say it, I must." He leaned closer, so she could feel the moist heat of the whisper in her ear. *"I've missed you."*

Her response to those words was devastating to her—*devastating*—for they uncovered a buried memory—of all the nights she had cried herself to sleep after their breakup, wishing it had all been a bad dream and her wonderful Mr. Edwards would come back and say those very words to her—that he was sorry and he'd missed her.

But suddenly, as quickly as the memory flashed in her mind, it disappeared again, because she had the good sense to remember that what happened between them had *not* been a bad dream. It had been very real, and she had to protect herself.

Annabelle raised her chin. "You're right about one thing. I don't want to hear it."

He leaned even closer. "But Annabelle, not a day has gone by that I haven't thought of you and wondered how you are. Sometimes I have dreams so real that I wake up in a sweat, thinking for days afterward that you were looking for me for some reason, or that you might even be in New York."

Annabelle closed her eyes, digging deep for the will to remember how cruel he really was. She would find it. She would.

"I have *not* been looking for you," she said, "and I was never in New York."

Though she could not deny that she had often looked for his face in a crowd over the past thirteen years.

With the back of a finger, Magnus stroked her arm lightly. His voice was gentle and soothing. "I'll say it a hundred times if I must. I *am* sorry, Annabelle, for hurting you. If I could go back, I would handle it all very differently."

Suddenly she couldn't speak. Her chest was heaving with a desperate need for air. A lump had formed in her throat and she struggled to swallow over it and force it back down, for she could not let herself be fooled by this blatant seduction.

She turned and faced him, imposing an iron will on herself. "But you can't go back, Magnus. What's done is done."

"Perhaps someday you will find it in yourself to forgive me."

"I highly doubt it."

His penetrating gaze did not waver. "I'm not the man I was thirteen years ago. I promise you that."

She frowned, wondering what was really going on in his mind. Was he truly sorry? Was he being sincere? And even if he was, would it make a difference? "You expect me to believe you, simply because you say it?"

"No, I hope you will be able to see it for yourself."

She looked him over from head to toe, still working hard to hold onto her caution, to be skeptical. "Because you have money? Is that it? A gallery? An expensive suit? Is that how I'm supposed to see that you've changed?" She walked away from him and swung around in the center of the office. "I'm afraid you're going to have to do better than that, Magnus, because I don't trust you. You could be the richest man in the world, and nothing you could say or do would ever change that."

He drew his head back as he digested her reply.

"I should go now," she said, before he could say another word.

He hesitated, as if he was not yet ready to let her go, then at last he escorted her through the office door.

They crossed the empty gallery, and Annabelle realized with a start that they hadn't even begun to talk about the art exhibition.

Perhaps it was just as well, she thought, because she was not sure she could survive seeing him again. It was too painful and unsettling.

She picked up her art case containing the three extra paintings she had brought.

He glanced down at the case. "But wait . . ."

Annabelle closed her eyes. He was not going to let her get away so easily after all.

"I know this is probably too much to ask," he said, "but I'm opening this gallery in a few weeks, and I would still like to include your painting—the one in my office." He glanced down at the case again. "But perhaps with your permission, I could look at those as well?"

Annabelle was momentarily befuddled after all that had just happened, but then she glanced around at the cream-colored walls and the shiny oak floor in this superb location, and was not about to let Magnus feel that he was holding her back from this. She had wanted to be indifferent, didn't she?

So she forced herself to hand the case over to him. "One look."

He nodded and carried it to the desk. Not entirely sure she had done the right thing, Annabelle stood back while he removed the first piece, which she called *Amber Grass*.

He held it at arm's length before him, silently studying it while Annabelle tried to forget that he was Magnus. Right now he was a gallery owner making a judgment about her paintings.

He set *Amber Grass* on the floor against the wall before withdrawing the next piece: *Autumn Forest*. Again he held it at arm's length, studying it for a long time while Annabelle waited.

"Do you have arrangements with any other artists to show their work?" she asked, glancing around suspiciously.

He didn't reply right away. He continued to look at *Autumn Forest*, then set it on the floor against the wall, next to the other one.

"Yes, I brought a few works done by some American artists. Have you heard of George Wright?"

He reached into the case for the last painting.

Surprised, Annabelle took a step forward. "George Wright? You're showing *his* work here?"

He was one of her favorite painters. He had a style of brushstroke like no one else, and he rebelled openly against convention.

"Yes," Magnus said, holding up the last painting. This one was a seascape that she called *Fierce Waters*.

Finally he turned to face her. "This one is the best."

"The seascape?"

"Yes. You have a gift with water."

Annabelle didn't know what to say. She was still staggered by the fact that Magnus had in his possession a painting by George Wright, and he was asking to include *her* work in the same exhibition.

"My home in South Carolina is on the coast," he said lightly, "and it has a spectacular view of the water." He set the painting down beside the others. "You would like it."

"Would I indeed?" she replied, not wanting him to think he knew her personal tastes.

But then she remembered telling him once that she wished she lived on the coast. Had he remembered that?

He sat on the desk, his hands curling around the edge of it. "The paintings are excellent, Annabelle. Can I show them? All of them?"

She took a moment to think about it. If she allowed him to show her paintings here, wouldn't that require more meetings or correspondence with him? She did not wish to have any connection with him again after today because she did not trust him.

But then she thought of George Wright. She imagined her work hanging on the same wall, then wondered if this was a ploy to lure her in . . .

"How long do you plan to stay in London?" she asked, wanting to understand what this would entail.

"I'm not certain. I've purchased two residences on Park Lane, so it depends how long the improvements take and how quickly I can turn them around."

She narrowed her gaze at him. "You came back to conquer London, I see."

"I suppose you could say that," he replied, his dark eyes gleaming with determination.

She experienced a spontaneous vision of Magnus buying the houses on either side of Whitby's London residence and turning them into brothels. Then she chided herself for entertaining such an outlandish thought. Surely he would never be so blatantly ruthless with his vengeance. Would he?

"Regarding the gallery, however," he said, changing his tone, "I might only be involved with it for a few more weeks. I'm looking for someone to manage it, and once it's established, I'll likely do what I do best."

"Sell it for a profit, too," she said.

He inclined his head somewhat apologetically. "It's what I do. And though I consider my galleries labors of love, I don't intend to stay in London forever, so it would be difficult to administer."

She was very glad to hear he didn't intend to stay in London.

"Well, I can see you've put a lot of work into this place," she said, glancing around.

"What can I say? I'm a worker."

She suspected he was trying to tell her he no longer coveted Whitby's position in society, that he had no respect for it and preferred his own. But she wasn't sure she believed that.

"It's probably futile to ask," he said, "but I don't suppose *you'd* be interested in managing the gallery for me?"

Yes, it was certainly futile.

"I have no experience," she replied.

"But you know art."

But she could not work for Magnus. "I'm sorry, I don't think so."

He grinned at her, and it was the first time today that she'd seen even the smallest hint of a smile. It was familiar and stirred those memories again, so she swept the recognition away.

"I just had to ask," he said.

"I'm flattered you thought I could do it," she replied, striving to sound businesslike.

"I have no doubt that you could."

The temperature of the room seemed to escalate suddenly as Annabelle stood before Magnus, who was still sitting on the desk, now paying her compliments.

He had paid her compliments once before, though, hadn't he? To seduce her and get what he wanted.

"But you haven't answered me about the paintings yet," he said. "Can I show them?"

Annabelle thought about it. Despite her hostility toward Magnus and her desire never to see him again, she knew this was an opportunity she could not refuse—to be shown in the same gallery as George Wright, when it was next to impossible to break into the London art world, especially for a woman.

She could not let her personal feelings keep her

from a dream such as that, could she? If she did, she would surely live to regret it.

Besides, Magnus had said he planned to hand the gallery over to someone else, so she would likely be dealing with that person after he returned to America.

After another moment's consideration, she finally gave him an answer. "Yes, you can show them."

Magnus slapped both his hands on the desk before he hopped off it, looking exceedingly pleased, while Annabelle wasn't so sure. "This is wonderful," he said. "I know your work will attract attention."

"No, George Wright will attract the attention."

"Not for long."

She wished she could take the compliment at face value, but alas she could not. Not coming from him.

"I'll escort you out," he said, walking past her.

When they reached the door, Annabelle stopped, feeling a sudden onslaught of anxiety over what she had just agreed to. She turned to face him. "Perhaps if there are any details to be discussed regarding the exhibition, we could correspond through letters, as I don't come to London very often."

It was a lie. She came all the time, and she suspected he knew it. She could see it in his eyes.

"Of course," he said nonetheless. "And I'll let

you know as soon as I find a manager. When I do, he will take over from there."

She stood in front of the door, waiting for him to open it.

"Thank you, Annabelle," he said again, and she wondered what he was thanking her for, exactly. The paintings? No, it was more than that, she suspected, but she did not wish to contemplate it further.

She simply nodded and walked out.

Chapter 10

~~~oGGo~~~

After Annabelle left the gallery, Magnus closed the door and stood for a moment with his hand still resting on the knob.

Well. That had not gone quite as swimmingly as he had hoped, but at least he'd broken the ice.

Leaning back against the door, he closed his eyes, feeling grateful for one thing at least—he finally knew what she looked like, after wondering for years how she might have changed.

Not surprisingly, she was just as beautiful as she had always been. Perhaps even more beautiful, for the years had given her a certain indefinable vigor, for lack of a better word. She seemed self-assured and more sophisticated than before.

But her eyes were still the same—wild and luminous, her figure still voluptuously attractive. The only difference was that her manner of dress was more conservative. She'd been wearing a sensible hat, and gone were the clumsy boys' boots.

He wondered if she still wore them in the country, when she was lugging her easel up and down steep hills, with her cow, Helen, plodding behind. Did she still have that cow? he wondered. He smiled affectionately at the thought of it, then his smile faded as he reminded himself he still had a steep mountain of his own to scale and conquer.

Pushing away from the door, he crossed the gallery to where her paintings leaned against the wall and crouched down to look at them again. By God, they were magnificent. He especially admired the creative mix of color—the blues and grays of the seascape, with hints of . . . Was it mauve?

He also had to marvel at how the water seemed to surge and swell before his eyes. How in God's name did she create such movement?

Then he found himself wondering why she had never shown her paintings to the public before now. What was she afraid of?

Rejection, most likely, which caused him some regret.

All that aside, she was without question miraculously gifted, and it only added to her allure. He was in awe of her, and he wanted her back in his arms, and eventually, someday, in his bed. For although there had been other women over the years, she was the only one he had ever loved.

But was it even possible? he wondered with a twinge of concern, striving to be realistic as he rose to his feet and returned to his office.

He glanced at the sofa cushion where she'd been sitting—she hadn't touched her tea—and recalled their conversation, how she had spoken to him with such hostility.

She had not forgiven him, but he was not surprised, given what he'd done to her and the number of years she'd harbored and nurtured her hurt. He had expected as much when he got out of bed that morning. He'd known there would be a quarrel of some sort.

He'd also known she would think he was here to exact further vengeance upon Whitby.

He'd told her he didn't give a damn about her brother—which was God's own truth—but he doubted she believed that, because there was a time when he very much *had* given a damn. Those five years after their breakup had been the darkest of his life. He had hated Whitby more than ever, and his bitterness had been all consuming, eating away at him like a disease. There were times when he'd become a villain himself, taunting his cousin, just to inflict pain on him where he felt pain was due.

And once, when Whitby was gravely ill, Magnus had actually hoped he would not recover. That was how dark those days had been.

If Magnus hadn't left for America when he had, he didn't know what would have become of him. He would surely have continued to wallow in his anger, on a downward course straight to hell.

But those days were over. After eight years in America, his life was no longer dismal. He'd made a success of himself, had learned to have hope, and because of that, he finally felt worthy of Annabelle.

Even though she had been unwavering in her antagonism today, he would press on. He would not give up. Rome wasn't built in a day, after all. He would simply have to be patient, and lay one precious brick at a time.

Annabelle returned to Century House that evening, exhausted after the three-hour train ride from London. Carrying her empty art case with her, she greeted Clarke, the butler, and went straight to her rooms to dress for dinner.

A short time later she was hurrying into the drawing room to join Whitby, Lily, and the children.

"Annabelle, you're back," Lily said cheerfully,

standing by the piano, holding John's hand, her youngest, who was only three. He ran to Annabelle, and she scooped him up into her arms.

"Auntie Annabelle!"

"Johnny!" she said. "Did you miss me today?"

"No."

"No!" Annabelle replied, laughing out loud.

"Father took us fishing!" Johnny explained, squirming out of Annabelle's arms, forcing her to set him down before she dropped him.

Annabelle gazed at Whitby, who was sitting on the other side of the room, across from young Eddie at the chess table. "You went to the lake?" she asked.

"Yes," Whitby replied. "It was a perfect day, wasn't it?"

"Perfect indeed," Eddie replied distractedly, moving a chess piece.

"I didn't want to go," Dorothy said in a haughty voice, for Dorothy—Lily and Whitby's only daughter as of yet—was a very grown-up four-year-old, who would never be caught dead touching a fish. She preferred her dolls and hair ribbons.

"So if you didn't go with the boys," Annabelle said, "what did you do today? Did you stay indoors?"

"No. I took Helen for a walk in the garden," Dorothy replied.

"Well, thank you very much. I'm sure Helen enjoyed the exercise."

Dorothy nodded proudly, then Annabelle moved to the sofa and sat down next to Johnny and Lily. Her thoughts drifted back to the fishing excursion.

"That old boat still floats?" she asked, realizing she hadn't been in it since that long-ago summer.

"Like a boat should," Whitby said. "We didn't have to bail, did we, boys?"

"What's a bail, Father?" Johnny asked.

"It's when the water leaks into the boat and you have to scoop it out with a bucket so you don't sink."

"I wouldn't like to sink," Johnny said.

Lily messed his hair. "I should think not!"

Lily and Annabelle shared an amused glance as Johnny slid off the sofa and went to join young James, who was sitting on the floor playing with his army of tin soldiers.

"How did everything go?" Lily asked in a quiet voice, though her eyes were brimming with curiosity.

Annabelle hesitated, glancing across at Whitby. "It went fine. He liked my other paintings, and he's going to include them in the exhibition."

"That's wonderful."

Annabelle then told Lily about the American artist, George Wright, and how it was an honor to be shown in the same gallery.

"But how was everything else?" Lily asked in an even quieter voice.

Annabelle wasn't sure where to begin. "It was rather nerve-racking. We talked about what happened years ago."

"You don't say."

"Yes, and he apologized to me, Lily. Can you believe that?"

Lily sat back. "I thought perhaps he might."

"Did you really?"

"Yes. Why would he come all this way and contact you unless he had something important to say?"

Annabelle gazed pensively toward the boys playing with their little army on the other side of the room. "I'm still not certain he came here just for the single purpose of apologizing. He seemed very determined, as if he were on a straight path toward something."

She thought about what he'd said to her, that he had missed her. Was it possible *she* was the something he wanted, and he was here in London to claim her? Could he be that presumptuous?

Yes, he probably could.

"He's purchased two buildings in London," Annabelle told Lily, attempting to distract herself from the idea of Magnus actually "claiming" her.

Lily's eyebrows lifted. "He must have money

beyond the allowance from Whitby. Did he say anything about that?"

"Yes, he said he doesn't want it anymore, and he intends to inform Whitby as such."

Lily gazed lovingly at her husband. "You're going to have to tell him everything, Annabelle. I can't keep it secret any longer. He knows me too well."

Annabelle watched her brother playing chess with his son. Eddie made a move, and Whitby shouted with laughter. "Brilliant, Eddie! I didn't see that coming!"

But there was something else he did not see coming, and she was not looking forward to explaining it.

Later that night, after the children had gone to bed, Annabelle returned to the drawing room with Lily and Whitby—as was their habit most evenings after dinner, when they would read or chat or play cards.

While Lily played the piano, Annabelle sat on the sofa with Whitby, but she wasn't really hearing the music, for her mind was occupied with thoughts about what had occurred that day and how she was going to tell Whitby what she had kept from him.

Taking a deep breath, she finally met her

brother's gaze. "There's something I need to tell you, and I hope you won't be angry."

Whitby sat back, his brow furrowing with concern.

"Over the past few weeks," she began, "I've received two letters from . . . a gallery owner. He wanted to include one of my paintings in an exhibition."

Her brother touched her arm. "That's *wonderful* news, Annabelle. Congratulations. But why would you think I would be angry?"

She bit her lip, then decided to cease her stalling and meet the problem head on. "Because the letters came from Magnus, and you're not going to like this, Whitby, but he has returned to London."

For a moment her brother stared at her as if he wasn't quite sure he'd heard her correctly, then his eyes darkened with worry and he looked across the room at Lily, who was tapping away on the piano.

Annabelle understood her brother's anxiety. He'd lost many loved ones in his lifetime—which was why he'd always been so protective of her—and he considered Magnus a serious danger.

"He wrote you letters while posing as a gallery owner?" Whitby asked.

Annabelle looked down at her hands upon her lap. "Well, he wasn't exactly posing. He really does own a gallery, and I went to see him today."

Whitby stared at her in disbelief. "Did you know it was him when you agreed to meet?"

"Yes, of course," she assured him. "I'm sorry I didn't tell you, but—"

Whitby cupped his forehead in a hand. "Why the hell didn't you, Annabelle? Who knows what could have happened? You shouldn't have gone there alone."

He stood up, looking as if he wanted to dash out of the house at that instant, find Magnus wherever he was, and confront him again, just like he had the last time.

All of a sudden the music stopped. Lily noticed her husband rise. "Is everything all right?" she asked.

"Magnus has returned," Whitby told her directly.

"Oh my," Lily replied.

For a long intense moment Annabelle's brother stared at his wife fixedly. "You knew, didn't you?"

Lily's lips parted. "Well . . ."

Annabelle felt immensely guilty for asking Lily to keep something so important from her husband, but that was apparently not Whitby's first concern. He strode to the window, contemplating what all this meant.

"He should not have come back. He is in breach of our agreement."

"Please, Whitby, sit down," Annabelle said. "Let me tell you what happened."

Thankfully, he returned to the sofa, and Lily sat across from them to listen in.

Annabelle decided to start at the beginning. "That summer that we spent together thirteen years ago, I painted Magnus in the boat fishing, and that's the painting he brought with him—the one he wanted to hang in the gallery."

"Wait a minute," Whitby said, holding up a hand. "You *painted* him? You never told me that."

"I didn't really want to talk about it."

He gazed in the other direction for a moment. "I saw that painting over his mantel once—on the day I offered him the money to leave England. *You* painted that?"

"Yes."

"It was one of the most beautiful paintings I'd ever seen, Annabelle," Whitby said. "I didn't recognize it as one of yours. Not that I don't think your work is exquisite, but it was different."

"I almost didn't recognize it myself," she said, "when I first saw it today."

Both Lily and Whitby waited in silence for her to continue. She took a moment to decide where to begin and what in particular she should tell them. It all seemed rather smudged together at the moment.

"When I met him today, he explained that he regretted the way he had treated me all those years ago, and that he hoped I could forgive him."

Whitby's jaw clenched visibly. "You didn't believe him, I hope." It was not a question, but rather a very strong suggestion.

"No, not really."

Where had that come from? It should have been a firm *Absolutely not*.

"Not *really*? You're not sure, Annabelle?" Whitby's tone dripped with disbelief.

Annabelle felt suddenly frazzled. "No . . . I mean of course I'm sure! And I told him so—that I could never trust him, not in a hundred years."

There was no mistaking the fact that Whitby's body relaxed significantly upon hearing that. His shoulders rose and fell, and his fist opened on his lap.

"I'm relieved to hear that, Annabelle. Did you get your painting back? He doesn't deserve to have it. We can hang it here. In a prominent place."

Nervous butterflies invaded her belly as she prepared to answer. "No, he still has it, and I left three more with him as well."

Whitby's hand slid up and down upon his thigh, as if he were trying to wipe something from his palm. "Why?"

"Because he is opening that gallery soon, and I want my work included in the exhibition."

Whitby chuckled bitterly, as if he had expected things to unfold exactly as they had. "But don't you see? That was his plan. He bought the gallery for the singular purpose of seducing you with it. That manipulative scoundrel."

Annabelle frowned as she fought to understand the reasons why her brother was so afraid for her, when he already knew she hated Magnus for breaking her heart.

"Tell me something," she said. "Why do you still hate him so much after all these years? I know you blame him for your brother's death, but everyone knows there was no concrete proof that—"

"Are you falling in love with him again, Annabelle? Is that what's happening here?"

She clenched her teeth together. "Of course not," she assured him. "I just want to know what I am dealing with. You believe he has returned for further vengeance upon us as a family—but vengeance for *what*? Surely he does not still harbor hatred because of what happened to his father. That was two lifetimes ago, and he seems to have moved on."

Whitby paused a moment before he spoke. "But you already know why Magnus has always been rejected here."

Annabelle sat with her back poker straight and squeezed her hands together tightly on her lap. "You told me that his father was dangerous, that he tried to harm your father when they were children. But how exactly?"

"Among other things, Magnus's father tried to set my father on fire."

Annabelle covered her mouth with a hand. "Surely not."

"The bed went up in flames, and my father suffered burns on his arms and legs, but thankfully managed to get out of the room alive."

Annabelle flinched at the cold, disquieting tone of her brother's voice. "But what did *Magnus* do?" she asked, needing more specific information. "Why was he also cut off from the family?"

Whitby raked a hand through his hair, his eyes clouding over with disdain. "From what I understand, no one even knew of Magnus's existence until he was nine. His birth was kept secret from us."

"How did you find out about him?"

Whitby sat forward, elbows on knees. "When Magnus's father died, his mother took it upon herself to demand financial support from us, and promised my brother John—who had just become earl that year and was only fourteen years old—that if he didn't give her what she wanted, she and Magnus would make all our lives a living hell. Then they did. Magnus threatened and even attacked John dozens of times over the next few years, and it didn't stop until John was dead."

Annabelle's blood chilled in her veins. "But Magnus would have only been a child."

"His father was a child when he lit my father's bed on fire. He was *mad*, Annabelle. He was jealous and hateful, and Magnus was the same. You know it yourself. You know what he did to you, how he used you. You know his heart is cold like ice."

She began to feel ill.

Whitby blinked slowly at her. "You were only an infant when Magnus came into our lives," he said.

"I was three when John died," she added. "I barely remember him. All my life you have been my only family. And now Lily and the children, of course."

Yes, Whitby had been her guardian as long as she could remember. Her protector. He had taken care of things when he learned how Magnus had used and discarded her, and he had held her while she wept.

Annabelle squeezed Whitby's hand. He was a good man, and now he was a husband and father. He loved his children with every inch of his being, and would gladly lay down his life for any one of them. There was no one in the world more devoted and loyal to those he loved, and Annabelle was thankful to be one of those fortunate people.

If she had to decide whom to trust—Whitby or Magnus—of course it would be Whitby. There was no question.

"Don't worry about me," she said. "The only

thing I care about is that my paintings will hang beside George Wright's paintings, and he's an artist I greatly admire. And I will *not* be seduced. I am not the foolish, trusting girl I once was. So I assure you, it will be impossible for Magnus to ever win back my esteem. Especially after what I've heard today."

Whitby closed his eyes and pinched the bridge of his nose, while Annabelle glanced uneasily at Lily, who shrugged helplessly.

They all sat in silence for a minute or two, until Whitby spoke. "There is still the issue of my contract with him. He is in breach."

"He knows it," Annabelle said. "But he told me he didn't want your money anymore. He's prepared to terminate the agreement."

Whitby looked up in surprise, as if he couldn't believe any of this and almost found it humorous on some strange, outlandish level.

"Well, it's not up to him, is it? Whether he likes it or not, the payments stop now."

Annabelle merely nodded.

"Where is this gallery he purchased?" Whitby asked.

"Two twelve Regent Street," Annabelle replied, knowing full well why Whitby wanted the address, but she was not going to stand in his way. If he had something to say to Magnus, he could say it. It was none of her affair. She didn't care. They were both grown men.

Though in truth, they had always been more like two bulls locking horns, ramming into each other at every opportunity.

Whitby stood. "I'll be traveling to London in the morning."

"I suspected as much," Annabelle replied.

He turned to leave, but Annabelle stopped him. "Wait, Whitby."

Her brother faced her, and she briefly mulled over what she wanted to say to him.

"You might find him different now," she said. "He has money."

Her brother stared at her briefly before he narrowed his gaze. Lily nervously cleared her throat.

"Rich or poor," Whitby replied, "I will *not* find him different." Then he turned and left the room.

Chapter 11

~~~~~

Magnus was leaning over a table he had purchased at an auction that morning, pushing hard upon the sander—back and forth, back and forth—taking pleasure in knowing that when he was finished, this piece would be exquisite. He would set the gallery cards upon it.

Feeling the strain in his back and arms, he straightened and swiped an arm across his brow. It was hard work, sanding paint off mahogany, but well worth it. And he'd always enjoyed working with his hands.

Just when he was about to lean back into it, the

gallery door opened, and who should walk in but Whitby.

Bloody hell, Magnus thought, setting the sander down and letting out a deep sigh of frustration, for he did not want to stop what he was doing, especially not to talk to his cousin, but he knew it was necessary. Best to get it over with.

He pulled off his gloves and tossed them onto the table, then sauntered across the gallery to address Whitby, who approached him from the other side.

They stopped in the center of the room and stood in silence facing each other, but after a very short time, Magnus grew tired of the bravado. He had no interest in this sort of thing, which was rather astounding. At one time he had lived for it—especially during the five years after his summer with Annabelle. His bitterness over that loss had simmered and raged inside him for a long time afterward, and his resentment toward Whitby had reached its peak.

Thank God he left for America when he had.

"I was expecting you today," he finally said to his cousin.

"Were you indeed?" Whitby replied.

"Yes. I suspected you'd want to discuss our contract. And I knew you would wish to have a word with me about Annabelle."

Whitby glared at him briefly before turning and wandering around the gallery, looking with a critical eye at the new wiring in the ceiling, the fresh paint on the walls . . .

"I will always be looking out for Annabelle," Whitby said, "as she is my sister."

"Not by blood," Magnus replied curtly, realizing it was a point he'd often revisited with a sense of relief—the fact that Annabelle was not born of the same ilk as Whitby and John and their insufferable father. Their grandfather, too. He could certainly not forget to include him.

Whitby merely glanced at Magnus, and ignored the comment. He walked to the front window and watched a few people walk by, then spoke with cool detachment. "A gallery. How out of the ordinary. You certainly chose a promising location."

"I always do."

Magnus watched his cousin saunter leisurely to the other side of the room, and recognized his intent to demonstrate how relaxed and confident he was—as if Whitby considered him a mere nuisance, nothing more.

Yet he had come all the way to London without wasting a moment, hadn't he? Perhaps Whitby was not as impervious as he pretended to be.

Not that it mattered, Magnus reminded himself. His cousin could leap off the back of a steamship, for all he cared. All he wanted to do right now was get back to his work.

Magnus glanced impatiently down at the

sander, which was sitting idle on the table . . .

"Look," he said, taking a step forward, "I've got things to do, so let us get through this, shall we? Yes, I've returned to England, and by doing so I have broken our contract, so why don't we render it void as of three weeks ago, the day I stepped off the ship? Feel free to have your solicitor draw up papers for me to sign."

Whitby faced him. "Just like that, you're going to give up ten thousand a year? I hope the visit was worth it."

"It was," Magnus replied with absolute honesty.

Whitby frowned. "Why? What could possibly be worth that much money?"

"Why I returned to England is none of your affair," Magnus replied.

"It's my affair when you break an agreement with me."

Magnus struggled to keep his impatience under control, for this conversation was going in circles when he just wanted to be done with it. "I told you I don't want your money anymore. In fact, I would like to repay all of it. I don't need anything from you."

"Except for Annabelle," Whitby said flatly.

All at once the tension in the gallery shot up to the ceiling.

Magnus felt the muscles in his forearms tighten beneath his sleeves, and when he spoke, his tone was distinctly firm. "But she doesn't belong to you, does she?"

Whitby's expression clouded over with a grave, stony warning. "She is my sister and therefore under my protection."

"But she can have no thoughts or conversations of her own? She's a woman now, Whitby. She can do as she pleases."

Whitby made no reply, but Magnus could see the displeasure in his eyes.

Oh, he was getting tired of this. He didn't come to England to fight with Whitby. He came for Annabelle, and that was all that mattered.

"Whitby," he said, rubbing the back of his neck, "is there anything else you wish to say to me? Because I have things to do."

Whitby's shoulders rose and fell as he pondered the question. "Yes, as a matter of fact, there is. I will have you know, Magnus, that my sister is off limits to you, and if you lay one hand on her or hurt her in any way, I will hunt you down and kill you. Do you understand?"

Magnus stiffened and swallowed hard over the bile rising up in his throat. God, he had thought things were going so well, but this was most assuredly out of line.

Evidently his cousin had not changed over the years. Not in the slightest.

"Do not attempt," Magnus said clearly and succinctly, "to tell me what I can and cannot do, Whitby. You do not control me, nor are you above me."

"Maybe not according to the American way, but in England I am very much above you."

Magnus clenched his hands into fists. He could barely comprehend how quickly his hatred toward Whitby awakened and shot to the surface.

But he would not be dragged back into the fight. That was behind him. He was here for Annabelle.

"If you will excuse me . . ." he firmly said.

Whitby walked to the door. "Don't say you weren't warned."

Bloody hell, that was it. He had tried to be civil, but there were limits to his forbearance, and he couldn't take this insufferable arrogance. Not anymore. Not on his own property.

He strode forward. "You still love to have the last word, don't you?"

Whitby raised a triumphant eyebrow at him and walked out, but as Magnus watched him go, he realized with a most disturbing uneasiness that where Whitby was concerned, he still loved to have it, too.

"What happened?" Annabelle asked, hurrying to meet her brother at the door the second he stepped inside the house.

Whitby smiled reassuringly. "Nothing of consequence. Magnus and I reached an agreement regarding our contract and his financial expectations."

Whitby handed his coat and hat over to the butler.

"That's it?" Annabelle asked, knowing there had to be more. She'd been waiting all day for the details, praying he was not going to return and tell her they had ended up in the street, rolling in the mud. It wasn't as if it hadn't happened before, or so she'd been told.

"You really want to hear it?" Whitby asked.

"Yes."

Was he daft? Of course she did.

Taking her by the arm, he escorted her through the entrance hall to the stairs. "As it happened, your name did come up, and I took the opportunity to inform Magnus that if he ever hurt you again in any way, he would have to answer to me."

Annabelle stopped on the stairs. "You didn't."

He stopped also, seeming surprised. "You didn't think I would fail to mention it, did you?"

Annabelle lowered her gaze. She understood why he felt compelled to speak to Magnus; they had their own issues. But she did not need Whitby to fight her battles anymore, and now she was worried that Magnus was going to change his mind about showing her paintings.

If any of them arrived on her doorstep in the next day or two, she would be extremely disappointed.

"I'm a woman now, Whitby," she said. "I told you I can take care of myself, and any connection I have with Magnus involves my paintings and his gallery and nothing more. You didn't have to tell him that."

Her brother looked taken aback. "And here I thought I was being your hero."

"I don't need a hero," she said irritably, then regretted her sudden moodiness. But ever since yesterday she'd been feeling anxious and edgy, as if the floor were going to collapse under her feet.

Whitby stood facing her on the stairs, one hand on the railing. "Well, I suppose I have nothing to worry about then."

"No, you don't," she said, despite her uncertain mood. "Except for your youngest son, who seems to have discovered what's inside the sugar bowl."

"Sugar," Whitby said matter-of-factly.

"Yes. All over his face and down between the sofa cushions."

Whitby gave her an affectionate look that suggested they exonerate each other, before he smiled and hurried up the stairs.

Annabelle went in the opposite direction, however, because she couldn't very well be around other people when her nerves were so disturbingly frayed.

For a full week Annabelle heard nothing from Magnus regarding the exhibition—not a single word—but neither did her paintings come hurling back at her, so she could only assume that no news was good news and everything was going ahead as planned.

She spent most of her time in her studio, working on a new painting—a waterfall surrounded by moss-covered rocks. She had sketched it a few months ago and was only now beginning the actual painting, though she was having some trouble with the water. It did not look real to her, and she could not help but recall her aunt Millicent criticizing her work once for not being more like a photograph.

"You painters are simply going to have to work harder," she had said, "or you might as well study how to use a camera. It's certainly quicker."

Annabelle nevertheless continued blocking in the colors of the waterfall.

At the start of the second week, while on her way downstairs for tea one afternoon, she met a footman carrying a silver salver with a letter upon it. It was from the Regent Street Gallery, and the mere sight of the address gave her heart palpitations, for this was all so much more complicated than just the gallery exhibition.

"Thank you," she replied, working hard to sound blasé, before turning back in the direction of her rooms to read the letter in private. She was turning the doorknob when she began to read:

Dear Miss Lawson,

It's been one week since our meeting, and I felt compelled to write and thank you for the opportunity to show your paintings in the gallery, and to inform you of my progress.

I have met with three other London artists who have agreed to be a part of the exhibition, and as of this morning, I now have in my careful possession all of the various works.

Tomorrow I will be speaking to a gentleman from the Times, *who will write something about the opening, so I am hard at work on the final details.*

I've enclosed an invitation for the opening on the evening of the twenty-seventh, and I hope you will choose to attend. All of the other English artists will be there.

Sincerely,
M. Wallis

A shiver of apprehension rippled through Annabelle's veins as she examined the invitation—an ivory card with a paintbrush done in watercolor in the top right-hand corner, and all the information printed in fine gold script just below.

She flipped it over, and on the back saw a list of all the artists. George Wright was named at the top, of course, and below in alphabetical order were the rest. Her name was in the middle.

She was ashamed to admit that despite all her fears and reservations about working with Magnus, she couldn't deny the fact that it was a thrill to see her name listed with so many fine artists.

But should she attend? she wondered uncertainly. If she did, she would have to see Magnus, when she did not want to see him ever again, not when she was so confused by the fact that he still affected her so intensely.

Annabelle sat down at her desk and reminded herself that this was a dream come true. How many years had she imagined her work being included in an actual London art show? And hadn't she already decided that she would not let her personal feelings hold her back?

All of a sudden the answer seemed clear. She should go. There would likely be a crowd anyway, and Magnus would be busy as the host. That would make it easy to avoid him.

But what would she wear? Good Lord, she had nothing, she thought, looking toward her dressing room. What did one wear to a gallery opening? A ball gown? Would it be that formal? No, surely not.

She checked the date again. At least she had time to acquire something. It was three weeks away. Plenty of time.

She breathed deeply and laid her open hand upon her chest. Three weeks. In three weeks her paintings were going to be exhibited in a London gallery.

Still barely able to believe it, she crossed to the window, not really seeing anything beyond the glass. She was too distracted.

Then it occurred to her that she should reply and let Magnus know she would be attending. Yes, that was the proper thing to do.

So she sat down at her desk and withdrew her personalized stationery from the top drawer, dipped her pen in ink, and began to write:

Dear Mr. Wallis,

I was pleased to hear of your progress with the gallery, and thank you for the invitation to the opening. I would be delighted to attend.

Sincerely,
Annabelle Lawson

She set down her pen and blew upon the ink, rereading what she had written.

. . . delighted to attend.

She sat back in her chair. *Delighted? Pleased to hear of your progress?*

She closed her eyes and blinked, as if that would bring reality back to her brain. This was Magnus she was writing to. In all her excitement, she had forgotten that rather sticky fact.

She felt her brow furrow with confusion.

Annabelle looked down at her reply again, and remembered their meeting one week ago at the gallery. She had been hostile toward him, aloof at best. Perhaps she should rewrite the note and try to convey that tone instead.

For a long time she considered it, then shook her head, wondering why she was giving this letter so much importance. It was a reply to an invitation, nothing more. If she were truly indifferent, she would not be analyzing it so carefully.

So with that, it was decided. No more doubts and uncertainties. She would send the trifling letter as it was.

Three days later Magnus sat down at his desk in the gallery office and read Annabelle's reply. She was coming. No. Even better, she would be *delighted* to come.

He leaned back in his chair until the front legs came clear off the floor and stretched his arms high over his head.

After his meeting with Whitby, he was sure he

had been hung out to dry. He'd imagined himself the topic of many heated conversations in the Whitby household—most of which would involve his misdeeds and flaws and general overall offensiveness. He'd even expected Annabelle to change her mind about letting him show her paintings. Every day, whenever a knock had sounded upon the gallery door, he'd expected it to be a footman, come to ask for them back.

But no footman had come, only this letter. This very satisfying letter.

He sat forward, the chair legs landing hard upon the oak floor. There were still so many things left to be done—one of which was the printing of the exhibition labels, and since the paintings were being offered for sale, he did need to understand Annabelle's expectations regarding price.

He supposed he could have asked her that in the last letter, but now he was glad he had not, for it gave him another excuse to write to her.

Dear Miss Lawson,

I will be placing exhibition labels on the walls next to each painting, and we must determine an asking price for each. It is my recommendation that you ask £200 for each of the three paintings you brought when you came to the gallery, and

£300 for The Fisherman. *Would that be acceptable to you? My commission is ten percent.*

M. Wallis

As soon as Annabelle read the letter, she dropped it onto her desk. Three hundred pounds? Surely he wasn't serious. She was no one special. She'd never sold a single painting in her entire life. She couldn't possibly ask that much.

She picked up her pen . . .

Dear Mr. Wallis,

While I am flattered by your confidence in my work, I wonder if a more modest price would be more appropriate. Perhaps £25 each, and £30 for The Fisherman?

A. Lawson

Magnus read her note and smiled. Dear, sweet Annabelle. She was modest, and completely oblivious to her talent as an artist. How could she not know?

Not that he was complaining. He was more than pleased that he would be the one to help her see it.

Yes, one brick at a time, carefully laid . . .

Dear Miss Lawson,

I received your reply in regards to the asking prices of your paintings, but I must plead your indulgence to trust me in this regard. I have seen many paintings come and go through my New York galleries, and I can assure you, these amounts are not unrealistic for works as exquisite as yours. If anything, I would like to ask more.

I am honored to be the one to show them for the first time, as I believe you have a rare talent. The gentleman from the Times was most impressed with your work, and singled you out among the others, and I was not at all surprised.

So please, I ask you, let me print those prices? Anything less would be unthinkable.

M. Wallis

Annabelle was sitting on the edge of her bed when she read the letter, and as soon as she finished it, she flopped backward, sinking into the soft feather mattress. Staring up at the ceiling, she wondered if she should pinch herself.

Were the paintings really that good? She had no idea. She felt totally incapable of judging her own work. All she felt when she looked at them was a frustration over the things she wanted to change.

She was never completely satisfied with any of her paintings and felt them nothing special at all, even after she was long finished with them.

Except perhaps for *The Fisherman*. She had not wanted to change a thing on that one—which had been a novel experience for her.

But still . . . £300? Could she possibly allow Magnus to ask that much?

She supposed he had an interest. He wouldn't want to ask something insignificant because he had a commission to earn. But nor would he want to ask anything outrageous, because if the paintings did not sell, he wouldn't earn a farthing.

But surely, if he was as wealthy as he appeared, his commissions were of no consequence. He had called his galleries labors of love, hadn't he? Yes, he had, and he had a great deal of experience.

Then it occurred to her—he couldn't be toying with her, could he? Flattering her as a means to an end? In a devious scheme to seduce her for some hidden purpose? To injure Whitby again?

Old fears and uncertainties came bubbling to the surface, because she *had* been flattered by all of this, and she caught herself chewing a fingernail.

Then again, if he *was* asking a high price just to flatter her, she would find out at the opening, wouldn't she? She would know very quickly if people thought the prices were unreasonable.

Annabelle sat up again and finally decided to

take a risk and let Magnus ask whatever he wished. As difficult as it was, she would trust him—at least in this regard. And she would use the gallery opening as a way to test him, to see if he had been deceiving her.

She walked to her desk and penned him a quick note to approve his suggested prices, then dressed to go and visit Madame Dubois in the village, who required Annabelle's presence for one last fitting of the dress she had designed for her. Annabelle could hardly wait to see it.

Chapter 12

On the night of the gallery opening, Magnus made his way through the crowd, greeting some of the guests as they arrived.

So far, only a half hour into the evening, it appeared to be a resounding success. There was a noisy hum of conversation and laughter, some of the most respected names in the art world were present, along with some very prominent members of society, including the Duke of Harlow, who was a well-known art enthusiast, and Baron St. Clair, one of the wealthiest men in London since striking it rich in the American railroad, of

all things. He was one of the few English aristocrats with whom Magnus felt he had anything in
common.

But despite the impressive showing of presti-
gious guests, Magnus felt no true satisfaction—for
the one guest who truly mattered had not yet arrived. He hoped she had not changed her mind.

Then the door swung open and there she was—
Annabelle—stepping into the gallery alone.

Magnus was jolted with a sense of urgency when
he saw her, and was pleasantly surprised she had
come alone, for he'd expected her to bring someone, perhaps even Whitby, which would have made
a blatant seduction considerably challenging. This,
however, was an unquestionable advantage.

She appeared nervous and flustered, so he interrupted the gentleman who was complimenting
him on his choice of champagne and shouldered
his way through the crowd to greet her.

"Good evening, Miss Lawson," he said, making
a conscious effort to speak in a businesslike manner, though beneath his surface politeness he was
struggling to harness a most uncompromising,
sexually aroused state of mind. How in the world
could he help it, when she looked so delectable in
an elegant, plum-colored evening gown that ac-
centuated the fullness of her breasts and the
tempting, lavish curve of her hips?

Quite frankly, it was an injustice that he'd never

seen her dressed this way before—in jewels and French heels and long, sleek black gloves. Even her fragrance aroused him. It was the sweet, spring perfume of lilacs.

"Good evening," she replied, handing her cloak over to the doorman.

Magnus waited for her to smooth out her skirt and take a perfunctory look around the room. "Can I offer you a glass of champagne?" he asked.

"Yes, thank you."

Magnus caught the eye of the waiter and signaled to him. An instant later Annabelle was lifting a champagne flute off the shiny brass tray.

"Please come in," he said, guiding her through the crowd. "There are some guests who have been waiting to meet you."

Annabelle allowed Magnus to lead her into the room, hoping no one could make out how nervous she was, for not only was she attempting to enter into the London art world—when in reality she was a thirty-four-year-old spinster aunt who lived in the country—but she was also interacting with the man who was, and would always be, her first love. Her only love, really, although those old feelings were now mixed with so many others—like anger, distrust, and trepidation.

As she followed him through the crowd, however, she realized with some anxiety that those off-putting feelings did not overrule the disturbing way she was reacting to him now—because seeing him again felt just like it had in the old days, when she would come to him at the lake after an agonizing week away from him and find him lounging back in the boat, looking handsome and virile. Unfortunately, the very minute she had laid eyes upon him tonight, her body had awakened the same way—with exhilaration and desire, and she did not understand how she could possibly be feeling that way. How could she forget the hatred that had crippled her all these years?

She noticed uneasily that her hands were trembling, so she strove to focus only on the gallery exhibition. She could not let him do this to her. She could not.

Magnus directed her to a group of gentlemen toward the back of the room, and they all stopped talking as soon as they noticed Annabelle. They studied her curiously, hesitantly, for there were not many women present, and one of the men in particular—older, with gray hair and spectacles—looked down the long length of his aristocratic nose at her before Magnus made the introduction.

"Harlow," he said, with a confident smile, "allow me to present Annabelle Lawson, my latest discovery. Miss Lawson, the Duke of Harlow."

Annabelle felt her face flush with surprise, then she gathered her composure and gracefully curtsied. "Your Grace, it is an honor."

The duke's eyes warmed instantly, his voice friendly and open as he spoke. "So this is the elusive new artist," he said as he bowed to Annabelle. "My dear, the honor is all mine. I am enchanted to meet such a remarkable talent."

Annabelle lowered her gaze. "Thank you, Your Grace."

He patted Magnus on the back. "My good man, you didn't mention she was not only gifted, but lovely as well. Miss Lawson, will you be so kind as to discuss your seascape with me? I just acquired it."

Annabelle sucked in a breath. "You did?"

"You sound surprised," he said.

She could feel Magnus's eyes on her, waiting for her reply.

"No, it's just so early in the evening. You must be confident in your tastes, Your Grace."

The duke seemed pleased with her answer, and offered his arm. "Shall we?"

Annabelle smiled and wondered if this would answer her question—whether Magnus had been merely flattering her with his extravagant asking prices.

She supposed he could have exerted some influence and worked something out with the duke as part of his scheme, but then she feared she was being overly suspicious to the point of absurdity.

But Magnus had always possessed a talent for knocking her off kilter, hadn't he?

The duke escorted Annabelle across the gallery to where her painting was hanging on the wall next to a few others, none of which she recognized. She and the duke discussed all of them in addition to hers, and Annabelle soon began to relax.

She eventually met the other three local artists who were present, and they were all friendly except for one, who was a member of the Royal Academy. He seemed rather vain about his own work, and spoke to her with a belittling tone.

"You may feel differently about Wright's work when you've gained more experience, Miss Lawson," he said to her, when she expressed her high regard for the American artist.

She did not bother to argue with him, for she could sense he was envious of Wright's talent. Instead, she turned her attention to the other gentlemen, who shared her appreciation, and enjoyed the delicious spiced shrimp *hors d'oeuvres*.

As the evening wore on, she realized that all her worries about seeing Magnus tonight were for naught, for he remained respectfully in other areas of the gallery, keeping his distance, leaving her to mingle on her own, and never once did he reveal that they had known each other before. He treated her exactly as he treated the other artists— with a professional reverence and respect.

She should have been relieved. She told herself she shouldn't even be noticing that he was ignoring her, but alas, she felt something very different, which was upsetting to say the least—for she was disappointed.

The sad truth was, she had been acutely aware of his location every single second during the night. Despite all the terrible things she knew about him, she'd had to fight to keep from glancing over at him constantly just for the mere pleasure of watching him talk, laugh, sip champagne, or run a hand through his hair.

Yes, she still thought him the handsomest man in the world, the most intriguing, the most irresistible, and she could not deny the foolish yearning for him to merely glance her way. She wanted the excitement, the thrill of his eyes meeting hers. And even though she had done everything in her power to convince herself she didn't care and was only here for the exhibition, she had to accept the fact that she would always be drawn to him, and she hated such weakness in herself—for wanting something that had once been so destructive.

Later, as the evening drew to a close and the guests began to disperse, Annabelle stood alone in front of *The Fisherman*, looking curiously at the little red mark on the exhibition label and feeling weary of the battle going on inside her head.

She glanced across the room to where Magnus was speaking to some of the guests, and as soon as their eyes met, she knew she was simply incapable of fighting the attraction anymore. She felt a powerful surge of longing course through her, and didn't have the strength to resist it. She had been suppressing her emotions for too long—thirteen years to be exact—and she was exhausted.

Whether he felt what she felt, she did not know. All she knew was that he was picking up two glasses of champagne and blazing a direct path toward her.

She took a deep, steadying breath, not sure what would happen if she ever completely let herself go free.

"You did well tonight," he said, handing over one of the glasses. "Let's make a celebratory toast." He raised his glass, and Annabelle joined him by doing the same. "To a successful opening and the launch of your career."

Annabelle drank to his toast, then endeavored to initiate some relaxed conversation, for she did not want him to know how shaky she felt just from the mere fact that he was standing beside her.

"You may find this hard to believe," she said, "but I never considered my art as a career. It has always been a hobby, though I've always dreamed it could be more."

"I don't find that hard to believe," he said. "Because I remember."

It was the first spoken reminder of the past, and it was unsettling, to say the least, so she tried to change the subject. She pointed at the red mark on the label. "I'm surprised we got that price, but I thought you said you would never part with it."

"I'm not parting with it."

Then she understood. "*You* bought it," she said with a grin.

His responding smile was infectious. "It was money well spent, to see you smile like that."

Her body tensed at the heat of the flirtation. If she was not careful, this was going to lead somewhere very dangerous.

"You didn't have to buy something you already own," she told him.

"Ah, but I didn't really own it. You had asked for it back, if you will recall. So now that I have purchased it, I will be its rightful owner, and no one will ever be able to take it from me. Besides," he added, "I get a commission on the sale."

"But it's *your* money."

He casually shrugged. "Now it's yours."

Annabelle shook her head at him. "I should refuse."

"Please don't. I'll sleep better this way."

Annabelle continued to look at the painting while she sipped her drink, realizing with some surprise that she was feeling more relaxed now that they had actually smiled at each other. It had to be the champagne. It was her third glass.

"But if you take this painting back to America,"

she said, "I'll never see it again. It feels strange to think of that."

"It will remain here in the gallery until then," he said. "You can visit it."

She nodded. "I wonder if I could paint another one like it." She tilted her head to the side. "Now that I see how I handled the brushstrokes, I think I might be able to do it."

"I'm sure you could."

A few gentlemen came to shake Magnus's hand and thank him for inviting them, and they complimented Annabelle on her work.

"See?" Magnus said after they were gone. "You'll be talked about."

A few others came to say good-night, and before long there were only a handful of guests left in the gallery and it was much quieter.

Annabelle and Magnus wandered around the room, admiring the paintings and discussing each of them at length. Then, surprisingly, their conversation shifted to another subject.

"I know that Whitby came to see you," Annabelle said frankly. "He told me what he said to you."

"Did he indeed?" Magnus replied, not seeming the least bit surprised. "Which part?"

"The part about me. That if you ever did anything to hurt me, you'd have to answer to him."

Magnus downed the rest of his champagne in

one gulp, then set the empty glass on a mahogany table and casually leaned a shoulder against the wall. His expression was playful and lighthearted, which surprised her.

"That's close, but not exactly it."

"What do you mean?" Annabelle asked.

"I mean, that's not exactly what he said. Let me see . . . If I remember correctly, he informed me that you were 'off limits' to me, and if I ever laid another hand on you, he would hunt me down and kill me."

Annabelle drew a breath. "Good Lord, he said those exact words?"

"He did indeed."

Of course she knew Whitby would never really kill anyone. It had just been a threat to emphasize how serious he was.

Even so, if he had said it, she would be extremely vexed with him. He could have foiled her opportunity to be included in this show.

But then again, this was Magnus. She had to be careful what she believed. She couldn't let her desires overtake her common sense, no matter how powerful they were.

"I suppose there is a slight difference in the meaning, isn't there?" she said, not wanting to reveal what she was thinking or feeling.

"It's rather subtle, but yes," he calmly replied.

"The 'killing' remark, though—that has a rather firmer message attached to it, don't you think?"

Then, without warning, she actually began to find this whole conversation comical, and was suddenly looking at the man who had taught her how to fish, the man who had laughed with her, the man who had been amused by her unconventional boots and had somehow understood the silly misfit she had always been. It almost knocked the wind out of her.

"Well, if you were to analyze the wording . . ." she said, losing the humor in her tone.

Their smiles slowly faded and Annabelle felt as if she were back on the picnic blanket with her head next to his, staring up at the sky and seeing the same shapes in the clouds.

Feeling anxious, she shifted her weight. Unfortunately, she was not accustomed to wearing heels, and she heard a resounding *crack* as her shoe gave way beneath her.

With a gasp, she grabbed for Magnus's arm to steady herself. "I think my heel just broke."

Magnus looked down, but her feet were hidden beneath her skirts. "Is it still attached to the shoe?"

She wiggled her foot. "Yes, but it appears to be dangling. Well, this is quite a pickle, isn't it?"

Magnus wrapped a hand around her gloved elbow to help her stay balanced, his voice calm and relaxed. "Not at all. I have glue in my office, and I can repair it right now."

Thankfully, they were standing adjacent to the office door, so they discreetly went inside. The room was dimly lit by one Tiffany lamp in the corner, and Magnus left the door open behind them.

He escorted her to the sofa, but remained standing in front of her while she stared up at his darkly handsome face—the chiseled jaw, the fine straight nose, the soft, full mouth . . .

"Perhaps you could hand the shoe to me," he quietly said, startling her out of what felt like a trance, for she was alone with him now.

"Oh, yes, of course."

As she slid it off with her other toe, a secret part of her wondered what would happen if he got down on a knee and removed it for her. She could envision his large hand wrapping around her ankle, cupping her heel, holding the arch of her foot.

"Here you are," she said with forced calm as she strained to hide her thoughts. She handed over the satin, lace-trimmed shoe.

Magnus went behind his large desk and opened the bottom drawer. "This is carpenters' glue." He withdrew a half-empty jar and set it on the desk. "It should do the trick until you can have the shoe repaired properly."

He remained standing, spreading the glue on the heel while Annabelle watched his hands. They had always been callused and rough-looking, and despite his wealth and prosperity and the fact that he was the owner of a very fine art gallery, they were surprisingly still the hands of a common worker.

She could not deny that it was that very quality about his hands that had always excited her.

Magnus pressed the heel back into place, then set the shoe on the desk. "There. We'll just have to give it some time to dry. Can I get you anything? Another glass of champagne?"

"No, thank you. I've already had quite enough."

Far too much, she thought with some unease, for surely she had to be in some kind of drunken stupor to be feeling so attracted to him after so many years of feeling nothing but the pain of his betrayal. Most confusing of all, she still felt that pain, right alongside the attraction. Which made no sense.

"Tea perhaps?" he suggested. "Or I could go fetch the tray with the shrimp that you seemed to like so much."

He had noticed. "Honestly, I couldn't eat another bite," she replied.

Just then an older couple appeared in the doorway, and the gentleman informed Magnus they were leaving. "It was a most enjoyable evening, Mr. Wallis. We appreciate the invitation."

"My pleasure, Stanford. Let me show you out."

Magnus turned to Annabelle and bowed slightly. "Will you excuse me for a moment?"

"Of course."

She watched him leave, listening to his laughter and conversation outside as she looked around the tastefully decorated office. There was another painting on the wall where *The Fisherman* had been hanging before. She didn't recognize it. Right in front of her on the coffee table was a vase of fresh chrysanthemums.

Her gaze then drifted to the large desk and ornate brown leather chair. The desktop was clear except for her lacy shoe and the jar of glue, and a basket containing a stack of letters and papers.

She leaned forward and glanced out into the gallery where Magnus was still conversing with the Stanford couple, and wondered how long he was going to be, because it was getting late, and she was beginning to feel more than a little uncomfortable with her all too intimate rapport with Magnus. Whitby would definitely not approve.

Besides, the room was clearing out, and she did not want to be the last person here.

Rising from the sofa, she limped on one foot to check her shoe. The glue wasn't completely dry, but at least the heel was attached. She could probably walk on it, if she kept most of her weight on her toe.

Annabelle set the shoe on the floor, and while she slid her foot into it, her gaze fell upon the basket of letters. One brief note was open on top, and before she knew what she was about, she was so overcome with curiosity about Magnus and everything he was doing here in London that she was reading it.

Mr. Wallis,

There's a problem with the wiring at Brownlow and Northington. Perhaps you could drop by in the morning.

George Smith

P.S. The electrical in the other building was finalized today.

Well, that didn't tell her much, except that Magnus was putting electricity into the two buildings he was renovating.

"I doubt it's dry," he said, startling her as he reentered the office.

She became instantly flustered, not because she'd been reading his correspondence—though she did feel a little guilty about that—but because he was handing her a red rose.

"What's this for?" she asked, presuming he'd

just picked it out of the bouquet outside the door. She lifted it to her nose and breathed in the fragrant scent.

"It's to thank you for coming tonight," he replied. "It wouldn't have been the same without you. Though I'm sorry about your shoe. Perhaps you should have worn your other boots—the ones you used to wear at the lake. Do you still have them?"

He seemed to remember everything. "I have a newer pair, but they're very similar."

They stood in the half-light gazing at one another for a quiet moment, until Annabelle began to feel afraid. *Yes, afraid.* It was the only way she could describe it.

She checked the time. Her driver would be waiting outside by now, thank goodness.

"I appreciate everything," she said shakily, struggling to smother the tension she was feeling. "But I really should be going."

Magnus's voice dropped to a slow, tantalizing hush. "Are you sure you wouldn't like to stay a bit longer?"

All at once Annabelle found herself unable to muster an appropriate reply. She imagined remaining here until all the guests were gone. What would occur?

Oh, she knew very well what would occur. They would end up on the sofa, and she'd be lucky to keep her garters in place.

Struck with a sudden alarm, she fortified her resolve.

"Yes, I'm sure."

He casually nodded. "But when will I see you again?"

Feeling the heady combination of his sexual appeal and the lingering effects of the champagne, Annabelle strove to make a firm reply.

"That's rather presumptuous, don't you think?"

Magnus discreetly glanced around to ensure no one was standing in the doorway behind him.

"Perhaps it is," he replied, his voice now a seductive whisper. "But I know you, Annabelle, and I know you can still feel the fire between us. So this can't be the end."

It was astounding, how potent sexual desire could be when it took hold with full force. It eclipsed all reason and sanity.

Thankfully, however, she did possess some degree of discipline, so she cleared her throat and endeavored to cool this madness—because that's exactly what it was. Madness.

"No, Magnus. I won't go there with you."

She simply could not venture into the fires of temptation and certain doom, because she could not trust this man. Her heart was still horribly scarred because of him.

Just then two other guests interrupted and thanked Magnus for the evening, and while he shook their hands, Annabelle managed to regain her sanity, realizing with a fright how quickly the situation had just spun out of control. A few minutes ago she had imagined herself lying with him on his sofa.

Touching her flushed cheek, she brushed past Magnus and started toward the door.

He followed, however, leaving the others standing where they were. "Wait, Annabelle, don't go."

"I have to." She met the doorman, who quickly retrieved her cloak from the front closet and held it up for her. She did not meet Magnus's gaze as she buttoned it. "Thank you for including my paintings in the show."

"You're welcome, but I will be in touch."

In touch?

"About the sales," he clarified, as if he knew the workings of her mind. She supposed he had been able to read her like a book.

Annabelle simply nodded. "I must go. My driver is waiting."

She turned to leave, limping to keep from breaking her shoe again. Magnus escorted her out onto the street where the coach was waiting.

"When are you going back to the country?" he asked, opening the door for her.

Annabelle climbed in and slid across the seat. "The day after tomorrow."

"Why don't you stay in London a little longer? We have to settle the sales, if nothing else."

The insistent fire in his eyes upset her balance, for it looked as if "settling the sales" was the last thing on his mind.

To be honest, it was the last thing on her mind, too, because the shocking truth was—she was still burning to touch him. He was the only man in the world she had ever truly desired, and now he had come back into her life and he wanted her.

He'd said there was still a fire between them, and it was true. It was raging hotter than ever before. But heaven help her, she could not be so foolish as to risk her heart. Not with him.

"You can send me a bank note," she said at last, struggling to grab hold of her cautious, sensible self. "I think that would be best. Driver!"

But Magnus was still standing there, holding the door open.

"I have to go," she said firmly, and she shut the door on him before he could say another word.

The coach lurched forward, and Annabelle turned in her seat to look out the window at Magnus, who remained on the sidewalk, watching her drive off.

As soon as he was out of sight, she faced forward again and held up a gloved hand to see how badly it was shaking.

Quite badly indeed.

Annabelle inhaled and held her breath, wondering if she could relax now that the gallery opening was behind her. Perhaps she'd survived the worst of it.

But then she pictured Magnus's face and heard his husky, alluring voice in her mind when he'd asked her to stay in London a little longer, and was forced to acknowledge the very disturbing possibility that the worst might still be ahead of her.

Chapter 13

The only thing that kept Annabelle sensible
through the night and into the next morning
was her constant focus on all the wretched things
she knew about Magnus. She thought of her
brother's aversion toward him, and the eminence
of his reputation as a villain in her family, and naturally, she thought of the way he had treated her
years ago.

But by doing that, she had to struggle to over-
look the fact that last night she had not found him
villainous in the least, nor did anyone else. He had
been charming and considerate, and made her

laugh and feel comfortable. Nothing he had said or done seemed to match the opinions everyone held of him. Which only served to confuse her while she ate her breakfast that morning.

Later, while sipping a second cup of coffee, Annabelle read the paper, but found herself distracted again by memories of the night before— her conversations with the Duke of Harlow and the other artists, the flavor of the champagne and the tang of the spiced shrimp, not to forget the image of Magnus repairing her shoe in his private, dimly lit office.

She thought of the letter she'd read, about the wiring in the buildings he'd purchased, then recalled that during their previous meeting, Magnus had told her that his properties were located at Park Lane.

Annabelle sat back in her chair and stared at the wall. The letter last night had mentioned the corner of Brownlow and Northington. That wasn't right.

Had Magnus lied to her?

For a moment she sat bewildered, wondering why he would lie about something like that, unless he had some darker purpose with his business ventures.

If that were true, she had to admit she would be vastly disappointed, because that morning, for the first time in thirteen years, she had actually let herself hope that she and everyone else had been wrong about Magnus all this time.

It was a wish she had never let herself acknowledge before now, because she was certain it was a foolish one, but after last night, she wasn't so sure.

Annabelle sighed and reminded herself that she could not fall into that trap. She could not be too quick to presume that Magnus's amiable behavior was completely sincere. She had to keep her head and continue to be cautious.

And although she did not want to be unreasonably suspicious, either, given his past transgressions, she couldn't help but question this. Whitby certainly would.

Consequently, two hours later she was stepping out of a hansom cab at the corner of Brownlow and Northington, looking up at the building Magnus had supposedly purchased, for she was determined to find answers.

The property was a large home with paned windows and a wrought-iron fence all around. In the front yard, a bricklayer was making improvements to the walk.

Annabelle's cab drove away, so she crossed the street to take a closer look. When she reached the gate, she read the plaque set into the ironwork: NORTHINGTON STREET ORPHANS' HOME FOR BOYS.

An orphans' home? She looked up at the second story windows, wondering what Magnus planned to do with the property. He'd explained he bought and sold buildings for a profit. Would he sell an orphanage out from under the boys who had found a home here?

It was exactly the kind of conclusion Whitby would come to. *His heart is cold as ice*, her brother had said.

Finding it all very unsettling, but not quite ready to make any drastic assumptions herself, Annabelle opened the creaky gate and approached the man who was on his knees, laying bricks. "Excuse me, do you work for Magnus Wallis?"

The man stood up and wiped his hands on his coveralls. "Yes, miss."

"I see you're making some improvements," she said. "Do you know if Mr. Wallis is intending to sell?"

The man wiped a finger under his nose and sniffled. "Oh no, miss, he doesn't own the place. He's just improving it. Having the whole place wired for electricity, and he's adding indoor plumbing as well. It's a changing world, wouldn't you say?"

Annabelle tried to clarify what the man was telling her. "But why would he make improvements to a building he doesn't own?"

"I reckon he's generous," the man replied. "Not like some people."

It was not what Annabelle had been expecting to hear, and she couldn't help feeling guilty for presuming the worst, when in fact Magnus appeared to be doing something quite charitable. He was renovating an orphans' home.

"Thank you for your help," she said to the man, smiling politely before she turned to leave.

"He's inside if you want to have a word with him," the man called after her. "He's checking the electric."

Annabelle stopped. Magnus was here? Now?

She felt an odd mixture of excitement and apprehension, and turned to look up at the windows, wondering if he'd already seen her out here on the walk, covertly interrogating his workers.

"Perhaps I will have a word with him," she replied, even though she knew she shouldn't. After last night, she should know better. But this charitable bequest—which seemed so out of character for a man whose heart was allegedly twisted—was petitioning her hopes.

Annabelle approached the front door and knocked, and was greeted by a plump older woman who was wiping her hands on her apron.

"I'm here to see Mr. Wallis," Annabelle said.

"Yes, come in. He's in the back garden. I'd take you, but I've got bread in the oven. Just go down that hall and there's a door at the end."

"Thank you," Annabelle replied.

There was a tingling in the pit of her stomach as she made her way toward the back of the house, but she tried to ignore it, for she was here only to ask him why he hadn't told her about what he was doing for this orphanage. Why had he kept it secret?

She reached the back door and stepped out onto a covered entrance, where her gaze fell instantly upon Magnus.

He was standing on the grass with his back to her, playing cricket with a group of boys. He'd taken off his jacket and was wearing a white shirt with the sleeves rolled up, along with a dark, patterned waistcoat. He was laughing at something, waiting for one of the boys to throw the ball.

They were all smiling and shouting, and soon Annabelle found herself smiling, too, laughing as a young lad fumbled with the ball until he fell over backward onto the ground.

Annabelle stood and watched for a few more minutes, until one of the boys pointed at her and said, "Who's the lady?"

Magnus turned. Annabelle felt a jolt when their eyes met, and her pulse began to pound even harder when he started walking toward her.

"That's it for me, boys," he said, his gaze intent upon Annabelle. "You'll have to finish the match on your own."

They all groaned, but quickly returned to their game.

"Well, this is a pleasant surprise," Magnus said, reaching the bottom step. He was slightly out of breath, and the hair around his face was damp with perspiration.

Annabelle inclined her head at him. "I hope you don't mind."

"Mind? I'm thrilled to see you, Annabelle." He climbed the steps. "How did you know I was here?"

She hesitated a moment before she answered. "I saw the note on your desk last night when I was putting on my shoe—the one asking you to check the wiring this morning. It gave the address, so I took a chance."

She refrained from telling him she'd wondered if it was all part of some dastardly master plan to harm her family.

"Well, I'm glad you did," he said. "Why don't we go inside?" He opened the door for her.

Annabelle entered and let him show her to the front parlor, where she could smell fresh paint on the walls. A few boys came bounding down the stairs, taking no notice of Annabelle and Magnus as they dashed toward the back door.

"Why didn't you tell me about this?" she asked when the house quieted down again.

"It didn't come up."

"But you told me you were making improvements to two buildings on Park Lane," she said.

He shrugged casually. "I am, and this is where the profits are going. Here, and to another girls' home across the river."

Annabelle's brow furrowed. This was not at all what she had expected. "I didn't realize you were such a generous philanthropist."

"I'm not really," he replied. "I just remember what it was like growing up in London, feeling like an orphan myself sometimes, having nothing."

Annabelle took a few steps closer to him, feeling as if there were many, many things she did not know about him. All she knew was what Whitby had always known.

"You never told me any of that before," she said, "when I knew you as Mr. Edwards."

Where had that come from? She shouldn't have said it.

His eyes were wistful, yet surprisingly tender. "There were a lot of things I didn't tell you."

She continued to gaze at him, waiting for more.

"I was only nine when my father died," he finally explained. "And my mother . . . Well, she wasn't much of one."

Just then two boys burst in through the front door, one shoving the other. "Bugger off!" the younger one said.

Magnus turned and watched them for a moment, and when the older one shoved the younger one again, he strode toward them. "Perhaps you could behave yourselves, gentlemen. There is a lady present." He put an authoritative hand on the older boy's shoulder. "Why don't you both go and join the cricket game out back. They're in need of a few extra players."

As soon as they were gone, Magnus returned to the parlor where Annabelle stood watching. "Boys like those two just need something to do."

She smiled and nodded in agreement.

"Can I offer you a ride home?" he asked.

"That would be very kind," Annabelle replied. "Thank you."

A short time later they were sitting across from each other on the soft cushions in Magnus's luxurious private coach, heading down the street.

Annabelle sat with her knees squeezed tightly together, her gloved hands clenched upon her lap while she looked out the window.

She could not believe that she was sitting here with Magnus—Magnus!—when for years of her quiet, uneventful life, she'd never thought she'd ever see him again.

Not to mention the fact that they had been lovers once. They had been intimate, then parted in the most brutal, excruciating way.

But strangely now, those unpleasant memories seemed almost like a bad dream, as if they had never really happened, and the real Magnus was the wonderful man she'd come to know as Mr. Edwards—the wonderful man before her, who had been such a charming host the night before, and was donating his business profits to orphanages.

Then Annabelle felt his gaze on her face. She turned her eyes from the window to look at him, slouched lazily on the red cushions across from her, his knees apart, one arm resting along the back of the seat.

All her womanly senses began to hum, for he was so impossibly handsome. And his eyes . . . He was staring at her as if he could see straight through to her soul, as if he *adored* her soul and knew her as well as only a lifelong friend could.

Annabelle sucked in a little breath and tried to deny the part of herself that felt happy—happy to be with him, the man who had for a brief time been her most precious friend.

"Would you like to see my buildings on Park Lane?" he asked, and somehow she knew that he recognized and understood her worries, and wanted only to put her at ease by distracting her.

He knew exactly what he was doing, she thought as she smiled and said yes, for the knots of tension in her shoulders began to unwind, and she stopped fighting so hard against the part of herself that was feeling happy. What was the point, after all? They were just going to look at a couple of buildings.

A few minutes later the coach pulled to a slow halt on the elegant residential street, and Magnus stepped out to assist Annabelle. She climbed out and looked up at a large home. A number of workers on tall ladders were applying stucco to the exterior.

"This one must be yours," she said, linking her arm through his when he offered it.

Magnus stood on the sidewalk beside her, looking up. "Yes, but when I bought it, it was two narrow, unkempt houses side by side."

Annabelle examined the full width of the structure. "You turned two houses into one larger home? I would never have guessed."

He pointed from one side to the other. "I redesigned the exterior for a unified appearance. On the inside I knocked out a few walls and installed all the modern conveniences."

"What extraordinary vision you must have had," Annabelle remarked, "to see the *potential* of what could be done."

Magnus placed his hand over hers on his arm and leaned close. "There is an old adage about architecture that says visionary buildings come into being only when the designer reaches far beyond what is there."

The idea stirred Annabelle's blood, and she smiled. "You have to see a blank canvas," she said.

"Exactly." He gestured toward the house. "It's almost finished. Would you like to see the inside?"

"I'd love to."

They climbed the cement steps to the front door and entered the wide entry hall, washed with abundant sunlight beaming in through an enormous front window. Annabelle looked up at the high ceiling, the chestnut millwork, and the magnificent dangling light fixture.

"It's so bright," she said. "And so modern with all these daring colors."

He'd used saffron and burgundy and persimmon, which was a refreshing departure from the sea of aesthetic conservatism that defined English art and design. It aroused Annabelle's creative sensibilities.

Magnus closed the door behind them and let her wander into the parlor on her own. "It's definitely a bold palette," he said.

"Bold, to be sure." She pointed at the far wall, where the fireplace was encased by a marble mantel and flanked by chestnut columns. "I love how you've chosen different shades of the same color for different walls."

He followed her in. "Not many people notice that, Annabelle. It's very subtle."

"You know me. I'm a painter. I'm obsessed with color."

He smiled and nodded, then let her lead the way to another room. She walked through the parlor to the library, and couldn't help admiring how the room was clearly masculine without any of the typical dark brown leather furniture and hunter green walls.

"Magnus, it's extraordinary. I've never seen anything like it."

He came to stand beside her. "I did my best to work with the architecture already on hand. Most of the molding and paneling is original, though I've added some as well."

"You can't tell the new from the old. It's seamless."

"I'm glad you think so. Would you like to go upstairs?"

Annabelle's first reaction was to think of the bedrooms and worry that it would be completely inappropriate to say yes, but since there was no furniture in the house, she decided it would be only *slightly* inappropriate. Besides, she wanted to see what he'd done with the rest of the house.

They climbed the curved staircase and reached the second floor, and Magnus took Annabelle by the arm. "Now close your eyes," he said, leaning close again. "I have a feeling you're going to like what I'm about to show you."

She did as he asked and allowed him to lead her down the corridor. A door creaked open, and Magnus guided her into another room.

"Open your eyes."

Annabelle opened them and found herself gazing upon a veritable temple of hygiene—the most luxurious bathroom she'd ever seen, complete with a hooded bath and spray shower encased in mahogany, a private water closet with a mahogany seat and matching cistern with hand-carved panels. The floors were polished marble. Gleaming tiles adorned the walls, and the water cabinet contained a basin of painted porcelain.

Awestruck, she walked all the way in. "This is spectacular!"

"I'm pleased you like it," he replied, casually leaning a shoulder against the doorjamb.

Annabelle went to touch the shiny brass fittings on the water basin. "I can't imagine how you could design all this with such care, then put the house up for sale and let someone else live here. Aren't you ever tempted to move in to the buildings yourself?"

He chuckled. "I like where I live."

"Do you have a bathroom like this in your home?"

He wet his lips. "I do, actually. In both homes."

To some people it might have seemed as if Magnus was boasting to impress, but Annabelle didn't get that feeling. He was simply being honest with her; he enjoyed his work and wanted to share it with her, for he knew she would appreciate it.

Which she did. Very much. How lucky he was, to be involved in such a creative profession.

All at once she was acutely aware of his manly presence in the doorway while he watched her wander around.

Laboring to redirect her interest back to the renovations instead of the man in the doorway, she continued to admire the fixtures.

"You've come a long way, Magnus," she said pensively. "You've done well for yourself. You have everything."

His voice was calm, unemotional. "Not *quite* everything."

Annabelle knew instantly that he was referring to *her*—that *she* was the one thing he didn't have—and when the initial shock of his declaration wore off, her body responded with a burning surge of attraction.

Not knowing what to say, and wishing she could not be so easily beguiled, she turned her gaze in the other direction. But Magnus wouldn't let her look away. He pushed off the doorjamb and sauntered toward her, stopping in front of her, so close she could smell his musky fragrance in the air.

"Would you like to see the bedroom?" he asked in a soft, silky voice.

Annabelle's pulse quickened at the suggestion, and a flash memory of the day he had touched her intimately on the beach flew through her mind.

He was too close, too persuasive and enticing, and the mere mention of the word "bedroom" made her weak in the knees.

Oh, she was in trouble now, she thought, because she almost wished the house *was* furnished.

She could certainly entertain a few fantasies about being in a bedroom alone with him.

She took a deep breath and shook herself. This would not do. She had to remain vigilant.

"That would be very nice," she said, with a surprising degree of aplomb.

He stared at her intently for a moment, as if studying her thoughts, then he slowly blinked and turned to lead the way down the corridor. "It's this way."

Annabelle followed him into the large room at the end of the hall, and after seeing all the bold colors throughout the house, the restrained bedchamber came as a surprise, and perhaps a bit of a relief, for it was a soothing, dignified cream with polished, honey oak floors.

He faced her and inclined his head, and his voice was soothing as well. "I'm not sure where the bed should go. Any ideas?"

Annabelle smiled. "Here, I believe." She moved to stand against one of the walls and gestured with her hands. "A floor-to-ceiling headboard would be nice. The owner could sit up and look out the window at the trees across the street."

Magnus crossed to stand beside her, facing the window. They both imagined themselves sitting up on the imaginary pillows. "I think you're right. Here would be perfect."

Annabelle watched the leafy trees blowing in the wind outside, and felt surprisingly calm and at ease. Then she turned her gaze to Magnus, who had been watching her profile.

He was so familiar, like a well-worn shoe. But much, much better looking . . .

Soon, the world diminished to a quiet heartbeat as his eyes held hers, and Annabelle wished desperately that things were different—that last night she had met him for the first time, that she had never suffered a broken heart because of him, and that her brother did not despise and distrust him.

Because God help her, she found him so immensely exciting in every way, and he awakened her senses like no other person on the planet. She didn't want to go home. She wanted to spend the rest of the day with him and go on talking about his buildings and what he would do next. She wanted to know everything about his life now that things were so different for him. She wanted to hear about his activities in America. What was the weather like? Did his galleries bring in many patrons? Was he happy?

But something stopped her from asking all those questions. Perhaps she feared that if she let herself drift into his existence, she would never be able to escape.

"I should be getting home," she said abruptly, before she had a chance to change her mind.

The disappointment in his eyes was almost tangible, but she did not allow herself to be swayed by it. It was vital that she continue to be prudent.

"Of course," he replied, offering his arm. "I've kept you too long."

Soon they were climbing back into his coach and settling in for the ride.

It had been a magical morning, Magnus thought as he sat across from Annabelle on the coach and admired the dazzling blue of her eyes. From the very first day he had met her on the train, he'd been swept away by her lively, vivacious nature, and today he was pleased to discover that she had not lost that zest for life. She'd been excited by his renovations, and her enthusiasm was contagious.

But she had always inspired him, hadn't she? And he knew that if it weren't for her, he would never have gone to America to better himself. He wouldn't have bothered, and he had her to thank for the new direction his life had taken.

Soon they entered Annabelle's residential district, and he knew the coach ride would come to an end. Hence, he resolved at last to give in to the need to be closer to her, and slid smoothly across the small distance between them. He positioned himself next to her and stretched an arm across the back of the seat.

Annabelle gazed at him questioningly, but with a hint of a smile that pleased him, for it was an honest smile. It was the smile that belonged to the young woman he had met on the train, the woman who had stood on a beach and painted him in a boat.

"I'm glad you came to see me this morning," he said.

"I'm glad, too," she replied. "I *think*."

Magnus chuckled, then ran a finger up her arm, from her wrist to the inside of her elbow, his heart thundering in his chest as he strove to control his desires—for what he really wanted to do was ease her onto her back here in the shady confines of the coach and feel her soft, lush body beneath his own.

Her breathing changed, and he was pleased when he sensed a slight surrender. Since it was not in his nature to ignore an opportunity, he spoke frankly.

"Annabelle, I know you're having a hard time trusting me again, but I wish you would give me another chance. Why don't we have dinner together tomorrow evening?"

She looked him in the eye, as if studying him, searching for answers. "I'm not sure that would be a good idea."

"Please consider it. We could start fresh and get to know each other again. I'm sure you'll see that I'm not the man you always believed I was."

She looked down at her tightly clasped hands in her lap. "Magnus, I have spent the past thirteen years trying to get over what you did to me, and though I am grateful for what you did for me in the gallery, and I enjoyed myself with you this morning, I'm not sure I'm ready to let you back into my life."

"But Annabelle—"

She shook her head. "It's not that I want to hold a grudge against you, or that I am unable to accept your apology. The problem is that I am afraid of getting hurt again. Love and the notion of handing my heart over to *anyone* makes me uneasy. I just can't do it. Not yet."

Magnus couldn't move. A pain even more excruciating than he had felt that day outside the bank throbbed inside his chest as he listened to Annabelle speak and he contemplated what he had done to her. He'd felt remorse many, many times over the years, but never as deeply as he felt it now, looking into her eyes and realizing what he had cost her. He wanted so badly to fix it. If only he could go back.

"I'm so sorry, Annabelle," he said, then he couldn't think anymore. He needed her to know how much he regretted the years they'd spent apart, and how desperately and passionately he still loved her.

He leaned closer to tell her with a kiss.

A surge of relief coursed through him when her soft lips parted in response and she took his face in her hands. He had dreamed of this for so many lonely years, but never dared to imagine it would happen.

Astonished at the overwhelming violence of his feelings—for he wanted her more than life itself—he curled his fingers around her gloved hands, inching closer to her on the seat, deepening the kiss. He wanted to take this further, to claim her for his own once and for all and never let her go again, but he knew he could not. She was a wounded creature, and he had to be patient, or he would scare her away forever.

Drawing back from the kiss, he touched his forehead to hers. "You don't need to protect yourself from me, Annabelle. You have my word, I will never hurt you again."

She shook her head, old fears and uncertainties resurfacing in her voice. "But how can I trust your word? I trusted you once before and you betrayed me. Besides that, you're still my brother's enemy. That has not changed."

"But that shouldn't matter because he's wrong about me," Magnus replied, more than a little frustrated by his cousin's persistent influence upon her. "He's *always* been wrong."

Annabelle's cheeks became flushed with red; her eyes revealed an inner turmoil. "But how can I take your word over his, when I've known him all my life, and I know he is a decent, honorable man? I don't know the same of you."

She looked down at the floor, seeming angry all of a sudden. Whether that anger was directed at herself or at him, he did not know.

"This shouldn't be happening," she said.

No . . . She was retreating . . .

So he kissed her again, deeper this time, and surprisingly, she surrendered to him once more, parting her lips and moaning softly as he took her into a full embrace.

It was all the assurance he needed. She *did* still have feelings for him, even though she was doing her best to resist them.

He felt the coach slowing and knew they'd reached her brother's residence, so he gradually withdrew from the kiss.

"Tomorrow night?" he asked, feeling revived and rejuvenated. There was hope. He knew there was.

A shadow of fear filled her eyes. "No. I'm expected back in the country tomorrow."

"Don't go. Stay another day."

"Magnus, please. I can't do this."

The coach rolled to a stop, and before he had a chance to get up and assist her out, she climbed over him and got out on her own, then stood at the open door.

"You *can* do it, Annabelle. Just give me one night."

She stared uncertainly at him. "Thank you for the ride."

Then she shut the door in his face and ran off.

He considered going after her, but what if Whitby was at home? No. Magnus knew if he engaged in a confrontation with her brother, it would not help matters. It would spoil everything, for that situation was particularly volatile.

So the coach lurched forward, and Magnus let his head tip back upon the seat, wondering how he was going to survive another day not knowing if she would ever find the courage to trust him again.

And for the first time in many years, he felt the roar of his old resentment toward Whitby awakening inside him—like a sleeping lion he wished would keep still.

Annabelle slept late the next morning, for she had barely slept a wink during the night. She'd been too shaken by what happened the day before and the way she'd felt when Magnus kissed her—weak and utterly swept away. She had done what she'd promised herself she would not do. She had lowered her guard.

Resigning herself to the fact that nothing could be done to change it now, Annabelle rose from bed and rang for Josephine, who brought her a breakfast tray with her usual morning meal—a boiled egg, tea, and toast.

She was setting the tray on Annabelle's lap when she said, "There's a letter for you, Miss Lawson. It came this morning."

Annabelle inched back against the pillows, trying not to sound too anxious or surprised, although she certainly was, for she suspected the letter might be from Magnus.

Was it a bank note?

That was wishful thinking.

"Where is it?" she asked.

"I have it here, miss." Josephine reached into her pocket, withdrew the letter and handed it over.

Unable to eat now that she was staring at a note from the Regent Street Gallery, Annabelle accepted it, then excused Josephine. As soon as the door closed behind the maid, she tore at the seal and unfolded the letter.

Surprisingly enough, it *was* a bank note—for the full sum he owed her—but there was more . . .

Dear Annabelle,

I know you plan to leave for the country today, but I could not bear to leave things as they were when we parted in front of your brother's house yesterday.

I know you have not forgiven me for what happened between us years ago, and I concede that it is your right. But please believe me when I say that I have suffered every day of my life for how I wronged you.

I know it is far too much to ask, but please . . . a second chance?

If only you would stay in London one more day. Please, Annabelle? We enjoyed each other's company yesterday, did we not? We could enjoy ourselves like that again.

I am in hell today, Annabelle, aching for you. I want you here with me where you are meant to be—in my arms, in my bed, in my life.

I will remain at my hotel all day if you should choose to see me. I sincerely hope you will.

Yours,
Magnus

By the time Annabelle finished reading the letter, her heart was pounding so fast she could barely breathe. She'd never read anything like it in her entire life. He was pleading with her. Pleading! And she, in turn, was desperate for him—desperate for his touch, his kiss, and so much more.

She had truly been swept away.

She set her uneaten breakfast tray aside and touched her bare toes to the cold floor. She slid off the bed and reached for her dressing gown, pulling it on as she strode to the window, which looked down onto the tiny, fenced-in garden out back.

She wondered, after all that had happened, if she could ever truly trust Magnus. There had been so much water under the bridge, and she would always worry that her desire for him had prevailed over her good sense.

She supposed the real problem was that she was torn between her unstoppable passion for one man and her deep devotion to another—the adoptive brother who had raised her. A man she had always trusted. And wasn't trust at the heart of all this? Whitby was warning her to stay away from Magnus. He believed him unscrupulous.

Annabelle didn't know what she believed, and that frightened her. She feared she was losing her mind.

Wanting suddenly to return to her home where she felt safe and secure and could think about this, free from Magnus's dangerous temptations, Annabelle picked up her pen and withdrew a sheet of paper from her desk drawer.

Dear Magnus,

I'm sorry, but I must go home to my family today. Please do not wait for me. I can't see you. I need time to think.

Annabelle

Glancing over at her egg on the breakfast tray and giving up all thoughts of eating, Annabelle sealed the letter and rang for her maid again. A moment later Josephine knocked and entered.

"Josephine, please send a footman to deliver this letter to the Grand Hotel," Annabelle instructed.

"Yes, Miss Lawson. Would you like me to take the breakfast tray?"

Annabelle stood up. "Yes, I'm not hungry. And when you're finished with that, go and pack your things. I want to go home, and I don't want to miss the midday train."

"Yes, Miss Lawson."

Josephine took the tray and left the room, while Annabelle quickly went to retrieve her traveling case.

Passengers were already boarding the train by the time Annabelle and Josephine arrived at the station and purchased their tickets.

"I'll be so glad to get home," Annabelle said, leading the way along the platform, walking the length of the train to reach their proper carriage.

"But you enjoyed yourself at the gallery opening, didn't you, Miss Lawson?" Josephine said, hurrying to keep up. "Everyone liked your paintings."

Annabelle smiled over her shoulder at her maid. "Yes, I suppose I did. It was a very successful evening."

They finally reached the carriage where they were to be seated, and Annabelle stopped to check her reticule for the tickets. But something caught her eye—or rather, someone. The station door flew open and a man came darting out, stopping abruptly on the platform.

The world seemed to disappear for a moment as Annabelle focused on him. For it was Magnus—

here to say good-bye, or to stop her from leaving, or to plead with her one more time for another chance.

The fact that her maid was now looking at him, too, did nothing to wrench Annabelle out of her stupor, because heaven help her, she could not take her eyes off him.

He was so darkly handsome in his open black coat, the collar of his white shirt contrasting sharply with his thick, wavy black hair. Despite everything, he was the most captivating man she had ever known. In all her life, no one had even come close.

His eyes met Annabelle's across the distance of the platform, and he merely stood there, seeming almost arrested himself.

Annabelle fought to understand the workings of her mind and body. She wanted to escape his power over her. She wanted to go home where she was safe with the family who loved her, but she couldn't move. She could barely breathe, for that matter.

Josephine faced her again. "Miss Lawson? Are we still going home?"

The words took a moment to register in Annabelle's mind. Somehow the young maid understood what was happening, though Annabelle had never confessed anything to her. She supposed it was rather obvious.

As the train blew steam not far from where they stood, Magnus continued to hold Annabelle in his gaze.

That was the moment she knew—there was no way on earth she could turn from him now and step on that train.

She would have liked to say she had thought it out and come to the conscious conclusion that she *could* trust Magnus, or that she had chosen her own happiness over her loyalty to her brother, or simply that she deserved some passion and pleasure in her life.

But none of those things entered her mind. She was aware only of her blood pounding through her veins and the noisy rush of lust that dashed like fire through her body, urging her to go to him, damn the consequences.

"No, we're not going home," she said. "Not today."

Somehow, practical thoughts found their way to the fore, and she gave her maid clear instructions. "Take the bags and return our tickets. Then use those funds to obtain transportation back to the house."

Then, without another word to Josephine, Annabelle started off across the platform toward Magnus.

Chapter 14

❦

Annabelle walked the length of the train, and Magnus began walking, too. They met face-to-face not far from a uniformed guard standing at the train steps, staring curiously at them.

"Is your coach waiting?" Annabelle asked.

Magnus made no reply. He simply held out his hand, and she took it.

Before she knew what she was about, she was scrambling to keep up with him, while he led her through the crowded station.

A moment later they were crossing the street and he was ushering her into the privacy of his coach. Magnus tapped the outside to signal the driver, then climbed in beside her, slammed the door, and drew the curtains.

It was instantly dim. He sat for a second or two, staring at the floor as if searching for his bearings, then turned to Annabelle and enfolded her in his arms in one smooth, sweeping motion. He buried his lips in the crook of her neck and held her for a long, shuddering moment, while her gloved fingers dug into the thick wool of his coat.

Then at last his lips found hers in a deep devouring kiss, and Annabelle could have wept with joy.

The coach lurched forward and they were knocked off balance, their mouths jerking apart. They both seized the opportunity to pause and look at each other, and it seemed impossible to believe what was happening.

What was she doing?

Then all at once his lips were upon hers again as the coach rattled down the street. The feel of his body beneath her roving hands forced Annabelle's wild and careless desires beyond the lines of reason.

"Thank God, Annabelle . . ." he whispered, kissing her neck and stroking her everywhere as he eased her onto her back on the seat.

He said nothing else, but just the sound of her name on his lips was enough. He was her lover, her only lover, and she had missed this so much.

How had she lived without it for so long? How had she survived?

Then he was on top of her, settling himself between her thighs in the tight, difficult confines of the coach. He slid his hands under her behind, shifting her, and they moved awkwardly, struggling to find a comfortable position on the seat. When his erection pressed against her womanhood, however, comfort seemed unimportant. Annabelle thrust her hips, and Magnus let out a husky growl.

She took his face in her hands and relished the pulsing heat of his mouth, while he tugged her skirts up and slid his hand inside her drawers.

Annabelle sucked in a breath at the thrill of his touch. Using his whole hand, he stroked the creamy heat that tingled and drove her mad with need, then he pulled back to look at her.

"You're still a virgin," he whispered.

"Yes," she replied.

He closed his eyes and rested his forehead upon hers, his touch growing slower, gentler. Annabelle sighed as he stroked her, and soon her body was trembling and all her muscles were clenching tight with breathtaking madness. She grabbed hold of his coat, squeezing the fabric in her fists as pleasure throbbed and pulsed through her. All she wanted was more, despite the fact that her brain was screaming at her to think . . .

Then her body relaxed and went limp. Pulling off

her gloves, she ran her own hand over his trousers and felt his erection. Yearning to touch him as she had never done before, she reached inside.

He closed his eyes and rolled slightly to the side to allow her better access, but movement was awkward on the narrow seat. If only they had more room.

A moment later, drowsy with desire, Magnus opened his eyes and wrapped his large hand around her slender wrist.

"You'd better stop. You're going to make me lose control."

"But I want you to," she replied, kissing his neck, inhaling the musky scent of his skin, thinking this was the most wicked thing she'd ever done, and she wanted to do so much more. She felt no need to hold anything back, which gave her a moment's pause.

This was Magnus, and she had vowed not to give in to him. She was so afraid of another heartbreak like the last time . . .

But when he kissed her, his tongue plunged into her mouth and she had to have this pleasure. At any price. She wanted sex. And why shouldn't she have it? She was thirty-four. What could she possibly be saving herself for?

The carriage bounced over an unexpected bump, and Magnus dragged his lips from hers. He grimaced as if straining to regain control, then leaned toward the window.

Pulling the curtain aside with a finger, he

looked out, then sat back. "We're close to my hotel. Will you come in?"

Annabelle hesitated. Should she?

He kissed her again, and continued to kiss her until the coach slowed and rolled to a stop, at which time they both quickly sat up. Annabelle pushed her skirts down to cover her exposed legs, while Magnus buttoned his coat. He combed his fingers through his hair.

"Are you all right?" he asked, taking her hand in his and kissing it.

She couldn't speak. She was shaking. All she could do was nod.

"Will you come in, Annabelle?" he asked a second time.

"Yes."

Was she really going to do this?

He picked her gloves up off the floor and handed them to her. "Put these on."

She did as he asked.

"When I open the door, step out and go inside, straight up to room twenty-one. Here's the key. I'll follow a minute later."

She nodded and accepted the key from him. He opened the coach door and she got out, then he closed the door behind her, remaining inside.

Annabelle hurried through the lobby of the hotel and straight up the stairs, as if she were a guest and knew exactly where she was going and what she was doing, though she hadn't a clue. She knew what room, of course, but the rest of it?

She found room twenty-one and glanced up and down the corridor before she inserted the key into the lock and turned it.

Pushing the door open, still worrying that she was making a terrible, terrible mistake, she entered the large, luxurious suite. A brass bed was dressed with a crimson and gold cover and enough pillows to drown in. The drapes were open, and a vase of fresh flowers was placed on a table in front of the window. Annabelle could smell their clean, summery scent.

She walked all the way in and touched Magnus's shaving supplies on the washstand. She glanced toward the dressing room and imagined his clothes hanging inside. She wanted to touch and smell them—she could barely believe she was here in his room!—but before she had the chance, she heard a noise and turned.

There he was, standing in the open doorway, seeming out of breath, as if he had just run up the stairs.

He was so handsome, so achingly beautiful, he almost brought her to tears.

He gazed at her for a moment. "I was afraid you'd change your mind and leave before I got here."

She shook her head. "No."

His shoulders seemed to relax, and he came in

and closed the door behind him, locked it, then walked to the window and pulled the drapes shut.

Sauntering toward her in the smoky light cutting through the crack between the curtains, he unbuttoned his overcoat and shrugged out of it, tossing it onto an armchair by the bed. He reached Annabelle and took her face in his hands.

"You can trust me," he said. "We won't do anything you don't want to do."

She knew what he was telling her. He was saying that she should not be afraid, because he would not take her virginity if she did not wish it.

Nonetheless, she was very afraid.

Struggling to overcome it—for she did not want to act a fool with him—she guided his hands away from her face and down over the top of her bodice to her breasts.

He gazed at her uncertainly for a moment. She was uncertain herself. She didn't know what she was doing, only that she wanted him to touch her. The rest, she would deal with as it came.

He took her face in his hands again and pulled her close for another kiss. She let out a little moan, while he backed her up against the side of the bed, stopping only to quickly remove his jacket, waistcoat, and shirt.

While he unbuttoned her bodice, she gazed in awe at his chest, smooth and muscular, then slid her open hand across his shoulder and down to the coarse hair below his navel. She followed the line of hair down into his trousers again, and wrapped her whole hand around him, swirling her thumb over the silky soft tip.

Oh, she was beyond hope. She never imagined she would experience this with Magnus, the man she had loved and lost. She felt faint and dizzy with longing. She wanted all of him—urgently—so she pulled her hand out from inside his pants and stripped off the rest of her clothes.

She stood before him, naked, letting him look at her, which he did, for a prolonged moment.

Then Annabelle stepped forward and wrapped her arms around his neck, and the next thing she knew, he had swept her off her feet and was laying her upon the soft bed.

"Finally," she whispered, her body burning as he came down heavy upon her. "Make love to me, Magnus."

He held her close, his body pulsing with gentle swivels and thrusts. "I want to, Annabelle, you know I do, but I want to do this right. I don't want you to regret anything."

"I won't."

In truth, she was not certain she would be completely comfortable with it afterward, because she was still so unsure of so many things, but she didn't want to worry about that now. All she wanted was this pleasure.

"Show me what to do," she said, completely unable to keep her passions at bay.

He rolled to the side and removed the rest of his clothing. The next thing she knew, he was easing himself between her thighs, nudging her legs apart.

"Bend your knees," he whispered, as the tip of his erection came to rest exactly where it should.

They both went still, staring at one another.

Annabelle's heart was pounding. She had no idea what to expect.

"You're nervous," he whispered.

"Just a little."

"Maybe we should wait."

Annabelle touched her finger to his lips. "No, I don't want to wait."

His chest heaved against hers as he contemplated what was happening. "If we do this," he said, "I promise to do right by you."

She knew what he was saying. He was telling her he would marry her.

Or if she wished it, he would leave her alone?

Annabelle closed her eyes. She didn't know what she wanted outside of this moment.

"Just make love to me," she pleaded, shaking those thoughts away, because she was ravenous for his body and would not be distracted.

He nodded and positioned himself.

Pressing his hips firmly between her thighs, he pushed into the throbbing heat of her flesh.

Annabelle felt the pain of the invasion and squeezed her eyes shut.

He paused, then pushed again, and she barely noticed she was digging her fingernails into his back.

"Relax," he said, kissing her on the cheek.

"Easier said than done."

He kissed the tip of her nose, then down the side of her neck. "I'll help you."

Annabelle lay still, trying to calm her racing heart while he took a nipple into his mouth. He flicked his tongue, and she gasped with a strange, delicious agony. He teased each breast, bringing her to such heights of pleasure, she wondered what more there could be.

But then he took himself farther down, kissing her flat belly until she quivered beneath his touch, remembering what he had done to her once before . . .

"Stop me before you climax," he instructed, kissing her inner thighs. Then he plunged his mouth and tongue into her burning depths, and she cried out in delight.

"Stop," she said in a panic before even a full minute had passed, because she wanted to do as he'd asked, and she was dangerously close to the peak of the mountain.

But oh, it was difficult to stop him.

She took hold of his upper arms and pulled him toward her. Tasting herself on his lips when he kissed her, she was overcome with a passion so fierce, she pushed her hips against his, feeling the silky tip of his shaft slide into her.

"You've relaxed," he whispered into her neck, his voice rough with desire.

She nodded, feeling the pain mount as he pushed deeper still.

"Are you all the way in?" she asked shakily, hoping he was, because she didn't think she could accommodate much more of him.

"I'm only halfway there."

He pulled out, and surprisingly, she pushed against him until he slid back inside. It was like her body had a will of its own.

"Am I hurting you?" he asked, his breath hot and moist in her ear, sending gooseflesh up and down her legs.

"Yes, but don't stop."

He continued to push and withdraw, while Annabelle clutched onto his shoulders, and eventually the pain began to subside with each slick, slow penetration. Then Magnus rose up on his hands and stared down at her.

"I'm all the way in."

Annabelle exhaled with relief and gave herself up to the miracle of what he was doing to her. She began to move with him, thrusting in the dim afternoon light, her whole body surging with wantonness and desire.

Everything seemed to come naturally, and when he lowered his weight upon her again—his stomach hot and sticky upon hers—she held him as close as she could, running her hands up and down the hard muscles of his back as they tensed and relaxed.

Soon they were both drenched in sweat and Annabelle threw her head back on the pillow. Tingling sensation shot from where they were joined, outward to the farthest reaches of her body, and at last she climaxed.

Crying out, she slammed her hands down upon the blankets and squeezed them in her fists.

She realized with both fear and joy that her life was never, ever going to be the same after this. Everything was going to change, because she had just experienced heaven.

And how, after today, would she ever be able to live without it?

Lying in silence on top of Annabelle, feeling his heart pounding against hers, Magnus withdrew from the tight fire of her body and rolled to the side. He stared up at the ceiling.

He was in shock. He had just made love to Annabelle, and it hadn't been a dream.

He laid his open hand upon his chest over his heart, and for the first time in his life he could have wept. It scared the devil out of him—for he was not accustomed to such sentimental weakness. The difficult circumstances of his life, especially during his childhood, had required him to be tough and impervious.

Not wanting to turn his head on the pillow and look at her—for he was certain she would be regretting what they'd done—he reached for her hand instead. When her fingers curled around his, he closed his eyes, relieved by that small offering, then finally turned toward her.

She was lying with her eyes closed, her hand pressed over her forehead as if she were troubled.

His gut wrenched and he braced himself. "Annabelle," he whispered.

He wanted to tell her he loved her. He wanted to say it right then and there, but knew he had to tread carefully.

She took her hand off her head and opened her eyes. "I can't believe we just did that."

"Please, I beg of you," he said. "Do not let yourself regret it."

She chuckled, but there was a hint of bitterness in it. "I don't know what I feel, Magnus. I *should* be regretting it, because I'm a respectable woman who just made love to a man who is not my husband, a man who is my brother's enemy, in a hotel room in the afternoon, no less. But all I'm thinking about is the fact that it was the most amazing thing I've ever done."

He gathered her hand in his, brought her fingers to his lips and kissed the soft pad of each one. He did not want this moment to end.

"I can't believe what it felt like," she continued. "I had no idea."

He leaned up on one elbow and stared at her freckled face for a moment before he kissed her. Her eyes were still closed when he came away, and she was smiling.

"You surprise me," he said.

She opened her eyes. "Why? Because I was morally deficient just now, and I don't even care?"

He knew she was attempting to make a joke, but he didn't laugh because he could see the anxiety in her expression, the uncertainty about her future. Instead, he ran his hand over her hair and wondered if it was possible that one day she could fall in love with him again like she had the first time. If one day she would be free of all her doubts and reservations.

"It certainly was amazing," he said. "I've never wanted anyone the way I wanted you today."

For a long moment she stared up into his eyes, then glanced away. "I'm getting cold. Can we get into the bed?"

He sat back and pulled the covers down, and they both slid between the sheets, lying on their sides facing each other.

"Is it always that enjoyable?" Annabelle asked.

"Every time is different, but for you, I suspect it will only get better."

"Better? That hardly seems possible."

"It won't hurt next time," he told her. "And there are other positions one can try."

He hoped to God they were talking about positions they could try together, because he could not bear to think of her doing this with another man. Ever. She was his now.

Annabelle laughed, but then her expression grew serious. "This is strange, Magnus."

"Why?"

She wet her lips. "Because I'm lying here with *you*. I trusted you enough to get into a private coach with you. I trusted you to be gentle with me just now, and you were, and I'm completely at ease, naked in your bed. Sometimes I wonder if there are two of you."

"Perhaps there are," he replied. "The man I was before I met you, and the man I am today."

She gazed at him pensively while their conversation was interrupted by the sound of laughter and footsteps in the corridor, followed by the closing of a door, then silence.

Annabelle reached up to touch his lips. He simply lay there, letting her explore his face with her gentle, caressing finger.

"Can a person really change so much?" she asked, wanting it to be true.

"I believe so. Especially if that person has something to live for. A hope. A desire."

"I must not have been enough of a desire for you the first time, thirteen years ago."

He took hold of her hand and kissed her palm. "Yes, you were, Annabelle, but I did not feel worthy of you. Everything changed when I went to America."

She rolled onto her back and draped a slender arm across her forehead. "It must be a remarkable place."

"It wasn't just the country," he said. "I could have gone anywhere and the effect would have been the same. I just had to break away from the life I knew—when I was always keeping my head down—and become the man I wanted to be."

Annabelle's eyes darkened with emotion. "There is so much I don't know about you, Magnus. Why were you always keeping your head down?"

He paused a moment before he spoke, for he had never talked to anyone about his childhood. "Because I was treated with cruelty and brutality by people who had heard the stories about my father."

"But Whitby has always insisted that you were a villain and bullied his brother, and that you caused his death."

Magnus shook his head. "That's not true. John was the one who started the fights, and Whitby would always come along to help finish them—at least until I learned to defend myself. And the afternoon John died, I was long gone. We had fought that day, yes, but he had ridden off afterward."

Annabelle sat up. "But what about your mother demanding money from him?"

He shrugged. "I know she asked John to take me in after my father died, but he refused."

"Whitby says your mother threatened John."

Magnus inhaled deeply. He didn't like talking about this, didn't like to think about his mother's odious conduct, or the fact that in this regard, Whitby was probably telling the truth.

"I wasn't aware of her threatening him," he said with a sigh, "though knowing her, she probably did. That would explain why John picked fights with me, wouldn't it?"

Magnus found it strange that he could feel so numb upon hearing this. He supposed he'd shoveled a great deal of dirt over his age-old bitterness.

"Sometimes I just don't know what to believe," Annabelle said. "I trust my brother. He wouldn't lie about things. But my feelings for you are so . . ."

She didn't finish. She merely closed her eyes and shook her head, as if she didn't know which way was up.

Magnus, however, *did* know. He leaned on one elbow and resolved to say what needed to be said.

"All of that is in the past, Annabelle. I've left it

behind, and I need you to do that, too. Come back to America with me. As my wife."

She blinked repeatedly, her face going pale before she replied. "Please don't ask me that now, Magnus. This has all happened so fast."

"But what were you thinking when you saw me at the station and decided to come away with me? Surely something had changed."

He had hoped she'd realized she still loved him, and was willing to move forward. In a way, he had wanted her to choose him over her brother.

"To be honest, I wasn't thinking beyond the moment," she said.

It was not what he'd wanted to hear.

When he raked a hand through his hair in frustration, Annabelle sat up, hugging the covers to her chest. "Please don't make demands on me, Magnus. Not now. This is all so very confusing, and I can't be impulsive about a decision that will affect the rest of my life. This morning I wouldn't even have believed I would be in your bed with you. I *still* can't believe it."

He slowly rolled away from her and sat up. He thought about how angry she had been with him when she first came to see him at his gallery. She had hated him then, and it was barely a month ago.

He said nothing for a long time, then picked his trousers up off the floor and pulled them on.

"Are you angry?" Annabelle asked.

He shook his head, strode to the window and pulled the drapes aside to look out. "No, but I suppose I am waiting for the axe to fall, one way or another."

He remembered something of the sort once before, when he was a boy. He recalled the stories his father used to tell him to distract him from the hunger pains in his belly when there had been no food in the house. He used to talk of a fairy-tale life that might someday be his.

But then his ailing father died and his mother had dropped the axe. She told him the truth about that fairy-tale family—that they had tossed out one of their own sons—Magnus's father—and banished him to hell because he had been a disappointment.

He had not been good enough for them. He'd been weak. Sick. Not normal.

And his mother had told him that they didn't want him, either.

Magnus heard the bedclothes rustling, Annabelle's tiny feet touching the floor and padding toward him. When he turned, she was standing before him, wrapped in the sheet.

"I just want us to enjoy ourselves," she said, the fresh afternoon sun bathing her in soft light, gilding the highlights of her wild, unruly hair. "I'm not ready to think about tomorrow, much less the rest of my life."

He touched her then, because he couldn't resist the rosy pink of her flesh, her freckled cheeks still aglow from their lovemaking. Gently, he traced the slender beauty of her neck and delicate shoulders, then the line of her collarbone, marveling at the silky warmth of her skin under his fingertips.

Watching her eyelids fall closed under the teasing lightness of his touch, he recalled that he had once told himself he would do anything to have her—so if that meant making love to her tirelessly until she finally surrendered to him heart, body, and soul, he would indeed make love to her tirelessly, with or without promises.

"Look at me," she whispered, her eyes still closed, her breasts rising and falling with breathless yearnings. "I'm trembling. How do you do this to me?"

He shuddered with anticipation and need, and answered her with a kiss that quickened his blood like nothing he'd ever known. Then, driven by lust, by the consuming need to possess her, he swept her off her tiny feet and carried her back to the bed.

Chapter 15

◦◦◦◦◦

Forty-eight hours later Annabelle woke naked in Magnus's bed, wondering if it was possible for a person to die from too much sex.

She sat up groggily and tried to make sense of the sheets, which were tangled chaotically at the foot of the bed. The pretty crimson and gold cover had been tossed aside early that morning and was piled on the floor near the window, while their clothes were strewn everywhere.

And her hair ... Well, it looked like some strange little creature had built a nest at the back of her head.

She yawned and nudged Magnus, who was naked as well, lying on his stomach, stretched out in a careless sprawl, snoring. Her gaze drifted over his sleeping form, the corded muscles of his back and buttocks, the wavy black hair spilling heedlessly across his face, his well-built, broad-shouldered frame taking up more than half the bed. He was a gorgeous specimen of manhood, she reflected with a sluggish, blissful smile, and even now, after two days of lovemaking, she was certain she could still manage a little more.

If it weren't for the niggling sense of responsibility to make contact with her family and assure them she was still among the living, she most definitely would.

She nudged him again. "Magnus, wake up. They're going to think we died in here."

"Who?" he asked, still half asleep, his lips puckered against the pillow.

"The hotel staff, that's who." She swung her legs to the floor. "And my maid has probably contacted the police by now and reported me missing."

"Surely not. She saw you go off with me."

"Precisely," Annabelle replied, smacking her tongue against the dry roof of her mouth.

She walked to the table by the window to pour herself a glass of water, but discovered she was rather sore in southerly regions and had to waddle like a duck.

"Come back to bed," Magnus said without opening his eyes or moving.

"No, I can't come back. You've done me in."

Hearing that, he rolled over at last. "You've done me in as well, woman. Do you think I'm made of steel?"

"There are times you appear to be," she replied with a smile.

"Well, not now. I'm spent."

"You need food."

"Food. I'd forgotten about food."

She waddled back to the bed and lay down on her back, her body crossing diagonally over his. "Maybe we should get dressed and go out."

He lifted his head off the pillow. "But you'd have to comb your hair."

"Where is a lady's maid when she is most needed?"

Magnus dropped his head back down. "What's her name? Josephine? Maybe you should let her go. She's been hopelessly ineffective. Look at this place. Your corset is hanging off the curtain rod, for God's sake." He pointed. "Look at that."

"You're absolutely right. I will fire her tomorrow."

Two minutes later Annabelle had forgotten about her responsibility to her family, and both she and Magnus were snoring again.

* * *

"I can't be just your lover," Magnus told Annabelle that night, his voice heavy with desire as he made love to her slowly and gently, sliding in and out with great care and attention to detail. "I must be more than that. I need to be your husband, Annabelle. For life."

She inhaled sharply at the sound of those words and the scorching heat of his penetration. *Your husband for life.* To be given that guarantee—that he would be hers and she would be his and they would share pleasure like this forever—it was beyond her imagination.

She cried out, a muffled sound of indulgence as her fingers dug into his back and her legs squeezed around his hips. He withdrew partially, then thrust back inside.

"Don't stop," she pleaded, voracious for him, needing more of this rapturous pleasure he offered.

"Marry me," he said.

She wanted to say yes. She wanted to scream it, but she couldn't think. All she could comprehend was ecstasy and sensation, and somewhere inside her mind something was telling her to wait—to be sensible, not to make a decision in such a wild state of emotion and arousal.

Was it her fear speaking to her? Or her common sense?

"Annabelle, I love you," he whispered in her

ear, his breath hot as flame, his intense physical rhythm incomprehensible.

"I love you, too," she replied. "I don't care about anything else."

His movements stilled and he drew back, just far enough to look her in the eye. "Then marry me. It's the right thing."

"I don't know, Magnus."

"Just trust me. You know you can."

There it was. That which was holding her back . . .

"I know I *want* to."

He slid all the way in, pushing firmly while swiveling his hips. "You want to trust me?" he asked. "Or you want to marry me?"

She considered it for a moment, but was losing herself in the pulsation of a mounting orgasm. "Both. I want both. *Yes.*"

Then the world outside of Annabelle's mind and body disappeared, and she gave into her desires once and for all, welcoming the force of Magnus's climax as he finally groaned and poured into her.

He collapsed upon her, heavy and exhausted, and lay there for a moment until their breathing returned to normal and their bodies regained their natural rhythms. Then he gently rolled off her and took her into his arms, holding her close with a different kind of tenderness, until the sun rose in the morning and light spread across their glistening, sated bodies.

Annabelle woke from a deep sleep as if an alarm bell had gone off inside her head. Groggy and disoriented, she sat bolt upright and looked around.

The suite was quiet except for the ticking of the clock and a cart with a squeaky wheel rolling by outside the door. Light was pouring in through the crack between the drapes, and the room was still a mess. She had no idea what day it was.

She gazed down at Magnus asleep beside her, naked under a single white sheet, one arm draped over his face, and suddenly remembered what had occurred the night before. He had been making love to her, and somewhere in the wild, spinning fury of her passions, she had agreed to become his wife.

All at once the old familiar doubts and fears came rushing back at her, and she wasn't sure she could move. She managed only to bury her forehead in a hand.

What had she done? She should have taken more time to think about the consequences of her decision, but she supposed she hadn't exactly been thinking with her brain.

"Good morning," Magnus said, his hand coming to rest upon her back.

Annabelle hesitated before she lifted her head to look down at him. "Good morning."

For a long quiet moment he studied her face. He tossed an arm up under his head, and somehow she knew he understood what she was feeling. How could he not? He must have been expecting this.

His fingers began to brush lightly across her back. "Don't worry," he said.

Annabelle swallowed with difficulty. "How can I not? We've been out of our minds with lust the past few days, and last night I agreed to marry you. What will Whitby say when he finds out?"

Magnus's eyes clouded over with momentary displeasure, but it vanished quickly as he continued to rub her back. "It won't matter what he says. We're together now, Annabelle, and I won't let anything or anyone tear us apart."

Still feeling unsure, she rested a chin on her knee and gazed pensively toward the window.

"Come here." He urged her back down to lie beside him.

Annabelle rested her head on his shoulder, and the heat of his body warmed hers.

As she lay there, she contemplated the misgivings still hammering away in her mind, and suddenly a far worse fear overcame her.

She imagined taking Whitby's side and telling Magnus she could not marry him. She imagined saying good-bye to Magnus, never making love to him again, never seeing him again—and quite frankly the thought of that was worse than death.

Nothing seemed to matter now but the joy he gave her. When he was holding her close in his arms like this, she didn't care about the past or what other people thought. She didn't want to be suspicious and worry that he was using her to hurt Whitby. She wanted to believe in him. She wanted to believe that he was telling her the truth—that he had come back to London for *her*, and revenge upon Whitby had nothing to do with it.

When it came right down to it, all she cared about was this crazy, mad love, and every instinct in her body was pushing her to trust him. Maybe that was all that mattered.

She leaned up on an elbow and looked down at him with love. "I don't want anything to come between us, either," she said.

Magnus took her face in his hands. "I'll make you happy, Annabelle. I promise. You'll never want for anything."

"I don't need anything except for you."

His eyes flashed with desire, and he pulled her down for a kiss, but Annabelle laid a hand on his chest to stop things before the kiss progressed to something more.

"We can't start this again," she said with a smile, "because we have to get up and get dressed. I'll need to go home today, Magnus."

He settled back, disappointed. "Why?"

"Because I have to tell them."

His chest rose and fell with a deep intake of breath. "Why do you have to go back there? Why don't we just leave? You could write to them from New York."

"No, I could never do that. They're my family and I care for them—Whitby, Lily, and the children. I can't leave without saying good-bye."

He sat up against the brass frame of the bed, his dark eyes sweeping over her face with a measure of discontent.

"You don't have to come," she said.

"Oh, yes I do. I will not have you going alone, as if you are ashamed of me. We must stand together."

"It wouldn't be like that," she assured him.

Magnus looked away toward the window. "*He* might think so. Or he might think I'm afraid to face him. He'll certainly try to change your mind."

Annabelle felt a chill come over the room with this change in Magnus's mood. She wished he would look at her. "It shouldn't matter what Whitby thinks," she said. "And nothing will change my mind."

Magnus looked off into the distance as if he hadn't heard her, then finally returned his gaze to her face. His eyes warmed, and she was relieved.

"You're right," he said. "It doesn't matter. I am only thinking of you. I hate that you must do something so difficult. If you like, *I* could do it. I could go and face him alone."

Annabelle tried to imagine that, but could not. Whitby probably wouldn't even believe that she had consented to marry Magnus. Whitby would think it a lie, or that Magnus had kidnapped her or some such foolishness.

She squeezed Magnus's hand. "No, you were right the first time. We must stand together. And I'm going to do my best to convince him that he's wrong about you."

Magnus merely nodded, and Annabelle's stomach began to churn with a slow mounting dread. She rested a hand on her belly, thinking she would be very glad when this day was over.

Century House in Bedfordshire was hailed by some as one of the most majestic palaces in England, and though Annabelle had lived there all her life, she never failed to be moved by its magnificence whenever she returned after time away.

The coach rolled past the ornamental fountain and came to a smooth stop at the front entrance. Annabelle glanced briefly at Magnus, who was looking out the window in the opposite direction of the house.

He does not want to be here.

"Shall we?" she said nonetheless.

"Of course," he replied. "Allow me."

He climbed out of the coach and offered his hand to Annabelle to assist her down. She started off toward the front entrance, but stopped and turned when she realized he was not following. He was still standing beside the coach, his dark eyes moving slowly from left to right across the front of the house.

"I haven't seen this place in eight years," he said, "and I've certainly never made it past the front doors."

Annabelle was uncomfortably aware of a change in him. There was no warmth in his eyes, no flirtatious spark or seductive appeal. Nevertheless, she spoke with confidence. "You'll make it past them today."

He nodded and followed behind her.

They walked up the steps and were met at the door by Clarke, the butler, who politely greeted Annabelle, but when he recognized Magnus, his expression turned to shock.

Annabelle removed her gloves as she spoke. "Mr. Wallis is my guest here today, Clarke. We wish to speak to Whitby, if you will please inform him."

The butler stared perplexedly at her before he closed the door behind them and recovered his aplomb. "As you wish, Miss Lawson," he said.

"Please tell him we will be in the gilded drawing room," she added.

Clarke bowed at the waist before he turned to

go. Annabelle could see the panic in his gait. It was not something she had ever seen before.

When she faced Magnus, he did not look pleased.

"It's this way," she said, wanting only to get through all this as quickly as possible.

They climbed the stairs, and Magnus looked up at the enormous ancestral portraits on the walls, some dating back as far as the fifteenth century. He was barely watching where his feet were going.

When they reached the top and entered the drawing room with its ornately carved, gilded ceiling, Annabelle watched him with a mild sense of trepidation. His eyes scanned over everything— from the massive gilt-framed mirror over the fireplace, to the Chippendale furniture, the statues, the harp, the grand piano, the gold wall sconces, and the tall tree ferns.

"You could feed half the orphans in London for a month with what it must have cost to furnish this one room alone," he said bluntly.

Annabelle didn't know what to say.

"It's a far cry from the place where I grew up," he added, approaching the eight-foot portrait of his grandfather on the wall and looking up at it. "There he is."

The derision in his voice was unmistakable.

Annabelle approached Magnus and linked her arm through his, seeking to remind him that the man in the portrait was part of the past and it was time to leave all that behind. Isn't that what he'd tried to tell her when he asked her to return to America with him as his wife?

"I never knew him," she said, looking up at the portrait. "He died long before I was born."

"Which was probably fortunate for you, because I doubt he would have taken you in."

Startled by the severity in Magnus's tone, Annabelle shot a surprised glance at him.

His expression gentled. "I'm sorry." He shook his head at himself. "That was thoughtless of me. I just never expected to see the inside of this house. It brings back old memories."

He took her into his arms and held her, calming her misgivings with the affection in his embrace.

Just then someone cleared his throat in the doorway, and both Annabelle and Magnus stepped apart. It was her brother.

Annabelle took an anxious step forward. "Whitby . . ."

He appeared horror-struck. "What in God's name . . . ?"

Annabelle gestured toward Magnus. "I've brought someone."

Whitby remained in the doorway. "I can see that for myself, Annabelle."

There was a long drawn-out silence while

Annabelle's gut began to churn and her heart hammered against her ribs. These two men—both of whom she loved—despised each other. They had fought as children, each blaming the other for unfortunate circumstances in their lives, and Annabelle wasn't sure it would ever be possible to change that.

She glanced anxiously at Magnus, who stood motionless, facing Whitby. "Why don't we all sit down?" she suggested.

After a moment's hesitation, her brother slowly entered the room, and Annabelle took a seat at one end of the sofa. As soon as she was settled, Magnus sat beside her, while Whitby took the facing chair.

"Where have you been?" her brother asked, sounding more than a little displeased. "We expected you home sooner."

She squeezed her hands together on her lap. "I'm sorry about that. I was . . . detained."

Whitby's piercing gaze flicked to Magnus. "Detained."

Magnus said nothing. He merely crossed one leg over the other and let Annabelle do the talking. She was very glad of that.

"Yes," she said, resolving to be firm and forthright, for there was no point dancing around the issue. "You see . . . Magnus and I have spent the past few days together and we have come to realize that . . . that we are still in love."

How foolish she must sound to Whitby, who no doubt could not believe his ears. She even sounded foolish to herself.

Whitby's tolerance seemed to snap like a tangible thing in the room. Annabelle almost feared the ceiling was going to come crashing down on their heads.

"I'm sorry, Whitby, but I hope you can understand," she said.

"Understand, Annabelle?" To her utter surprise, he spoke not with anger, but with gentle pleading, as if Magnus were not even there. "How can I? I've watched you go through your adult life without hope or optimism because of what he did to you. All this time, you've hated him."

"Only because I was hurt," she explained, though she did not feel confident. She felt ridiculous, for she had changed her opinions—opinions she'd held for thirteen years—virtually overnight, even after Whitby had warned her that Magnus would try to seduce her. Which he certainly had done, quite effectively.

Whitby wet his lips and shifted in his chair. He appeared shaken, but determined to convince her that she was making a mistake and was merely confused.

Meanwhile, Magnus was watching all of it, sitting back with quiet fortitude.

"No, Annabelle, you forget," Whitby said. "Do you not remember the lies you could not forgive?"

"I do remember that," she said, "but it was a long time ago, and I'm a different person now and so is he." Magnus gave her an encouraging nod, and she was so very, very thankful he was here, because she wanted to be with him. She did. She could not let anything change her mind.

Whitby, however, watched the exchange from where he sat across from them, and all his gentle pleading flew out the window. He stood up. "Annabelle, you're not stupid. Use your *head*."

She shot him an exasperated look. "I *am* using it."

"No, I don't believe you are."

She stared dumbfounded at her brother. "You need to give him a chance, Whitby. He's not the villain you think he is. There have been misunderstandings, and he regrets what happened between us. He never *wanted* to hurt me."

She looked at Magnus then, needing him to intervene, to defend what she was saying.

He recognized her entreaty, and turned to Whitby. "Indeed I am not the villain here. And I do regret what happened between Annabelle and me. But you have played a part in her unhappiness, too, Whitby. Annabelle has felt trapped here, as if she owes something to you because your family took her in. She needs to feel that she is free."

"Is this true, Annabelle?" Whitby asked.

She paused. "You have been very kind to me, Whitby, which makes it difficult to do something that will disappoint you."

Whitby shook his head at Magnus. "I'm not going to apologize for being *kind* to her."

"Well, *I* have apologized to her," Magnus said, "and she has forgiven me."

Whitby's face screwed into a disbelieving grimace. "You can't be serious, Annabelle! You believe him? Tell me you were not so gullible. You assured me you were not."

"I was not gullible, Whitby. It's the truth. He is not the man you think he is." She fidgeted and cleared her throat, striving to maintain a confident tone. "I think it's time you stopped hating Magnus so much, and put the past to rest."

"Put it to rest." Whitby shook his head and strode to the other side of the room.

Annabelle felt like she was suffocating. She glanced desperately at Magnus, but he was sitting forward, watching her brother.

Finally, Whitby faced them again. "What do you mean to tell me today, Annabelle? Why did you bring him here?"

She sensed he already knew the answer to that question, but he needed to hear it just the same.

"We are engaged," she said, feeling her heart break at what should have been the happiest moment of her life.

The ensuing silence carried enough weight to crush the house.

Annabelle sat motionless, immobile. She was aware of Magnus beside her, waiting for Whitby to oppose the engagement, and she wasn't sure what would happen after that.

Whitby strode closer. "Can't you see? He came back here to use you again, so he could finally feel he has won."

"No, you're wrong," she replied, hearing her voice break because it was not something she wanted to hear, not after she'd suffered so much, fighting against her doubts and fears.

"It's just because you are lonely," Whitby spat. "You are not thinking clearly because you are desperate for a marriage of your own."

Her lips fell open. "I am not desperate."

At that moment Magnus stood, tall and ominous in the room. "I think I've heard enough."

"I beg your pardon?" Whitby said bitterly.

"Shall I repeat it for you, cousin? *I have heard enough.*"

Whitby slowly blinked. "May I remind you of the fact, sir, that you are not welcome here."

Annabelle stood also. "Yes, he is. It's my home, too, and he's my guest."

But they both ignored her.

"Your sister is coming with me," Magnus said. "She has agreed to become my wife, and I will be taking her back to America with me."

Whitby spoke through clenched teeth. "You will do no such thing."

Annabelle stood there stunned as she watched them, not knowing what to do or say.

"I will do exactly as I please," Magnus shot back. "She belongs to me now."

"I don't belong to either of you!" Annabelle cried out, but again they both ignored her. They were glaring at each other like a couple of angry wolves.

"You insufferable bastard," Whitby said, his voice low, but brimming with a dangerous, repressed fury.

The grandfather clock chimed once, and before Annabelle had a chance to say another word, they both simultaneously charged at each other.

Chapter 16

Magnus and Whitby grabbed hold of each other in the drawing room, knocked over a plant, then slammed hard up against a tapestry on the wall. The heavy fabric jostled as they shoved each other, then they hurled back to the middle of the room, shouting as they fell against a table, knocking over a lamp, which smashed on the floor. They fell beside the broken glass and rolled in the other direction, grunting and cursing until Annabelle shouted, "Stop it! Both of you!"

Whitby pinned Magnus down and punched him in the jaw, then Magnus sat up and bashed his forehead against Whitby's. Her brother fell backward.

"Stop!" Annabelle shouted again, and suddenly Lily was beside her, grabbing her husband under the arms and scrambling to pull him off Magnus.

"What's going on!" she shouted in disbelief.

The sound of his pregnant wife's voice seemed to arrest Whitby on the spot. He sat back on the floor, cupping his forehead.

Magnus staggered to his feet and wiped the back of his hand across his bleeding lip. He was out of breath and panting.

Magnus jabbed a finger at him. "I'm warning you, Whitby. Don't even try to come between us. We'll be leaving for America tomorrow, and don't expect to visit, because you won't be welcome in my house."

Shocked and shaken, Annabelle turned to her brother and sister-in-law, who were waiting for her to say something.

All the weight of the world descended upon her at that moment, and she wasn't sure she could find the words to speak.

Then Magnus's arm curled around her waist and he closed his eyes and pressed his face against her cheek, and she found herself holding tight to him. She wrapped her arms around his neck.

She looked back down at Whitby and Lily and felt

a wretchedness of heart she'd never imagined possible. "I'm sorry," she said. "I'm going with him."

With that, she and Magnus left the drawing room.

They made it only as far as the staircase, however, before Annabelle stopped and took hold of the railing, her anger finally spilling over the edge of her composure. "What in the name of God was that?"

The fire from the struggle was still burning in Magnus's eyes. "What do you mean? He insulted you."

"How?"

"He said you were lonely and desperate."

Annabelle shook her head at him and descended the stairs, hearing him follow fast behind her.

"That wasn't about me," she said accusingly. "It was about you seizing the opportunity to fight him. You were waiting for it."

They were practically sailing down the stairs now.

"Oh no you don't," he said. "Don't try to make it seem like it was me. I sat there calmly through all of that. It was your brother who wanted to fight from the first minute he set eyes on me. He wanted to crush me, like always."

Annabelle walked quickly across the entrance hall, her strides snapping her skirts between her legs. "You think it's him and he thinks it's you. I'm sick of it."

Magnus followed her out the front door and down the steps to the coach. She climbed in and sat down, and he climbed in beside her, slamming the door shut, but the coach didn't move.

"How can you be angry at me?" he asked. "I was a bystander."

"Oh, yes, you were very unassuming when you smashed him up against the tapestry!"

"I did it for you, Annabelle. I was defending your choice to marry me. I was not going to let him stop us."

"But I saw the fury in your eyes! You were out of control, and all this time you've been promising me that Whitby no longer has any power over you—that you had left all that behind, and the only reason you came back to England was for me. I believed you. I trusted that you were telling me the truth."

"Don't do this, Annabelle," he said. "Don't let yourself. You're so ridiculously loyal to him! Just because he took you in and raised you does not mean you have to live your life only to make him proud. You must find your own way and your own happiness. Be true to yourself. You don't owe him your whole future."

"It's not as easy as that. I trust him to know what is best for me and what will make me happy, when I don't really trust myself."

"Or me," he said.

She did not reply.

"Say it, Annabelle. I am the reason you don't trust yourself."

"Yes!" she shouted. "I made an error in judgement years ago. I was fooled. Duped. And after what just happened, how can I not still have doubts? How can I believe that there is not some truth to what Whitby just said—that you want me because you want to feel you have won. You simply want to take something from *him.*"

His eyes darkened with frustration. "That's not true. You're letting him influence you. Trust your heart, Annabelle. You know I love you."

"But you were still fighting the same battle today that you always were! What has changed?"

Magnus sat forward and wiped his lip again, examining the blood on his hand.

"Whitby is not a bad man," she told him. "He only wants me to be safe and happy, and I don't think either of you really knows why you hate the other."

That statement caused him to lift his head and look at her with dismay. "I know very well why I hate him, Annabelle."

"Why?"

"Because he has always taken pleasure in making my life a living hell! He has deprived me of my birthright, beaten me to a pulp on numerous occasions, spread cruel gossip about my father and me, causing us to be treated as outcasts and lunatics. As a child, I was spit upon in the streets, kicked and beaten by those who enjoyed thrashing a fallen aristocrat. But it was my father I pitied the most, because he died a broken man. That is why I will always hate your brother—for continuing his grandfather's legacy of heartlessness."

Stunned by his outburst, Annabelle could feel her throat closing up. "But you told me you didn't care about Whitby anymore, that that was behind you. How can I trust completely that there is not a part of you that *is* using me? Do you even know it yourself? I saw the satisfaction in your eyes when you told him I belonged to *you* now, not him. At that moment, I was nothing more than a weapon to use against him. And I can see the hatred in your eyes now. I just heard it in your voice."

She looked out the coach window toward the horizon over the treetops in the distance.

"You can't blame me for hating Whitby," Magnus said. "But it has nothing to do with you."

"But that's just it! I do blame you for hating him. It's not his fault you and your father were cut off from the family. Your father *was* dangerous. He tried to light his own brother on fire."

The shock of hearing that seemed to stir Magnus's anger all over again. "That's a blatant lie! My father was not dangerous. He was sick and weak.

That is the reason why my grandfather didn't want him. He lacked the appropriate stature of an aristocrat."

Annabelle felt her brows pull together in a frown. "That's not what Whitby believes."

Magnus shrugged and looked off in the other direction, as if what Whitby believed was of no consequence to him.

Hope sparked anew in Annabelle's veins. "I feel a great need to get to the bottom of this."

He shook his head at her, as if he was puzzled by that desire. "Why? It's in the past."

"It is not in the past, because you are still bitter about it."

"I'm bitter that you won't trust me!" he shouted, raking a hand through his hair in frustration. "You continue to trust Whitby over me, when what I need is for you to take a leap of faith. Just believe in me *now*. Forget about the past."

Annabelle shifted uneasily on the cushioned seat. "Perhaps I could talk to Whitby and tell him you think there's been a mistake," she said. "He might listen to me."

Magnus took hold of her shoulders. "Annabelle, it was a long time ago. It doesn't matter. Just trust me now and come away with me."

"I can't."

"Why? What are you looking for? Concrete proof that you can trust me? Because you will

never get that. The trust has to come from here."
He touched her chest, over her heart.

Annabelle gazed at him in despair. "But there is
so much to be sorted out here."

"Annabelle, I'm asking you . . . Don't confuse
all this with your fear of letting yourself love me.
Just look in your heart."

He regarded her intently with eyes dark and be-
seeching, and she did as he asked. She *did* look
into her heart, where she felt passion and love and
hope and desire. She wanted Magnus with every
breath in her body. She wanted to spend the rest of
her life with him.

But he was asking her to take a blind leap of
faith and simply believe him, when she could not.
She was afraid to, especially when there were still
so many unanswered questions.

She wished it was not so, but she needed something more than Magnus's word—his word
against Whitby's—to hang her trust upon.

She lowered her gaze, knowing it was going to
kill her to say this, and it was going to kill him to
hear it . . .

"I'm sorry, but I *can't*."

Magnus tipped his head back on the upholstery
and stared up at the dark ceiling of the coach.
"You're going to trust Whitby's word over mine?"
They sat in silence for a moment. "Don't do this,
Annabelle. Come with me now."

"No, not like this. Don't make me choose between you and them when I'm not ready. If it's me you love, you'll be patient." She crossed in front of him to climb out of the coach.

"Where are you going?" he asked.

"Back inside."

"Please tell me you're going to collect your things."

She opened the door and stepped out. "No. I can't go with you, Magnus."

She backed away from him, toward the house.

He climbed out of the coach, too. "*Please*, don't go back in there."

"I have to. I need to fix this."

"You can't fix anything!" he shouted. "Even if you find out there had been a mistake and my father was wronged, it won't give you what you are looking for. Why can't you accept that?"

She stopped and sucked in a breath, overcome suddenly by self-doubt, but then she kept going, because she simply could not take that leap of faith. She wished she could, but she could not.

He called to her one more time. "Annabelle!"

But she kept going.

Magnus pressed the heels of his hands to his forehead, then strode back to the coach and pounded his fist against the outside of it over and over. He grunted with fury and frustration as he kicked a wheel, then got back inside, slammed the door and shouted at the coachman to drive off.

Gathering her skirts in her fists, Annabelle strode purposefully up the stairs and returned to the drawing room, where Whitby and Lily were standing together in front of the window. Whitby was holding a cloth to his forehead.

She stopped in the doorway, and Lily immediately came hurrying across the room to hug her.

"Oh, Annabelle."

When they stepped apart, Annabelle gazed at her brother, who was still standing at the window. He must have seen what had occurred out front.

"Thank God," he said, lowering the cloth and tossing it onto the marble table beside him. "I'm relieved you had the good sense to come back."

Annabelle loved her brother, and she knew he only wanted what was best for her, but she had never, ever been more angry with him.

"I have not come back," she said, "at least not the way you think."

He shook his head at her, as if he couldn't get over her foolishness, then turned and faced the window.

Annabelle strode toward him. "How *could* you, Whitby?"

He faced her again. "How could *I*? You were the one who brought an enemy into our home and told me you wanted to marry him. Marry him,

Annabelle! Of all the men in England, you had to choose *him*!"

Annabelle tried to explain. "I fought it every step of the way—honest, I did—but then I just couldn't. I am in love with him."

Whitby's eyes fumed with shock and dismay. "So you are determined? You're going to choose that scoundrel over us?"

"I have not yet made that decision," she said. "I am still . . . *unsure*." And that was putting it mildly.

He seemed to relax at hearing that. "So you still have some reservations about him?"

Annabelle paused, nodding her head. "How can I help but have reservations? I've had a broken heart since I was twenty-one. I'm not capable of trusting *any* man." She sank into a chair and buried her face in her hands. "Heaven help me, I'm still such a misfit."

Whitby crossed toward her and touched her shoulder. "You're not a misfit, Annabelle. You're just cautious, and wisely so."

"I'm not so sure. I love him, Whitby. Why can't I just trust him? Why must I live in constant fear that the rug is going to be pulled out from under me, with no warning whatsoever?"

"Because that's what happened the last time."

Her brother's eyes softened with compassion, which Annabelle greatly appreciated at that moment, when she felt so very alone and was worrying that she'd just made the biggest mistake of her life, walking away from the man she loved.

She sighed heavily. "Maybe it would help if I understood more about his father being sent away," she said, still fearing that Magnus was right—that she was using the past as an excuse, giving it more importance than it deserved because she was simply afraid of letting herself love him.

Whether or not that was the case, she did not know, so all she could do was press on. "Magnus truly believes they were wronged."

"That's not what I know about it," Whitby said.

He appeared less angry now, and she wondered if it was possible that he might take pity on her and help her.

"Well, it's your word against his," she told him, "and I'm tired of all the questions, Whitby. I need to feel as if I know what I'm doing."

But even if she did know the truth, would she *ever* feel completely sure?

Annabelle spent the rest of the day questioning various members of the household about Whitby's grandfather and his twin sons, and everyone who worked in the house said the same thing Whitby had always said—that the boy had been sent away because he'd been violent and dangerous.

One woman had even said that Magnus's father had "the devil in him," which had done nothing to improve Annabelle's optimism.

Of course, there were very few servants who had actually worked in the house when Magnus's father lived there, and it was so long ago that no one even remembered what he looked like.

Annabelle had the distinct feeling that people merely believed what they'd heard through gossip over the years, and that the story had essentially taken on mythic proportions.

So when all her questions turned up no new information, she spent the evening in her studio, distracting herself from the stresses of her life by working on the painting of the waterfall.

She still could not seem to get the reflections in the water to look real, so she finally gave up, chocking it up to the fact that she was too anxious to concentrate.

That night, Annabelle went to bed feeling certain that she was wasting her time on this futile search. What was the point of it, after all, when Magnus said he didn't care about the past? What difference would all this make once they got to America, if she went with him? What had happened to his father had nothing to do with their lives now. If she was going to give her whole heart to Magnus, she was going to have to do as he'd asked and somehow find the courage to take that blind leap of faith.

Just then a quiet knock sounded at her door, and she leaned up on both elbows. "Come in."

The door creaked open, and there stood her brother, holding a kerosene lamp. He was still wearing his dinner jacket, but his shirt was open at the collar, his tie loose around his neck.

"I'm sorry to wake you," he said.

"You didn't. I wasn't sleeping."

He hesitated a moment. "I need to speak to you."

Annabelle sat up.

He closed the door behind him, walked to the bed and set down the lamp, then pulled a chair up and took a seat.

"Today, after you told me that Magnus believed his father was wronged," Whitby said, "I began thinking about it, and I remember whispers and gossip when I was growing up. Gossip about my grandfather."

Annabelle's pulse began to beat. "Pertaining to what?"

Whitby ran a hand through his hair. "Evidently, there was a parlor maid who worked here in the house, and she and my grandfather were intimate lovers, and they almost ran away together."

"It sounds scandalous," Annabelle remarked.

"This maid was let go after a few years, but I

seem to recall hearing that she was sent away at the same time Magnus's father was."

A disturbing notion suddenly occurred to Annabelle. *"Was she the mother?"*

Whitby held up a hand and shook his head. "No, no. Nothing like that. Magnus's father and my father were definitely twins, that is certain."

Annabelle was not sure where her brother was heading with this, until he reached into his waistcoat pocket and handed her a folded note. "But perhaps this woman knows something and can give you some insight into what happened. If she's still alive, that is. I have no idea."

Annabelle unfolded the note and read the woman's name, Rose Michaels, along with a London address.

"I don't know if her family still lives there," Whitby said, "but it was all I could find in the employment records."

Annabelle tossed the covers aside and slid to the edge of the bed. "How can I ever thank you?"

He stood and took her hand. "Don't be so grateful. I still don't trust Magnus, and I'm hoping this woman will prove me right. I just want *you* to be sure of your decision, whatever it turns out to be."

She wrapped her arms around him, and he held her briefly before he drew away. There was a note of warning in his voice when he spoke.

"All I ask is that you be careful, Annabelle. Don't let your emotions rule your head. But God forbid, if you do, and you decide to go with Magnus, please know that you can always come home to us. We will be here for you no matter what."

"Thank you, Whitby. It is good to know."

He turned to leave, but stopped in the doorway. "You should also know that if that man ever hurts you again, I swear I will cross the ocean to make him pay. I promise you that, Annabelle."

And she knew that if circumstances warranted it, her brother would make good on that promise.

His head in a fog, Magnus entered his hotel room and looked around.

The maids had been there. The bedclothes were in order, the drapes were open, and everything was tidy. It was almost as if Annabelle had never been there.

Closing the door behind him and dropping the hotel key on a table, he slowly walked to the bed and rested a hand on the brass frame. He rested the other hand on his stomach, because he felt ill, as if he'd been shot back there into those dark times when he wanted to crush Whitby, to blame him for his pain. He'd thought he was over that, but today had been very grim.

He was ashamed of himself—for his shocking, appalling behavior in Annabelle's drawing room.

He had tried to crush Whitby again. He had felt such intense bitterness toward him.

Why had he even bothered to come back to subject himself to this? He felt wretched, like that rejected boy who had been kicked and beaten and called the spawn of a madman.

He regretted coming back. He should not have come. Not even for Annabelle. She was too entrenched in that world. He wanted to leave right now, to go home to America.

But God, oh, God. He could not. Because he still wanted Annabelle with every inch of his soul, even though the likelihood of his ever truly having her seemed slim, because she simply could not trust him.

Granted, she had said she wanted to fix things, but he didn't want her to go poking around in the past, finding out things he might not even want to know.

What if she discovered something that would confirm what Whitby had always said, and it would make Annabelle fear and loathe him more than she ever had before—just as everyone else had all his life?

In all honesty, he was afraid of what she would find, because how well had he really known his father, after all? For all he knew, maybe his father *had* been a madman.

Chapter 17

Annabelle knocked firmly upon Rose Michaels's door and was greeted by an attractive woman in gold spectacles. Her gray hair was swept up into a loose knot, and she appeared to be in her sixties.

"Good afternoon," she said.

Annabelle smiled politely. "Good afternoon. I'm looking for someone who lived here quite a few years ago, and I'm wondering if you might know her. Her name is Rose Michaels."

Annabelle saw recognition flash through the woman's eyes before she gave a melancholy smile. "Rose was my mother. But she died seven years ago."

Annabelle sighed and bit her lip.

"Is there anything I can do to help you?" the woman asked.

Annabelle wondered again if it was possible for *anyone* to help her. She was standing at a stranger's house, looking for answers about Magnus—a man who had no connection to these people. Rose Michaels was a ghost. She had never even met him.

"No," Annabelle said, waving her hand in a dismissive gesture as she turned to leave. "I'm sorry to have bothered you."

"Wait, dear . . ." The woman took an anxious step forward. "How did you know my mother?"

Annabelle stopped on the front walk and turned around. "I didn't. My brother—the Earl of Whitby—gave me her name, because she once worked as a maid at Century House in Bedfordshire, and I wanted to ask her some questions about that. But it was such a long time ago."

The woman's eyes narrowed curiously. "Your brother is the Earl of Whitby?"

"Yes. Well, actually, I was adopted, but he is like a true brother to me."

The woman nodded her understanding. "I can guess what you wanted to speak to my mother about, but I am curious as to *why*, after all these years."

Annabelle swallowed nervously. This was very awkward. A scandalous affair was not something one spoke about to a stranger.

At the same time, it was important that she learn the truth, and she sensed that this woman knew something.

"Would you like to come inside?" she asked.

Annabelle hesitated, then accepted the woman's kindness.

"I'm Hannah Pascoe," she said. "And you are . . . ?"

"Annabelle Lawson."

They shook hands, then went into the parlor and sat down.

"I'm looking for information about the former earl's son, Robert Wallis," Annabelle said. "He was the younger of twins, and he would have been just a boy when your mother worked at Century House. The older twin was the heir to—"

"I know who he is," Mrs. Pascoe interjected. "He was the boy they sent away. The one they kept secret."

Annabelle sucked in a breath. "So you *do* know about that."

"Only what my mother told me, but she asked me never to speak of it." She stood up, strolled to the mantel and took down a framed photograph, which she handed to Annabelle. "This is what she looked like a few years before she died. That's

when she spoke to me about what happened at
Century House. I suppose she had begun to long
for certain things in her past, or perhaps she just
wanted someone to know."

"*Long* for certain things?"

Mrs. Pascoe shrugged noncommittally. "She
told me your brother's grandfather was the great
love of her life, and she never really recovered
from the heartbreak of being sent away. She
dreamed of him until the day she died."

Annabelle stood up, reached for the picture,
and looked at Rose's face. She was an elderly
woman, and it was difficult to imagine what she
would have looked like so many years ago.

Annabelle handed the picture back. "I believe I
understand how she must have felt, because the
reason I am asking about this is that I have met the
man who is Robert's son, who has also been ostra-
cized from the family."

Mrs. Pascoe stared in silence at her for a moment, then turned and set the photograph back
upon the mantel. "And you're in love with him."

Annabelle managed a smile. The woman was
very astute. "Yes, I am. But I don't know what to
do, because no one trusts him, and I'm not sure
that I should, either." She paused and looked
hopelessly at the picture of Rose, then cupped her
forehead in a hand. "Oh, I don't even know why
I'm here and what I hope to accomplish. *I'm* the

one who needs fixing, not him, and not this feud between him and my brother."

"If you really love this man," Mrs. Pascoe said, "your heart should know whether or not you can trust him. What happened to his father should have nothing to do with it."

Annabelle smiled wretchedly. "You're not the first person to tell me that, and I know you're right. The real problem is that I still fear that his love is not real, and that he is lying to me about everything and I'm going to end up with my heart broken again."

Mrs. Pascoe inclined her head.

Annabelle swallowed hard, and felt a need to shift her focus back toward something she could sink her teeth into, something that *could* provide answers, because all the rest of it was still so muddy in her brain.

"The last person I asked," she said, "told me that Robert had the devil inside of him."

Mrs. Pascoe sat down again, and her voice was sullen, but sympathetic. "The devil? No, that's not true."

Annabelle faced her. "What do you know about it, Mrs. Pascoe?"

For a long, tense moment, the woman was quiet, then at last she spoke. "Perhaps you had better sit down. This might take a while, and I don't think it will be easy for you to hear."

Despite all her attempts to convince herself that none of this really mattered because it was in the past, Annabelle was overcome with curiosity, so she returned to her chair and sat down to listen.

Chapter 18

 ~~~∽◯◯∽~~~

Dear Magnus,

I have just returned from a most fascinating meeting with a woman who knew of your father, and I have much to tell you. Could you come to the house in Mayfair as soon as you receive this letter? I will be waiting for you.

Annabelle

Magnus stood next to his coach on the street outside Whitby's London residence, gazing up at the large stone mansion. He had stood here in this spot many times as a boy and later as a young man, always an outsider wondering what the house looked like on the inside. He had longed for acceptance then, and wanted what Whitby had been blessed with—a family who wanted him.

He felt a dim flicker of the old familiar feeling of isolation and loneliness, but knew it was merely the memory of those days, for he no longer cared that he was an outsider. In fact, he preferred it this way. He had no interest in being accepted by the people of this world, and no longer cared what this house looked like on the inside. All he cared about was Annabelle.

Besides, he had two homes in America that were just as fine. Finer even, for he'd worked hard to attain them. He had *earned* them.

But Magnus was not here to revisit his difficult youth. He was here to see Annabelle, because she'd asked him to come.

He would listen to what she had to say about his father. If the information was damning, he would ask her not to judge him by his father's deeds.

Magnus hoped she would be able to do that, and come away with him regardless, though after what happened the other day, he doubted that would be possible for her. She was not likely to take a risk with him. She'd become far too cautious and guarded.

But that was his fault, he supposed, and perhaps he deserved this. He was now reaping what he had sown.

He closed his eyes and stood listening to the wind in the trees. Deciding that he'd done enough speculating, he stepped away from his coach and started off across the street.

He reached the door and knocked, and was more than a little surprised when the butler greeted him warmly. "Good afternoon, sir. Please come in."

Magnus crossed the threshold, and while the butler took his coat, he glanced across the main entrance hall and found himself looking at the large portrait of Whitby and his wife and children.

Then unexpectedly, despite his reflections about not wanting what Whitby had, Magnus experienced a stabbing sensation in his gut. Maybe he didn't need Whitby's possessions, but he did need Annabelle at his side. He wanted a portrait just like that one in his own home back in America.

"Allow me to show you to the drawing room, Mr. Wallis," the butler said. "Miss Lawson has been waiting for you."

Magnus followed the butler up the stairs to the second floor and was shown into the room. He stopped just inside, his gaze falling upon Annabelle as the doors closed behind him. She was standing in front of the window, wearing a sky blue gown with white lace at the collar, and she was smiling at him.

No—more than smiling. She was beaming. Her eyes were glimmering with happiness; she looked like she could barely contain the joy that was bursting within her.

Instantly, he felt joyous as well. How could he not? She looked more beautiful than ever, smiling at him in that way, and he felt certain that she was going to say yes. That she had missed him the past few days just as desperately as he had missed her, and that she was ecstatic just to see him.

He took an anxious step forward. He wanted to close the distance between them and take her into his arms and promise her the world if she would let him give it to her . . .

But all at once something stopped him. A movement to his left. Another presence in the room.

Magnus turned his gaze and saw Whitby rising slowly from the chair in front of the fireplace.

The elation Magnus had just experienced seemed to fall flat on the floor at his feet, and his whole body stiffened defensively.

"Magnus," Whitby said, his tone cool.

Magnus glanced uncertainly at Annabelle, not sure what he was facing here.

Perhaps she recognized his unease, for she came forward to welcome him. "Magnus, I'm so glad you're here." She gestured toward the sofa. "Won't you sit down?"

So much for taking her into his arms, he thought, with a hint of annoyance at having his desires so swiftly curtailed. This was to be a formal meeting, evidently.

Whitby crossed the room to sit in a chair opposite the sofa, while Annabelle sat down beside Magnus. She smiled again, which caused him to look questioningly at Whitby, who was not smiling. Not in the slightest. He looked as somber as ever, which was why Magnus did not know what to expect.

When Annabelle finally spoke, her voice was quiet and shaky. "As you know," she said, "I've been asking questions about your father and why he was sent away, as I felt a need to understand this feud between you and my brother."

Magnus glanced at Whitby. His cousin merely stared back at him, revealing nothing.

"This may be difficult for you to hear, Magnus," she continued, "and I apologize in advance."

Difficult to hear?

He felt as if the air in the room were getting thinner. He turned to Whitby. "Do you already know what she is about to tell me?"

"Yes," he replied flatly, and Magnus clenched his jaw. He hated this. He hated being at a disadvantage.

Annabelle sat forward and continued. "I found a woman who is the daughter of a maid who was employed by your grandfather at Century House seventy-five years ago, when your father was born. She was intimate with your grandfather for five years, before she was forced to leave for that reason."

Perhaps he was overly skeptical, but Magnus couldn't help doubting the credibility of the source. "You found one of my grandfather's jilted lovers, and you're going to believe what she says?"

Annabelle squeezed her hands together on her lap, and Magnus instantly regretted his tone. But how could he help it? He had been accused of everything nasty and disagreeable all his life, and it was almost impossible not to become defensive. Especially with Whitby listening to all this in noteworthy silence.

"She couldn't say anything," Annabelle said shakily, "because she died seven years ago. It was her daughter I spoke to, but she knew a great deal about what happened to your father. May I describe it to you?"

He gazed into Annabelle's eyes and recognized her discomfort. Her brow was furrowed, her face flushed. She wished to tell him something that was obviously going to be unpleasant, and she was dreading it.

"Yes, Annabelle," he said, more gently this time. "You may certainly tell me."

The tension in her body diminished slightly.

"This woman, Rose Michaels, was deeply in love with your grandfather, and she knew why he sent his son away."

Magnus braced himself for whatever was coming.

"Your father was not dangerous," Annabelle said. "You were right about that. What happened was tragic and disturbing, and he was indeed greatly wronged, just as you have been. You've been right all along, and Whitby knows it."

Magnus's gaze darted to his cousin, who was still sitting at his ease in the chair. He simply nodded at Magnus, then gestured with a hand toward Annabelle.

Magnus returned his attention to her, feeling oddly disconnected from his body while he waited for the rest of the story.

"According to Rose Michaels," Annabelle said, "your father was in fact your grandfather's favorite son. He was the gentler of the two boys, and perhaps because he was the younger one and would not have the advantages of his older brother—the heir—your grandfather doted on him. He spent more time with him, and he loved him very much."

Annabelle's gentle expression darkened, however, with sadness and regret. "But there was an accident when he was four. Your grandfather had taken him into the stables one afternoon, and he was kicked by a horse."

Magnus felt his brows draw together with horror over hearing such a thing. "Kicked?"

Annabelle glanced uncertainly at Whitby, who said, "Tell him the rest, Annabelle."

She slid closer to Magnus. "Your father's skull was cracked and he was never the same after that. He had seizures, and this is where the tragedy occurred. Rose Michaels said that your grandfather was so disturbed by the sight of the seizures that he kept your father hidden most of the time, so no one would know. Perhaps he feared an asylum, or perhaps he was ashamed. It's difficult to know."

"That's why he sent him away?" Magnus asked, barely able to believe what he was hearing.

"Yes. And it's very likely he was having a seizure the night he knocked over the lamp that caused the fire."

Shock held Magnus immobile. "But why would he be cut off in every way? Why did my grandfather not at least take care of him financially?"

"He did provide for him somewhat. He paid for the cottage where he was raised, and the woman who cared for him."

"But he received nothing after that, when he moved to London."

Annabelle's eyes glistened with tears and an unspoken apology. "I'm sorry. I know it was not enough. It was unfair, and I wish I could change how your father was treated. I was heartbroken to hear it, and there is nothing I can say to make it right."

"But why would he do that to the son he doted on?" Magnus asked, still shaken by all of it. "How could he have been so callous?"

"I don't know. Perhaps it was guilt. He couldn't bear to watch him suffer."

"It sounds to me like he was worried about appearances. He didn't want a lunatic in the family."

A flood of memories came at Magnus suddenly—all the times his father had locked himself in a room and hid himself away. No wonder he had been ashamed and afraid to let anyone see the truth. He had been banished from his family because of it.

Magnus sat forward and dropped his forehead to the heels of his hands. It was an unforgivable injustice. His father had been abandoned for no fault of his own and removed from his home, torn from his family and made out to be something he was not. He was never cruel or violent. The only cruelty had been in the heart of Magnus's grandfather, who had valued appearances over the love of his son.

Magnus lifted his head and looked at his cousin. "Did you know about this?"

"Of course not. Not before today."

They continued to sit in silence for a moment, until Whitby finally spoke. "You and your father were indeed wronged, Magnus, and I offer my most sincere apologies. I have every intention of making it right."

"Making it right?" Magnus ground out. "How can anyone make it right? My father is dead, and he lived a miserable life. So pardon me for pointing out that there is no way in hell you—or anyone else—can fix that."

Whitby dropped his gaze, his face drawn and pale. "I cannot argue. All I can offer is my deepest regrets for the way you have been treated. If I had known . . ."

Magnus stood up. "You should have known, Whitby. If Annabelle could find out the truth so easily, why couldn't you? Or your brother, John?"

"We had no reason to doubt what we'd always been told, and from what I had seen of your behavior—"

"*My* behavior? Fighting with your brother? Did you ever stop to think that he picked the fights with *me*?"

Just then he felt Annabelle's hand curl around his. "Magnus, I know you're angry, and you have every right to be. This must be a shock to you, but please sit down. There is so much more to say."

He labored to control his breathing, then slowly did as she asked.

Annabelle was quiet for a moment, presumably to let the news settle in. Then she reached for his hand. "Magnus, I called you here today to tell you the truth about your father, but also to inform you that Whitby is now open to the possibility that you may not have been at fault regarding John's death."

"And what, pray tell, changed his mind about that?" Magnus asked.

Whitby sighed. "Because I trust Annabelle. I trust her instincts. She was right about you telling the truth about your father, wasn't she?"

Annabelle shared an affectionate smile with her brother.

"Magnus," she said, "let us now tell you how Whitby wishes to make amends for everything. I know that no one can change the past, but we can at least affect the future."

She looked toward her brother, as if they had rehearsed this speech and it was his turn to speak.

"There is a property near Peterborough," Whitby said. "It's been in our family for five generations, and it's an impressive country house with a number of prosperous tenant farmers. I would like you to have it."

Magnus turned his gaze back to Annabelle, who appeared pleased and proud.

Whitby continued. "I would also be honored if you would allow me to introduce you into society. I can put in a word for you at my club, and I can arrange a full social calendar for you, and you will likely receive a number of the very best invitations before the week is out. It is my wish to see you fully restored to your rightful position, Magnus. It's the least I can do."

Magnus felt Annabelle squeeze his hand, and looked into her eyes. He had never seen her look so happy. She wanted this for him. She wanted him to take the house and join Whitby in his club.

Feeling almost numb, he shook his head in dismay. *"Do you even know me at all?"*

Annabelle's smile vanished instantly. "What do you mean?"

"I don't wish to sound ungrateful, Annabelle, but do you think I would want what your brother is offering?"

She blinked a few times, and her voice revealed her surprise. "But you have always felt cheated out of your birthright . . ."

"Not any longer," he replied angrily. "I am not the man I once was. How many times do I have to explain that to you? Did you not see it over the past few weeks? But I suppose you did not. You did not see deeply enough to truly believe I was not a monster. You had to go running around to hear it from other people. From strangers."

Her lips parted as she stumbled over words, in the end saying nothing.

Magnus shook his head at her. "I came back here so you could see the man I have become, but you still see only the man I once was. The man who broke your heart." He raised a hand, gesturing around the room. "And I don't want this." He turned his gaze to his cousin. "I beg your pardon, Whitby. I realize your intentions are honorable and I thank you for your concern, but you must understand that I do not wish to become a member of your club, nor do I want the house in the country. I want to go back to America where I can work and enjoy the challenge of it. I don't want this life."

"But you are entitled to this," Annabelle said, her voice revealing shock and bewilderment, and Magnus felt the distance between them rise up suddenly like an ocean tide. Annabelle was entrenched in this world. Unlike him, she had not been born into it, but she had been raised within it, and her perspective was, in truth, very limited.

He was surprised and disappointed as he sat there staring across at her, because that was what he had always loved about her—the fact that she was not really one of them. He'd always admired her unconventionality, and had connected with her because she seemed to be an outsider, like him. She had not cared that he was a mere bank clerk when they met on the train so very long ago. He'd always believed they were similar creatures, and that she'd loved him for what he was on the inside.

But now, looking into her eyes and seeing her

desire to pull him into this world with her, he never felt more disconnected.

He had been wrong. They were not the same, and she did not know the real man he was deep down.

Magnus stood. Both Annabelle and Whitby stared speechlessly at him.

"Annabelle," he said, "I must thank you for finally discovering the truth about my father. I am glad to know it. And Whitby, I appreciate what you wanted to do here today, but I'm afraid I must turn down what you offer."

He turned and started toward the door.

"But Magnus!" Annabelle said, rising to her feet as well.

He stopped and faced her, but she couldn't seem to find any words. She merely stared at him, with eyes wide as saucers, looking utterly dumbfounded.

"Good day," he said, feeling only a suffocating need to get out of that room. He bowed slightly at the waist before he turned again and walked out.

He had already received his coat from the butler and was making his way across the street to his coach when he heard Annabelle call his name again.

"Magnus! Wait!"

He stopped in front of his coach and shut his eyes, wishing she would just let him go. He didn't want to talk to her right now. He didn't want to explain himself, because he wasn't sure he could. He didn't even know how he felt about everything he'd just heard.

Nevertheless, he turned and waited.

She paused while a carriage crossed the street in front of her, before she picked up her skirts and dashed across. "Where are you going? Why did you leave so quickly?"

"Because I don't belong in there, and I couldn't sit and listen to Whitby offer me charity on a platter, as if what he was going to give me was the only thing that would make me worthy of your trust."

"That's not how it was," she said.

"No? That's how it looked to me. I'd never seen you so happy, Annabelle. All the reservations you had were gone because suddenly your brother approved of me and I was going to have social precedence as the grandson of an earl. I was going to be a respectable, honorable gentleman, sipping tea in drawing rooms—as if those things would erase what I had done to you. But nothing can erase it, Annabelle. *It happened.* I *was* that loathesome man who broke your heart, and that past we share is never going to disappear. What I need is for you to move past it and forgive me."

"But you don't understand. When I learned the truth, I wanted you to have what you should never have been denied."

"I never wanted that when I came back for you,

but you couldn't believe it. You had to try to fix the past, when all anyone can do is live with it and learn from it."

He turned toward his coach and stepped inside.

"Wait a minute!" Annabelle shouted. "You can't blame me for not trusting you. What did you expect?"

He sat down, but couldn't leave because Annabelle was holding the door open, preventing him from closing it. "I don't know."

She finally let go of the door and stepped back. "Will you go back to America?"

"It's my home now," he replied.

"When?"

He paused, staring at her. "Tomorrow. I've already handed my properties over to my solicitor."

Rage found its way into her voice as she swiped violently at her tears. "So that's it? You're just going to leave? Why am I not surprised?"

He looked into her eyes, which glistened with tears, and realized with aching remorse that she was still so very angry with him over what had happened all those years ago, and she almost seemed to be taking some perverse pleasure in being right. *That he was doing exactly what she'd predicted he would do.* That she had been right all along not to trust him, or any other man, for that matter.

But how many times had he told her he was sorry, and why couldn't it ever be enough? All his life he had felt unworthy, and now she was looking at him as if he were a disappointing wretch. It took him straight back to the loathing he'd endured in his youth.

So, he had been right. Annabelle solving the mysteries of the past had not changed a thing.

God, he couldn't do it anymore. He couldn't go on waiting for her acceptance and forgiveness. It was time he found his own pride, with or without Annabelle's belief in him.

"I have to go," he said, tightening his grip on the door handle. He just wanted to get out of there.

He shut the door and sat back in the seat, resisting the urge to look out the window at Annabelle, because God help him, despite everything, he still loved her.

Chapter 19

❧

"**Y**ou don't think he'll really leave, do you?" Annabelle asked Lily late that night while they sat on Annabelle's bed.

"I don't know," Lily replied. "The only time I ever saw you together was the other day in the country, when he fought with Whitby."

Annabelle slid off the bed and padded across the floor to the fireplace to warm her hands. "You must think me a fool, then. All you saw was the man everyone has always described—angry, vengeful Cousin Magnus."

Lily sighed heavily. "I don't think you're a fool,

Annabelle. You saw something in him that no one else did, and because of that, you uncovered the truth about this family's past, and you proved that mistakes in judgment had been made. Even Whitby believes it now—that Magnus was not all bad, that he had been wronged and he had a right to be angry."

"But despite what happened to his father," Annabelle said, "Magnus is still Magnus. It doesn't erase what he did to me thirteen years ago, or the fact that he just walked out on me again. Knowing the truth about the very distant past doesn't change what exists today. He told me it wouldn't. I should have listened."

Lily merely shrugged at her. "I don't have the answers, Annabelle. Only you can decide what you believe."

"That's the problem." Annabelle returned to the bed. "What scares me is the fact that nothing he could ever do or say could ever have made me trust him, because I am simply not capable of it. I'm deficient."

"No, you're not."

"Oh, what does it matter anyway? He left me standing there in the street today and told me he was going to return to America, apparently forgetting that he'd proposed marriage."

"But did he officially withdraw his proposal?" Lily asked, running a hand over her swollen belly.

"From what you told me, it doesn't sound like he did. Perhaps in his mind you were just having an argument and he has no intentions of leaving England without you."

Annabelle flopped onto the bed. "If he leaves on that ship in the morning, abandoning me a second time, that should answer the question."

For a long moment Annabelle stared at the ceiling in silence, wondering what she should do. Should she wait and see if he would leave without her, or should she search for the courage to take that difficult leap of faith, and do whatever it took to try and stop him?

Through the night, Magnus wrote four letters to Annabelle, and in each and every one he apologized for something—for closing the coach door on her and driving away, for not taking the house her brother had offered, for saying things that hurt her—but when he read over each letter, he chastised himself for doing it again. For crawling back to her and pleading with her to accept him.

It was what he'd been doing all his life—longing for acceptance into a family that didn't want him, until he had finally grown to hate them.

Would he grow to hate Annabelle eventually, if he spent his entire future striving to earn her trust? Never feeling good enough?

In the end he did not send a letter.

So it was with a heavy heart that he left his hotel room the next morning, traveled to the docks and boarded the ship, checking over his shoulder as he crossed the gangplank, gazing into the sea of faces on the dock, searching for her, wondering if she had come to stop him from leaving, or to tell him to wait for her, that she was coming with him . . .

When he stepped on board the ship, a porter showed him to his stateroom and saw that his trunks were delivered. Then Magnus sat down on the bed and held his gloves in his hand, tapping them upon his knee.

He felt rather nauseous, and the ship hadn't even left the dock yet.

He checked his timepiece. They wouldn't depart for another fifteen minutes. Perhaps he would go up on deck and look over the rail . . .

A minute later he was heading down the corridor and pushing through the doors to the sunny upper deck. He walked to the rail and wrapped both hands around it, leaning over to peer down at the crowd on the dock. People were waving to the others beside him, who were smiling and blowing kisses in return.

He experienced a burning panic suddenly, as if he'd just swallowed a red-hot lump of coal. Maybe he should get off the ship. It had been just an argument, after all. Perhaps he was being too hasty and stubborn.

Feeling his breath come short, he scanned the crowd again, then checked his timepiece.

Five more minutes.

Should he get off? he wondered again. Was there time?

He swallowed hard and leaned farther over the rail to see if the gangplank had been lowered yet. It had not. He could still change his mind.

Then he saw a movement in the crowd. Someone running. A woman. He sucked in a quick breath and watched her shoulder her way through the tight crowd toward the gangplank. He couldn't get a clear view of her, but her hair was just like Annabelle's.

Magnus was off like a shot, running for the upper deck doors and flying down the steps, taking two at a time, darting down the corridor that led to the outer door.

If it was Annabelle, he would tell her he was sorry. He would get down on his knees and thank God in heaven that she had come, and he'd pull her into his arms and never let her go again. Pride be damned. He would do whatever it took just to have her with him. What had he been thinking, leaving her again after he had come so far?

He stopped suddenly, however, when he reached the main door and found himself staring not at Annabelle, but at another woman. She was just stepping on board, flushed and apologetic for being late.

Then the gangplank was hoisted away and set down on the dock, the doors were closed behind the woman, and a whistle blew somewhere behind Magnus. He stood there breathing hard, feeling as if he were floating in a haze or a bad dream, staring at the ship door, tightly closed.

"Can I help you, sir?" a porter asked, blocking Magnus's view of the door.

"I beg your pardon?" he replied.

"Is there a problem? Are you waiting for someone?"

Yes, he was. But she wasn't coming.

He stared blankly at the young man and knew that this was one of those moments in life. It was a fork in the road. Should he get off the ship? Or should he return to his cabin and settle in for the voyage?

He imagined what would happen if he got off. He would return to the Whitby mansion in Mayfair and plead with Annabelle yet again . . .

The porter was still staring at him, waiting for his answer.

Magnus steadied his voice. "No. I'm not waiting for anyone."

With that, he turned away from the door and headed back to his stateroom alone, fearing that in about an hour, he was going to be cursing himself and regretting his godforsaken stubborn pride.

* * *

It was with a burning sense of panic that Annabelle came running onto the dock with barely a minute to spare before the ship left.

She had awakened that morning determined to stop Magnus. She'd dressed at lightning speed, skipped breakfast, and dashed out the front door, terrified she was going to lose him forever because she'd been too afraid to take the blind leap he'd wanted her to take.

But when she arrived at his hotel, he had already checked out, and the desk clerk assured her quite emphatically that he was bound for America that very morning.

That should have been enough, Annabelle thought miserably, as she pushed her way through the crowd on the dock, after first going to the wrong pier and getting lost. It should have been the answer she needed—that Magnus was abandoning her yet again, and she had been a fool to believe there was hope.

But it had *not* been enough. She was desperate to see him, without the slightest care for her pride or her fears. She had not been able to let go of the tiny fragment of hope that still flickered within her—that yes, he loved her and she could trust him. That she'd always been able to trust him.

It couldn't be over yet, she thought as she reached the gangplank. It couldn't.

But then a porter blew his whistle and waved

his arms over his head, and the gangplank was lifted away from the ship.

She stopped on the dock, watching, looking up at the people waving from the railings, searching for Magnus, unable to accept that he was actually on board.

She tried to make her way along the dock, shading her eyes from the sun as she looked for him. She walked the length of the ship, then found herself searching through the crowd on the dock, wondering if he had changed his mind and had never even stepped on board.

But she did not see him.

Not long afterward, the ship blew its horn and the ropes were drawn up and everyone was waving good-bye.

Annabelle stood among the crowd, watching in dismay as the ship steamed away from the dock. A cold, piercing agony spread through her like ice.

What a fool she was. She should have known better. How could she have put herself in this situation, to be rejected a second time?

And how could he have done this to her? How could he have made love to her with such tenderness and passion, then leave like this? It was unimaginable, and she didn't know how she would ever recover from such a betrayal a second time.

Somehow, feeling completely dead inside, she managed to turn around, walk back to her carriage and make her way home, though she remembered none of the trip.

When she arrived at the house, she asked the butler, "Did anyone pay a call? Was there a letter delivered?"

"No, Miss Lawson," he replied soberly.

She wondered if he knew whose letter she was hoping to receive. Either way, it did not matter.

Annabelle slowly climbed the stairs and went to her studio rather than her bedchamber, for she had no intention of flinging herself on her bed and crying like she had all those years ago. She would not do that again.

All she wanted to do now was distract herself from the persistent hope that Magnus had not even been on the ship to begin with, and would perhaps be knocking on her door within the hour . . .

She looked at the painting she had brought with her from the country—the waterfall surrounded by moss-covered rocks.

With her body moving in an oddly mechanical way, Annabelle donned her smock and squeezed some paint onto her palette, creating a few different shades of brown and adding black, green, and white. Then she picked up a brush.

But as she stared at the water flowing over the rocks, she knew in her heart that she was too frustrated to paint, and besides that—this piece wasn't right, and it would *never* be right. She wasn't happy with the brushstrokes around the rocks, and the mist at the bottom was all wrong, as were the shadows on the trees. It didn't look real.

She needed to change it. It wasn't even close to being finished. It was a mess.

She took a step forward, dipped her brush and lifted it, but froze with her hand an inch away from the canvas.

How could she paint now, when she was so angry because she had not been able to trust the one man who understood her eccentricities and aroused her passions?

He was the only real world she had ever known, she realized suddenly, with a raw new heartbreak. He was the only person who had ever made her feel alive.

But he had left her.

Overcome by a fierce swell of frustration, she turned her palette over in her hand and smacked it paint side down upon her canvas, smearing it back and forth over the waterfall, wanting only to destroy the painting, to turn it into a misfit, too. Just like her. She hated the way it was. She couldn't get it right. And she was so bloody, bloody angry!

After a few seconds she realized what she had done, and winced as she pulled her hand from the palette—which stuck to the canvas briefly before sliding down.

Annabelle quickly reached for it, to keep it from

falling onto the floor, not really caring that she had destroyed the painting. She hadn't liked it anyway, and it had felt so good to feel the thick paint smearing under the palette.

Finally, she peeled it back to see the anarchy she'd created . . .

It most certainly was a picture of anarchism. It was wild, unrecognizable mayhem—nothing but emptiness—just like her life without Magnus.

She stared at it for a moment, but then turned her back on it because she couldn't bear the loneliness it made her feel.

She set her brush and palette down on the table. Closing her eyes, she wondered if this creative agony was worth it. Perhaps she should give up painting altogether and give up being strange. She should replace these boots with a pretty pair of shoes, and get a lapdog like other spinsters her age.

No. What was she thinking? She could never replace these boots, nor could she stop painting. And she would always prefer her cow to a lapdog.

So she turned around and faced the canvas again, and strangely, sadly, when she looked at the waterfall, all she saw was Magnus.

Struck by the sight, she reflected upon the state of her life and the confusing collage of her emotions. She still couldn't believe he had left her. She had been so sure that everything was different this time.

She supposed it *had* been different. But it was all her fault for not being able to give him her whole heart, for thinking only of protecting herself and keeping her world safe, like her dull, uninteresting paintings.

Except for *The Fisherman*, of course. It was the one piece she was proud of, and she had painted it during the one and only time in her life that she had felt truly free to be herself.

Then suddenly, something prompted her to pick up her brush and palette—with its outlandish, muddled mixture of color—and approach the canvas.

She could still see Magnus in the waterfall.

Tilting her head this way and that, she dabbed at the image, moving the thick paint around to better capture what she was seeing.

She didn't even bother to try to make it look like a photograph. She was seeing something very different that morning, and she was holding the brush in a way she'd never held it before . . .

Three hours later, after wielding her brush swiftly and furiously without a single break to rest her arm, Annabelle stepped back and looked at the colors on the canvas.

For the first time in her life she felt satisfied setting down her brush.

Chapter 20

❦

One month later

The London Times

August 21, 1892
LOCAL ARTIST TURNS
LONDON ART WORLD
ON ITS EAR

The latest exhibition at the Duke of Harlow's Regent Street Gallery has been causing a stir among art enthusiasts here in England and as far as Paris, with the modern expressions of artist Annabelle Lawson. Miss Lawson has risked her reputation as a landscape realist to

349

produce a body of work so nonrepresentational
that one simply must stop to study the themes
of reflection and reality, so evident in the
artist's passionate brushwork. It cannot be denied that no English painter has yet dared to
challenge the aesthetic sensibilities of the public, and in so doing, has freed all future English
artists from the tedious constraints of competi-
tion with the camera . . .

The New World

November 1892

Chapter 21

With a glass of red wine in his hand, Magnus stepped out of his bedchamber onto the second-story veranda that lined the rear of his South Carolina mansion by the sea.

The sun was just setting over the water, and it was a warm evening for November. He could smell the saltwater in the air, hear the power of the surf on the beach.

A sailboat was visible in the distance, and he raised a hand to shade his eyes and watch it heel impossibly in the wind, until the sails were almost touching the waves. At the last minute it righted itself and turned toward the horizon.

Magnus took a slow sip of his wine, then sat down on the cushioned wicker chair. He lifted his feet onto the small table, crossing his legs at the ankles.

He sat here often in the evenings after dinner, watching the sun go down. It was his favorite time of day, and his staff knew not to bother him, for he worked hard from sunup to sundown and needed this time to rest and reflect.

Consequently he was surprised when his butler stepped through the door onto the veranda. "I beg your pardon, sir. I'm sorry to disturb you, but you have a visitor."

Magnus lifted his legs off the table. "Who is it, Bradley?"

"She didn't wish to give her name, sir, but she has an English accent."

Magnus knew that his butler was aware of what had occurred with Annabelle in England, though he never spoke about it directly. As a result, the comment caused Magnus to rise to his feet so fast he almost knocked over his chair.

"I didn't hear anyone arrive," he said.

"The surf is rather thunderous tonight, sir."

Magnus looked down at the waves crashing on the beach. "Yes. I suppose it is."

He set down his glass and straightened his tie,

then glanced at Bradley and saw an emotion in the man's eyes he'd never seen before.

Was it pity?

Magnus checked himself. Bloody hell. What was he doing, getting his hopes up like this again? How many times had he received a female caller and run downstairs hoping it would be Annabelle?

And had it ever been her? No. It was always some other woman, looking for a charitable donation, or someone visiting the area and looking for directions, and each time it happened, his anger toward Annabelle and everything that had occurred between them resurfaced.

He really needed to stop doing this, he told himself. It was over. Even if she did come back to him, he would not wish to rekindle anything. He would not wish to return to constantly having to prove himself to a woman who simply could not believe in him. He believed in himself, and that was enough. He had finally put the past to rest.

"Thank you, Bradley," he said, relaxing his shoulders and speaking in a calmer voice. "I'll see what she wants."

"She's in the library, sir."

Magnus entered the house through his bedchamber and made his way to the main staircase and down to the ground floor. He peered out the front window and saw a carriage outside, then went immediately to the library.

He hesitated outside the door, however, for despite all his self-imposed lectures on letting go of the memory of her, he wanted to savor this moment, because he knew that as soon as he walked through the door, the dream would be snuffed out again, as always.

He supposed certain elements of his past would never be resolved.

Finally taking a deep breath, he pushed the door open and entered. A woman wearing a colorful floral scarf over her head stood across the room with her back to him, looking out the window at the ocean, perhaps watching the sailboat that was now just a tiny speck on the horizon.

She must have heard him walk in, because she turned and faced him. When their eyes met, Magnus felt his blood rush to his brain.

It was her this time . . . It was Annabelle.

Neither of them said anything for a moment, but it wouldn't have mattered if she'd asked him a thousand questions at once, because he couldn't speak. He couldn't even think, he was so shocked by the vision of her, looking more beautiful than ever before, and so different.

Her clothes were not the same. The scarf over her head was wild and vibrant, and her dress was unfashionably loose with fringe at the cuffs. She wore no gloves, and her golden hair was spilling over her shoulders in wild, frizzy waves.

The sight of her made his breath catch in his throat, and he had to struggle to steel himself against the attraction he felt toward her—because he had to protect himself.

When he continued to stand there without speaking, Annabelle lowered the scarf and draped it over her shoulders. She took an uneasy step forward, as if she weren't sure she should have come. "You're surprised to see me."

He swallowed over the elephant in his throat. "Yes."

They continued to gaze at one another while the sound of the waves crashing outside filled the silence.

"How have you been?" he finally asked, because he could not be rude, but he maintained a cool tone.

"I've been well, thank you. I've been painting."

He saw her gaze move discreetly over the walls of the library.

"It's in the drawing room," he said, somehow knowing she was looking for *The Fisherman*. "Hanging over the fireplace."

She nodded. "I see. I wasn't sure if you would still have it."

"Why wouldn't I?" he replied, his voice still cool and detached.

Annabelle shifted her weight uncomfortably from one foot to the other. "Well, after what happened between us."

Beneath her surface politeness, he thought he detected a note of apology in her voice, but he couldn't be sure, because he remembered all too clearly how they had parted and what she had said to him. She had believed he'd only wanted to triumph over Whitby, that he never really loved her, and she had looked at him with disdain.

The bitter memory of how she had not been able to trust him—despite everything he'd done to prove that she could—made him steel himself again.

"What do you want, Annabelle?" he asked directly, deciding that he didn't want to play games or engage in small talk with her. It was too late for that.

She looked down at the floor before finally lifting her gaze to meet his. Her voice was steady, her chin held high. "You're angry with me."

He raised his hands at his sides. "Nothing has changed since we parted."

"May I inform you," she said, "that I've been angry with you, too, Magnus. You deserted me. After everything that happened between us, after I'd given myself to you, you left." Suddenly, she began spewing out every thought that must have been on her mind over the past few months.

"What if there had been a child?" she asked. "There wasn't, thank God, but what if there had been? Did you not wonder about that?"

"Yes, I wondered about it," he told her. "But I thought that if there had been, you would have contacted me. On the other hand, if you had chosen not to . . . Well, that wouldn't have come as any great surprise."

Her delicate brows drew together in a frown. "What do you mean by that?"

"It would have been consistent with every other aspect of our time together if you had not believed I would act honorably, or if you had not wished to marry me because you did not trust me enough to be a decent husband and father."

Her face softened slightly. "Is that what you thought?"

"Naturally, yes."

She turned and faced the window again, while Magnus stood waiting, still wondering why she was here. She hadn't really answered that question, had she?

He walked toward her and leaned a shoulder against the wall so he could look at her profile— her tiny nose, her deep-set blue eyes and full lips. The truth was, he still thought she was the most beautiful creature on the face of the earth, and being this close to her made his blood course through his veins like a damn raging river.

It aggravated him, because he didn't want to feel that way about her. He wanted only to remember how angry he had been over the past few months.

"Why did you leave England so quickly?" she asked, facing him. "Were you using me like the last time?"

"What a question!" he said, throwing his hands up in the air. "Of course I was not using you, but I'm not going to stand here and try to convince you of that until I'm blue in the face. If you can't believe it, or you don't already know enough about me—"

"I do believe you," she said flatly, and Magnus wondered if the earth had just shifted under his feet.

"I must be hearing things," he said with a bitter laugh.

She gave him a stern look. "I've thought about it a lot over the past couple of months, Magnus, and I've been able to at least recognize the fact that I *was* incapable of trusting you, but only because you had hurt me so deeply the first time. Maybe you can't understand that . . ."

Oh, but he did understand it—because he was feeling that way himself at this very moment. He was afraid to trust *her.*

"Then why didn't you write to me?" he asked.

She hesitated. "Because it took me a long time to figure out what I wanted to say, and to be honest, for a long time I was too angry with you for leaving. You didn't even *try* to resolve things between us."

"I didn't *try*?" he burst out. "I'd been trying to resolve things since the first day, but nothing I said or did made any difference to you."

"But you didn't have to leave the very next day. You could have at least waited."

Frustration heated his face. "For how long? You knew I had booked passage on the ship that morning, yet you didn't try to stop me. I even stood at the rail and watched for you, but all I could think of was the fact that you would never be able to trust me, that you would always think ill of me. And when you didn't show up at the dock, I had to force myself to let go of the hopeless need for your approval or forgiveness."

Annabelle's eyes filled with tears. "I *was* at the dock," she told him, her voice full of pain and regret. "But I went to the wrong place, and then I was too late."

He felt his body shudder as he drew in a sharp breath. "You were there?"

"Yes," she said. "Despite all my fears that I would be rejected again, I went there hoping I was wrong. I was going to plead with you to forgive me for not trusting you, and I was going to tell you I loved you. I wanted to prove to you that I could take the leap."

He shook his head skeptically. "But I was looking for you. I would have seen you."

"I got there just as the ship pulled away. I was there, Magnus."

He turned away from her and crossed to the middle of the room. "But for months I have believed otherwise. Why did you not come here sooner?"

"Because after you left, something changed in me, and I needed to understand it."

Magnus walked to the other window to look out, on the opposite side of the room from where she was standing.

Annabelle let out a frustrated sigh. "I know this may sound strange, but part of the reason I came here was to thank you."

"Why?"

"Because I didn't really know who I was until you left me," she explained. "Something in me exploded that day—all my anger, my frustrations, my passions. I'd always known I was living by rules that didn't suit me, but that I was afraid to break out and do anything risky. I've always thought myself a misfit, as you well know. But when I watched your ship leave, all those rules were broken. I was so angry, I didn't care about anything anymore. I was no longer afraid, because nothing seemed to matter, and it made me open my eyes to certain things."

He shook his head at her, and she crossed the room to the bookcase, bent forward and picked up her large portfolio. He hadn't noticed it there.

"Maybe you'll understand when you see what I brought you." She set the case on the table in the center of the room and withdrew a painting.

Magnus looked at it from where he stood at the window. "It's me."

Though how he knew that, he couldn't be sure. It was hardly a conventional portrait.

But rules of portraiture aside, it was astounding. He walked toward it and took it in his hands, holding it up to the light to study it.

It was as if he were looking at himself through rain-covered glass. Or perhaps water. Yes, water. Deep, choppy water. There was movement, too, as if he were forever changing with the swells.

"My God, Annabelle. When did you do this?"

"The day you left."

He studied the image of his face, then let his eyes wander to the outer edges. He looked at the colors, the shapes, the shadows and contrasts. One rock in particular caught his eye . . .

He pointed at it, in the top left corner. "Good Lord, you *were* angry, weren't you?"

She smiled faintly. "Yes, but it was the setting that enraged me. I think this is my aunt Millicent." She pointed at a rather bulbous boulder in the bottom corner, and Magnus chuckled despite himself.

"I believe I see the resemblance. That must be her nose."

Annabelle laughed, and despite all their arguing just now, it was the sweetest sound he could ever imagine.

They stood in the library for a long time, side by side, looking at the painting.

"It's extraordinary," Magnus finally said. "I've never seen anything like it. Has anyone else seen it?"

"Yes. Most of London. Paris, too."

He chuckled with disappointment. "That's a shame. I would have liked to be the first to exhibit it."

Annabelle smiled, but there was a deep sadness in her voice. "I'm sorry I didn't give it to you first, but I wasn't ready to show it to you, and I needed to . . ." She didn't seem to know what to say, so she returned to the window again.

"You needed to do *what*, Annabelle?"

She sighed. "To be free for a little while," she said. "I told Whitby and Lily that I needed to do something for myself, and they were happy for me and wished me well. So I went on my own to Paris and spent the past three months there, painting every day."

He put the portrait down and followed her. "You went to Paris? Did you show your work?"

"Yes, and I spent time with other artists who

shared my desire to paint in new ways. I was even included in an exhibition with Mary Cassatt."

His lips parted in surprise. "Extraordinary. You did well, Annabelle."

She shrugged, as if making light of it. "I'm surprised you hadn't heard about it. I thought you might have been keeping up with what was going on in the art world."

He shook his head. "I wasn't keeping up with anything. I retreated from all that after I returned. I still own my galleries, but I haven't set foot in either of them in quite some time. I suppose I needed a bit of a holiday."

She sighed and faced him. "Magnus . . ."

All at once he wanted to touch her face, her lips. Everything about her was magical and vibrant. She was like no other woman he had ever met, and she had been brave enough to go to Paris and show her work with Mary Cassatt. *Brava, Annabelle. Brava!*

But he resisted that emotional outburst and the surging rush of his desires, for he could not let himself give in so easily. She had not given him what he'd needed last time. He'd even begun to believe that his love for her had been a fantasy all along, that she was not—and never had been—the daring girl he remembered from his younger days.

But then she began to speak, and all he could hear in his mind was the sound of her voice in that fishing boat on the lake . . .

"Magnus," she said with her gaze downcast, "when you came back to London and I saw you for the first time at your gallery, I was not the person I am now."

"That sounds familiar," he said.

She smiled, but there were tears in her eyes. "I was so worn-out and unhappy, but you brought me back to life."

"But I was the one who killed your spirit in the first place," he said with regret.

"No. You just made me see that I had never really been living, and I really *needed* to explode four months ago. I needed to be pushed over the edge and be fearless with nothing to lose. I needed to learn that I could trust my instincts and take chances, that I could steer away from what was safe, and I did that through my paintings. Because of you. You unlocked something."

The physical world around them seemed to almost fade away as his eyes held hers and his heart began to beat very fast. "What are you saying, Annabelle? Why did you come here?"

She strode closer. "I came here to finally take that blind leap of faith with you, Magnus, and I'm praying with all my heart and soul that you will take my hand and leap, too. That you will forgive *me* this time, and find it in yourself to believe that I do love you. That I've loved you every day of my life." She walked to him and laid her open hands on his chest, and a shiver of need rippled through him. "And I would give anything to know that in spite of everything, you still love me. I want you back, Magnus. *Please.*"

She rose up on her toes and touched her lips lightly to his, and he was overcome by a love so potent that no amount of discipline or self-control proved powerful enough to stop him from taking her into his arms. Then he covered her mouth with his own.

Deepening the kiss, he pulled her as close as he could. Her lips were soft and warm and succulent as he swept his tongue inside, and all at once nothing mattered but his need to possess her. He picked her up and began carrying her out of the room.

"Where are you taking me?" she asked in a breathless voice, kissing his cheeks and mouth and neck as he headed toward the stairs.

"To my bed."

Burning with desire after months spent dreaming of making love to Magnus again, Annabelle gave no argument.

She held tight to his strong, broad shoulders as he climbed the stairs. He carried her down a wide corridor and through to his bedchamber, lined with dark oak walls and furnished with a massive mahogany bed. The room glowed pink from the sunset outside the window.

He laid her gently onto the soft bed, then came

down upon her, his body heavy and warm and insistent. She welcomed him with legs parted, thrusting her body close, sliding her hands down his back. She wanted him with every breath in her body, with every spark of passion coursing through her, and she couldn't wait a single moment longer. She had to have him, on any terms.

"Make love to me now, this instant," she pleaded. "Don't keep me waiting. I've waited long enough."

Obliging her reckless impatience, he didn't even take time to get undressed. He merely reached a hand down to unfasten his trousers, tugged her skirts out of the way, and entered her in a smooth, silky thrust that stole her breath.

Annabelle tossed her head back on the pillows and gasped, as pure unadulterated rapture suffused her senses. She loved this man, she desired him beyond all else in the world, and a sheer, mad need for everything he offered compelled her to lift her hips to deepen the awesome, satisfying penetration of his arousal.

"Oh, Magnus, please say you love me," she whispered, her breath coming short. "I can't lose you again." Leaning up on one elbow so he could look her in the eye, he drove into her with a steady pounding rhythm until her mind and body tingled with ecstasy, then at last he spoke, his voice a deep, husky seduction in itself.

"Of course I love you, you gorgeous misfit," he

said, pressing his lips to hers, kissing her profoundly with all the power of the thundering surf outside the window.

Annabelle smiled with wantonness. "Oh, thank God," she cried out, squeezing her legs around him, meeting his deep thrusts with her own insatiable hunger for fulfillment. "You'll never get rid of me now," she said.

Magnus drew back and smiled in response, his eyes dark and impassioned with seductive teasing. "I should hope not."

Then he drove deeper still, propping himself up on his hands. He was rigid inside her, filling her with exquisite sensual bliss, driving her to the ends of sanity. Annabelle dug her fingernails into the fine fabric of his waistcoat as feverish, orgasmic sensation raged and prevailed.

"Marry me this time, Annabelle," he said, just as the wave hit—when a powerful orgasm pounded through her.

"Yes," she whispered.

Then she felt the hot pulsing of his release, deep, deep inside herself. Magnus pushed hard and spoke her name, then he collapsed upon her, heavy and out of breath.

Holding him tight in her arms, delightfully exhausted, Annabelle marveled at the tears seeping from beneath her eyelids. "You forgive me?" she asked, her voice shaky with sentiment and love.

He gently withdrew and rolled to the side, resting his hand upon her cheek. "There is nothing to forgive, Annabelle. All that matters is that we're together now. Finally."

"Yes, finally." She touched his face also, running a finger over his strong cheekbone. "I've missed you."

"I have missed you, too—every wretched day of my life. But all that's over now, because you're here."

"Yes," she said with a tender smile. "I'm here, and I have never felt so happy, or so at home."

"Because this is your home. It will always be your home. Here with me."

"It's what I always dreamed of," she said.

Then he rolled onto her again and filled her once more with pleasure.

Epilogue

◦────୨◐୧────◦

"Is it almost finished?" Magnus asked, reaching the top of the hill where Annabelle stood before her easel, paintbrush in hand. The sun was shining brightly overhead without a single cloud in the sky, and the wind had picked up, cooling her cheeks.

"Yes." She stood back to look with a critical eye at what she had done. "Come and see it."

She set her palette and brush down on the ground, and held out her hand. Her husband came to stand at her side. Together, they looked at the painting—a bold mix of textures and colors, all sweeping together with swirling movement.

Annabelle tilted her head. She felt satisfied with this piece, for she truly believed she had captured—really captured—the passion and splendor of their seaside home.

Magnus slid his arm around her waist and continued to stare at the painting, while a breeze blew a part in his hair.

"I am in awe," he said quietly, resting a hand over his heart. "It makes me feel euphoric, Annabelle. Triumphant. It's the best thing you've ever done. I mean it."

Her eyes filled with tears as she smiled at him. "You say that about all my paintings."

He pulled her closer to him. "It's always true."

Annabelle returned her gaze to the painting and stared at it for a long time, feeling the genuine romance in the color of the sea, and the joyful warmth of the sunshine on the water. In the background, sailboats with bright spinnakers dotted the horizon, yet none of it was absolutely perceptible. All the images intermingled together to form a rich, colorful whole.

"You once said I would love this place," she said to her husband as she gazed toward the sea and felt the wind on her face, "and you were right. I've never been so happy, never knew it was possible. I feel at peace here, Magnus."

He took the hand that he still held over his heart

and touched it to her cheek. "You once felt trapped, Annabelle. Do you ever feel that way, now that you have made a commitment to be my wife till death do us part?"

She sighed and cupped his hand in hers. "Never. Because of you, I learned to be free. You pushed me to learn it. And now that I am free, I have been able to love you without reservation, holding nothing back. I am alive now, Magnus, when I didn't really know how to live before. But what about you? Are you happy now?"

He closed his eyes and inhaled deeply. "Yes, thanks to you. I will always be grateful that you found out the truth about my father, Annabelle, but more importantly because you made me see that we can all change and grow. You are a forgiving person, and I love you for that. I've learned to forgive, too."

He took her face in his hands and touched his lips gently to hers, then drew back and looked at the painting again.

"We shall never sell this one," he said, "even though it would bring in a small fortune, to be sure."

Annabelle rested her head on his shoulder. "Perhaps it could hang in the front room."

"I know a better place." His voice had become playful all of a sudden.

"Where?" she asked, though she suspected she already knew the answer.

"Our bedroom. Not over the headboard, but next to the bed, where we can see it."

She grinned mischievously. "But that might be a waste. We've never been interested in looking at paintings when we're in bed."

Magnus considered the issue carefully, then nodded and went to pack up her paints and brushes. "You're right, as always, but I suggest we at least try it out. Let's go hang this masterpiece, then slide under the covers and see what we end up doing."

Annabelle laughed, and feeling quite euphoric indeed, and overcome with a deep, loving desire for her husband, quickly went to fold up her easel.

No fooling! The best in romance comes from Avon Books...

♥♥

Promise Me Forever by Lorraine Heath

"Lorraine Heath steals your heart!"
—*New York Times* bestselling author Christina Dodd

A very proper lady rekindles the passion—and love—with the Earl of Sachse, a man she thought she'd lost in this latest by *USA Today* bestselling writer Lorraine Heath.

Sighs Matter by Marianne Stillings

"Marianne Stillings writes fun, sexy suspense!"
—*New York Times* bestselling author Carly Phillips

When Claire finds herself in danger she turns to a sexy detective she had vowed never to see again . . . even if they had engaged in a willing, mutual seduction.

The Viscount's Wicked Ways by Anne Mallory

"A fresh, vibrant talent who cannot be ignored."
—*Romantic Times* BOOKclub

The brooding Viscount Blackfield is a man any well-bred lady would shun. But Patience Harrington has never been a proper lady!

Angel in My Bed by Melody Thomas

"An author to watch!"
—*USA Today* bestselling author Karen Hawkins

Meg Farady believed her former life was behind her—until the man she believed had betrayed her came back into her life. And that man is...her husband!

Visit www.AuthorTracker.com for exclusive information on your favorite HarperCollins authors.

REL 0306

Available wherever books are sold or please call 1-800-331-3761 to order.

Avon Romantic Treasures

Unforgettable, enthralling love stories, sparkling with passion and adventure from Romance's bestselling authors

Avon Romances
the best in
exceptional authors and unforgettable novels!